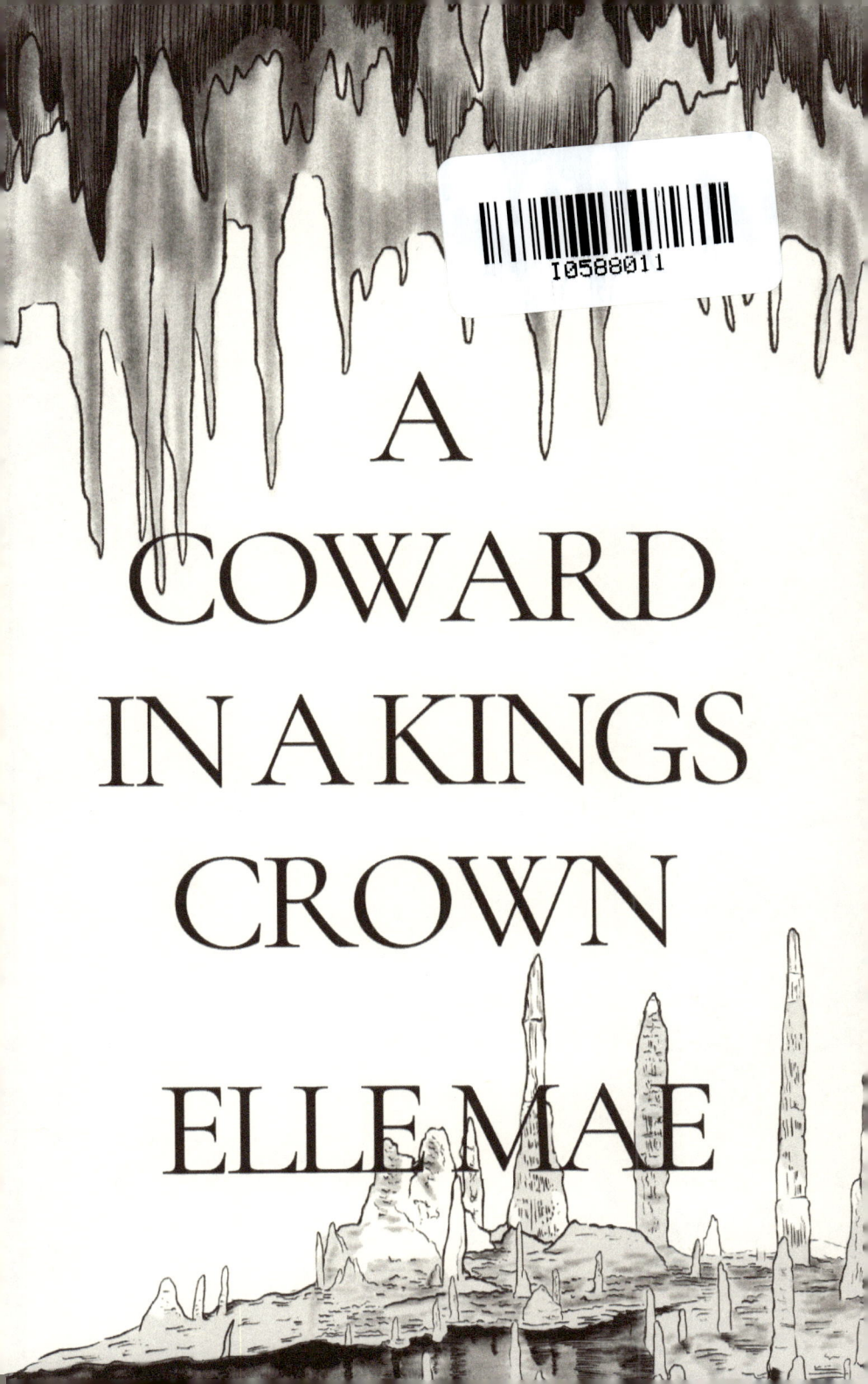

A COWARD IN A KINGS CROWN

ELLE MAE

ALSO BY ELLE MAE

Contract Bound: A Lesbian Vampire Romance

An Imposter in Warriors Clothing

The Price of Silence: Winterfell Academy Book 1

The Price of Silence: Winterfell Academy Book 2

TRIGGER WARNING

Before moving forward, please note that the themes in this
book can be dark and trigger some people. The themes can
include but are not limited to; sexual assault, death, gore,
domestic abuse, and violence.
If you need help, please reach out to the resources below.

National Suicide Prevention Lifeline
1-800-273-8255
https://suicidepreventionlifeline.org/

National Domestic Violence Hotline
1-800-799-7233
https://www.thehotline.org/

To my readers, thank you for your support!

I had been a good king, a great one even in comparison to the others. They turned their back on the world, content to never look back. They shirked their duties and watched as the world was taken over by those who had less than good intentions.

I had left the Other World many a time even though Nitri, the highest of all kings, had forbade it. I would sneak away when Nitri was preoccupied by his many slaves; he was easily distracted, and it made it a perfect time to complete my duties as a king… but it was only time before I was thrown out.

After I had given birth, he had cast me out like I had a disease. A punishment for having the child of a half breed, he said. Ever since he had locked us away from these worlds because of a forlorn love, we had been forbade from laying with them, forced to break our mating bonds. I didn't have one, until I visited the Dark King a decade ago. After that, my fate was sealed.

Even though I had lost my throne, the power of the universe still resonated inside me. Nitri had tried, but he could never strip away my power if the universe willed it. I was lucky the universe favored me so, or at least I thought it had.

Now my visits had turned permanent and I was able to live on land in the light kingdom, but those times would soon have to come to an end, and I would have to destroy not only my own child's life but the innocent, young light boy's as well.

The Light King, Acidos, was a black spot in an otherwise light world. I had been fooled by him for so long, given him so much power, so much knowledge of the Other World, and he had taken it and twisted it so cruelly.

And on his son no less.

I watched as Iniq ran in the grass alongside Baecos. Iniq shot sparks out of her hand in attempt to sway Baecos from chasing her, but the bright young boy knew better; he simply ran through knowing that the magic would do him no harm. They were not but three years old and yet the world had dealt them such a fate. Their minds could not comprehend the things—the cruel things—that waited for him.

Baecos. The poor boy.

The thoughts that had come out of Acidos were enough to make my stomach twist and my blood boil, but the universe had warned me. There was no stopping his plan; it was necessary for the fate of the world. The only thing I could do was ensure that Iniq would be there in the end to not only be strong enough to live through what Acidos had planned, but then to face Nitri.

"They are perfect for each other," Acidos commented from his place at my side.

His thoughts were unholy. He knew I could see the way he pictured his own son bleeding out on an altar. The way he fantasied about consuming his magic. I could see the way he licked his lips and his gaze narrowed in on his son as he tackled Iniq to the ground.

"You cannot play god, Acidos," I told him. I should have

never told him about Nitri's cruel games on his heirs. It was my own lapse of judgement that caused this. His son's blood is on my hands now.

"There is nothing I can do that the High Kings cannot." He let out a sigh. "The only difference is, I am barred from your world while you are now tied to mine."

"You kill that boy and I swear that I will kill you where you stand," I didn't let him know the universe forbade me from harming a hair on that evil man's skull—I had played around with the thought too many times before it showed me a picture of Iniq bloody and mangled at the ripe age of twelve. The universe was far crueler than the imposter of a king that stood before me. It wanted the bloodshed so it could craft the children into what they needed to be. Everything from now would be to push us to our final goal.

Acidos let out a booming laugh causing the children to bring their curious gaze to our spot in the grass.

"Oh, I won't kill him, Neia," he chided and rolled his gaze over to mine lazily. There was a smirk on his face. No, he would do much worse. The plan furled out in his mind with ease. My veins turned icy as I sought my own child's golden eyes.

The universe would make her suffer for its plan to work— they both would. And it would have to be I who put that plan in place. To turn the tide, to destroy the world for it to be reborn once more. Those sweet, poor children. Even though I knew of what Baecos would turn into, I could not hate the boy. After all, it was my own fault.

CHAPTER ONE
INIQ

As a human child, I had thought snakes were my worst fear. Their slimy scales and slitted eyes wrapped around my dreams and squeezed until I almost fainted. I was so caught up in my own fear that I could barely hear my human mother trying so desperately to save her child from the cold grip of the snakes body. Instead of her arms being comforting, they would turn cold and become so much more similar to a snake's than human skin.

I imagined this moment much like that. The only difference was as the golden-eyed snake stared down at me, my fears were driven by something much different.

Nitri, the King of kings, the ruler of all in this land and the only person who could determine my fate, stood in front of me. His long blond hair framed his face in a feminine way, even as his golden eyes were narrowed and his teeth were barred.

I had been nervous to meet him yet excited at the same time. My pitiful life was over. I had finished what had taken six lifetimes to do, and now I was here to claim my prize, but the prize was in a chokehold, much like the snake had put me through in my human childhood. Similar to the way Baecos's, the disgusting Light King that held me captive, hands had once gripped at my throat. Similar to the way the door tried to force me into this world, against my world.

My new fear was unlocked at the moment. It hurt more than it scared me because some part of me knew what I had to be feeling must have been the ultimate truth. Because why else would I have gone through all that I had to get here to be rewarded... with this?

Nitri didn't even look at me as I entered the room to meet him after six hundred years; his eyes were trained on the woman that shielded his lower half from me. She was a demon, a full blooded one like Spiris had explained to me on the way here. Her bright red eyes seemed to be dull, and her horns protruded out of her messy blonde hair that Nitri's hand was currently tangled in.

Even though I had heard from Spiris what the differences between full blooded demons and halfblooded demons like Cruor were, my mate and Fire King, I could sense none of this from the woman in front of me. Instead, it was the same woman I was before the door had opened for me, submitting to someone who didn't even deserve to breathe the same air as me. It was like a slap to the face and made me feel so alone yet seen at the same time, and I was terrified of what this meant.

"You made it," Nitri said with a grunt as his hips snapped into the woman in front of him. Her long dress was pulled up over her bare bottom, and she was thrown over the table that occupied the room.

The grand area that was normally reserved for the feeding of kings was hardly a place to be fucking someone in such a fashion. A once distinguished place now turned into a disgusting show of dominance in such a way, I couldn't help but believe that Nitri did this on purpose. He knew I was coming and wanted to show me the control he had over me, over the world. His hand in her hair, the way the room was littered with wait staff, and him not caring who saw him pound into a person who didn't even make a sound was an undeniable announcement.

I am the king, Nitri's eyes seemed to say. *And you will watch as I take whatever I want.*

I was fed up with people taking what they wanted. Tired of seeing the way they made people bend to their will. This whole time, I felt like I couldn't put a finger on the feeling until the red-eyed demon girl met my gaze and I saw one so similar to my own stare back at me.

"I'll come back," I murmured and turned back towards the large iron door Spiris held open for me. Only a moment had passed, but both of us froze when we saw what Nitri was doing. In this moment, I wished I had been successful in convincing him to loiter with me. It had been but half an hour since I had learned of his resurrection. I had so much to tell him, so much to make up for, so much to apologize for, and yet, he had insisted to meet the master of a king who was still pounding into his maid as Spiris and I locked gazes.

He regretted it too.

"No need," Nitri said, and the skin slapping stopped. I wanted to grimace at the meaning but held it in as I slowly turned back to face him.

The maid had fixed her dress already and scurried back to the line of other wait staff lined the halls of the dining room. Their eyes watched her as she did.

"And it wasn't a show of control," he said, repeating my own words back to me. A jolt went through me when I realized my mind was not safe around him. How could I expect the king to not have a handle on dark magic? Nitri fixed his all-black robes as he walked around the table and stood in front of me. "As a king, I have a duty to make sure my line continues. I have a daughter now, but as you may realize, having a daughter as an heir to a throne is far less than ideal."

His slim fingers reached out to grab a lock of my black hair.

I gripped onto the spark of courage that lit my insides and smacked away his hand. He cocked his head and narrowed his eyes at me as they ranked my form.

"I have come to take my throne." The words Spiris had coached me on felt unfamiliar in my mouth. The tone, the weight; it's like the words knew the truth.

"You are denied," Nitri said coolly. His hand gripped my chin and tipped my face up as if I was any woman that would bend to his control and not the new king in this castle. "That thing you feel inside you? That sinking feeling? It is right, you should listen to it."

He had sniffed out my fear like a cat hunting its prey and went in for the kill when I was least expecting it. I had come here with the expectation of me taking my throne and was met with a disgusting show, a reminder of the pain I went through. He had to have planned this to exploit my fear.

"You're weak, Iniq." He took the words out of my mouth. "Getting here was lucky, but I can ensure you going forward, you will not get close to the throne. I will not allow a weak-willed woman who isn't even a full magician to rule over the kingdoms that your mother built from scratch." He didn't give me time to digest the information he had given me. "It would be a disgrace to her and a disgusting sight."

He backed away, his cool fingers leaving my chin. A small, dangerous smile played at his lips.

"The next time I want to see you is on your death bed as your pitiful body wastes away."

The High Kings were a powerful group of demons who stood above the rest. The lived in their own little world as if running away from their own creation. Everything we touched, felt, smelt, was a product of Nitri's powers. He was the first King to have awoken into the darkness of the universe. I still do not know if it was Nitri's own loneliness that caused him to forge the other Kings, or if they were as much of a mystery as he was.

There are two other kings that rule over Fire and Water, and Earth and Air... the throne that was rightfully mine remained empty. They were supposed to rule as one, but the kings rarely congregated. Even though there was only a single king missing it became very apparent as I walked through the empty halls of the castle they had taken as their home, they were just as alone as I was and more divided than the outside world knew. Besides wait staff, the only other people that roamed this area were me and Spiris.

Spiris had been here since I was taken forcibly into Baecos's kingdom and my magic stripped from me. He was the one that concocted a one-hundred-year plan to help me escape. The one that made the loneliness that wracked my body for all these months lessen considerably, but every night as I ran from Baecos in my dream, I became aware of just how easy it would be to lose him again. His skin was harder now, his magic reserves larger, and his blood lust heightened, but he was not indestructible, and I was not willing to test it.

I wanted so badly to just enjoy life in the castle with him by my side, but there was a wedge between us that grew the longer I stayed in the castle. After the third week, it had become painfully obvious that there were things left unresolved that neither of us dared bring up. It made me antsy, like my arms and legs were on pins and needles.

The feeling made me wander more, made me seek out Nitri. I was running away, I knew that. Running away from him, cutting him off. Even after everything, I didn't know how I could face him after everything that happened with Baecos— everything that happened with Cruor.

Today, he had brushed my hair out of my face, a move that caused my heart to skip a beat and my breath to catch. The next moment, I was trying to feel for Nitri's signature in an attempt to stop the way he made me feel... I wasn't sure I could handle it. Wasn't sure if I wanted to test the fates again.

"Leave me," Nitri said simply once I entered the dining room he so seemed to love. Every time I had run into him, it was always in the same place. This time he was preparing to eat, the table was set, and all that was left was the food. He waved his hand and, in an instant, the table filled with enough food to feed Solis twice over and have some left for the hell hounds who have an uncontrollable appetite.

Swallowing thickly, I sat down in front of Nitri and began picking from the food at the table. An act that would cause me to stall if I was in the magical realm, but here I did it as an act of defiance and that only fueled me forward no matter how the pounding in my heart pulled me away from the table.

I ate mechanically as his deathly glare weighed on me.

"Spiris," I called and patted the seat next to me. His curly hair and black eyes entered my view with an apprehensive expression on his face.

"No slaves at the table," Nitri chastised, and the chair I had claimed for Spiris burst into wooden shards.

"Let up on the girl, Nitri," a smooth feminine voice called from the open door.

I looked to see a woman with short, pale blue hair that curled around her head. There were black horns coming out of her head, much like Nitri and Spiris, but she and Nitri had matching chains wrapped around them. Seeing their horns made me even more cognizant of the ones I might never get, if Nitri had his way.

Her golden eyes shined against her tawny skin, and the tattoos that marred her skin were placed in a way that made me envious of her bone structure. The magic coming out of her slim frame was undeniable. She was a king for sure, and from the look of the tattoos on her face, air and earth most likely her domain.

"Correct, young one," the girl praised and took the seat to my side that was still in one piece. "But I am not a woman."

A heat ran up the back of my neck as her eyes glanced over me rather than the table. Apparently mind reading was not just limited to the dark power as I had thought, and it was a terrible reminder that I would never be able to hide anything ever again.

"I am sorry," I told her. "You are just so pretty." I wanted to slap myself for swooning when Spiris was literally by my side; he was so close that I could feel the heat radiating off of him.

"I am genderless, they and them are more appropriate pronouns," they told me. "And do not fear, attraction is normal. I am but a god compared to your weak form."

I knew their words were not met as a jab, but the clench of my stomach came anyways.

"High King Faelin," Spiris greeted with a bow. Faelin gave Spiris a light smile.

"Glad to see you are finally reunited with your loved one," she greeted back. *Loved one.* My heart pounded even faster in my chest than I thought possible. We were so exposed, it made me feel even smaller and weaker than I once did.

"I guess we all came together for a meal," a wistful voice said from the doorway. I turned to see the last high king enter the room. He was much smaller in stature than I had expected a king to be as his black robes nearly looked to swallow him whole. His silver hair hung in straight strands against his pale skin. He met my gaze with a small smile. "Nice to meet you, Iniq. We have been waiting. I know Spiris was anxious to see you again."

I wanted to crawl up and die of embarrassment, but I quickly shoved that feeling far down in my stomach and sat up straight. *I would not be embarrassed*, I chanted to myself. *I belong here.*

Kneku grabbed a chair next the one Nitri had destroyed and sat next to me. Spiris had to move to accommodate the small king but remained firmly behind my chair, his hand brushing my side as if to ensure he was still there.

"While you are here, I expect you to follow the rules I have set forth for you," Nitri said as he conjured a wine glass filled with sparkling liquid and drank from it slowly. His eyes stayed on mine even as he tipped his head back to allow the liquid past his thin lips. "Stay in this castle. Do not bother me. And do not leave this realm."

"Telling her not to bother you is asking for her to seek you out even more," Kneku said. He had gathered his own food and lightly nibbled on a piece of bread before speaking again. "You saw how she was when Neia was still alive."

My heart stopped at the mention of *her* name. I knew it. I knew her. *My mother.* My eyes shot towards Nitri.

"Yes, your mother," he said with a dull tone.

"She was wonderful," Faelin said as they sipped from their glass.

"Until she was exiled," Nitri said. "For breaking the rules."

His words can be seen as a warning, or a dare if one looked from another angle.

"Such a harsh topic for dinner," Faelin said. "Let's rejoice that we have a suitor for the empty throne. The world will be right again once she ascends."

There was a pause around the table. Did they not know the extent of Nitri's anger? His unabridged hatred for me? They had to feel it. Every time I entered a room with him, it was like his eyes attacked me and the air in the room dropped drastically.

"She could leave her weak body. It would be the perfect solution," Kneku commented.

I couldn't tell which emotion was stronger: the surprise or the panic. They were on my side; they were fighting with me against the person who had created this universe. The person who could destroy us with a snap of his fingers. They had a death wish.

"This is why you came," Nitri said and smashed his glass on the table. The sparkling liquid splattered across the table and glass shattered. A maid came from out of nowhere to clean up the glass. Nitri grabbed her wrist harshly as she reached over the table to pick up the shards. A whimper escaped her lips as Nitri snapped her wrist in an unnatural direction.

I gasped. "Don't you hurt her."

"If you tell me what to do with my slaves, I will tell you what to do with yours, and I can promise you, Iniq, you will regret it," Nitri said with a growl and threw the girl's wrist away like it was a toy he had gotten tired of. With a wave of his hand, she was gone.

"He is *not* a slave," I fought back, the anger that seemed so dull the last few weeks coming to life. It was unnatural in my veins, and I couldn't help but think back to the time I had snapped a neck as easily as Nitri had snapped that demon's wrist.

"You come here to try and sway me," he accused, ignoring me completely. "And for what? A puny magician that can't even harness her darkness?"

"If she learns, she can stand on her own. She would be worthy," Faelin insisted. "Like her mother had planned, surely you will not let Neia's dying wish be in vein?"

"She brought that on herself!" Nitri growled and stood up, the chair behind him shattering into a million pieces just like the chair before. "By procreating with a disgusting half breed. By disobeying me. That was her own fault."

I had no words for the way his words echoed in my chest. I was shocked, angry, sad, and upset all at the same time. I had no other wish than to take him by the throat and demand he take his words back.

"We have a world to right, Nitri," Kneku said. "Learning to harness the dark will be easy for her."

"I don't give a damn about those magicians. I would rather they die in a burning fire than ever have to look at something so pitifully weak again. They were a mistake." Nitri straightened himself suddenly like he had only just realized what he was doing. His eyes still burned when he looked at me. "Learn to harness it, all of it, and then *maybe* I will give you an audience where you can plead your case."

"Nitri—" Faelin started, but they were cut off.

"I have spoken, Faelin," Nitri hissed. "Do not test me."

Suddenly he was gone in a flash of light leaving only me and the two other High Kings at my side. I had a feeling that convincing him to ascend me would be just about as hard as escaping Baecos had been.

CHAPTER TWO
SPIRIS

*I*t is said that those who are forced to come back from their final resting places, never fully come back. Like a dandelion, once destroyed, they scatter into millions of pieces. Imagine trying to find every single puff, trying to search in every nook and cranny, and having to put it painstakingly back into place.

That's what it was like to bring a soul back. It was possible, but there was always some part of the human that remained unaccounted for.

If they were lucky, it would be a small insignificant memory. The face of their dead mother, a childhood best friend, their own name, even. If they found themselves to be on the other side of that luck though, it was rumored that whole parts of their sleeves would be missing. Instead of the loving daughter you expected to revive from the dead, they would come back a monster. The person who once thought of everyone before themselves, now couldn't care less about a person, even if that meant their death. Friends turned to enemies. Feelings of love turned numb. Those that were the most dangerous didn't even realize that they were missing anything. Those people would blindly chase after one of the only feelings that they could feel.

The smile that played at Iniq's lips as she looked at the most powerful being in the universe as he warned her to never appear in his sight again was proof enough. After so many times of being forcefully pulled back from her resting place, she had to be missing something. I had been watching her when I had first come back from my own resting place. Every day I would sit by the only device that allowed us to see into other worlds, Eternity Fountain the kings called it, and watch as she ran for her life more than once. For the first few nights, I didn't dare sleep, and as a new demon, I would need it, but they assured me that after a while I would be able to pull from the universe around me and sleep would not be needed. I couldn't dare risk the chance of something happening to her. I knew that I couldn't help, but at least I thought that maybe, she would feel at ease if she knew that I had been watching.

She felt no such thing.

When she finally made it into this world, I raced to her, ignoring the words of the High King Kneku. He had warned me Nitri would punish my actions, that he would be furious I left the castle as a slave. I didn't care what would happen to me, the worst already had, and after so long, I couldn't bear to have her think of me as dead.

Things went downhill from there quickly. I wished that I would have waited because as soon as I had brought her back into the castle and we were met with Nitri taking advantage of the wait staff, I knew whatever relief that had filled her when she arrived here was gone. She would be back in the nightmare of Baecos's mansion, forced to watch as someone just like her stood in her place at the mercy of a High King. When Nitri met my eyes during that time, I knew it was my punishment.

And when she met my eyes after, I had been sure that there was something missing from her. It made sense, trauma did that to a person, but even as a magician, I felt it. Now as a demon under the roof of the High Kings, it was undeniable. She still did it, searched out danger any second she could. She would precisely provoke Nitri, and I had counted my blessing ten times over as I watched him play with the idea of killing her in his mind. He had the same facial expression now as all those times. It resembled a cat in waiting, his eyes watching her carefully, assigning her weakness. It was chilling.

"Nitri, do you hear how ridiculous you sound?" Iniq asked, the smile still on her face. Her half white and half black hair was pulled away from her face by two intricate braids that started at her temples, the rest in waves falling around her shoulders. Her skin was much healthier than before, but a smudge of purple under her eyes let anyone that looked know that she was having trouble sleeping. The nightmares still plagued her even after months of being in the king's domain, I wouldn't be surprised if it was Nitri's doing. He had a mysterious way about things. It had started with him pulling our wait staff from us, then hiding the king's robes from Neia's closet, and now I did not know how much longer he would live with the disobedience.

"My answer will not change," Nitri replied and took a sip of his tea. A lock of his long blond hair fell in front of his face as his head tipped down to the rim of the cup. Pitch black horns curled out of the sides of his head, and they were wrapped in intricate gold chains as was custom of the kings. His long blond lashes fluttered, and his golden eyes met mine for just a moment before lowering back down to his cup. Nitri's robes shadowed his body in black, leaving his pale skin seeming almost translucent.

I hated the way his eyes flitted over to me, feeling my chest rip open and my soul lying there bared for him to see.

The kings kept their powers from us—another order of Nitri after the dinner where they had sided with Iniq. Their interactions were close to none; we could barely find them no matter how hard we had searched. Only on occasion did they come, and it was never when we called. The only thing I was able to figure was that keeping things from Nitri was almost impossible. The High Kings could *see* things regardless of which powers they held. Nitri was a dangerous mix because as King of Kings, he had to hold every single power, so that meant on top of every exploitative elemental power he had, there was also no knowing how far his gaze reached.

"How can you expect me to learn when you refuse to teach me?" Iniq said with a growl. Did she know her eyes lit up when she dealt with this type of confrontation? Did she feel her body vibrate? I shifted in my place behind her chair and placed my hand lightly on her shoulder. She leaned into my touch and I heard her voice invade my mind.

I know, she said. *I know I shouldn't provoke him.*

If you know then why do you do it? I asked back. I felt her irritation through the bond.

"Why do you do it, Iniq?" Nitri asked, putting his cup down on the table and meeting Iniq's eyes, a smile of his own playing at his lips. This was the usual now, he would invade our minds without us even knowing. "You should listen to your slave, he's smarter than the other bunch. They are only good for procreation and cleaning, sometimes barely a thought passes through their measly little heads."

"Don't you call him that," Iniq spit at Nitri.

"It is okay," I said in a whisper to her.

"It is not, Spiris," Iniq snapped at me and shrugged off my hand from her shoulder. "You know very well how I feel about that."

"I will not change how this world works for the opinion of one magician, child," Nitri said, his voice taking on a dangerous tone. *Child.* I knew that hit a sore spot in Iniq, even without her projecting her feelings on to me. But to be fair, we were all children compared to Nitri. I was not sure even the other kings knew how old Nitri was from the information I had carved out of Kneku he was present when they awoke as kings. Faelin was silent, never daring again to feel Nitri's wrath.

"A King," she corrected. "A king you refuse to ascend. A king you refuse to teach. A king you refuse to even acknowledge unless cornered."

"Just because you were birthed from a King does not give you the right to claim their title. You have to *earn it*. And from what I have seen you are far from worthy," Nitri said. Iniq was about to open her mouth and fight back but Nitri raised his hand, and Iniq's jaw snapped shut with an audible snap. *An air power*, I noted. "You were too stupid to learn how to use your powers wisely the first time, and only after countless deaths and a memory seal were you finally able to finish the one thing we asked of you. Do not test me like this again, even giving you the continued chance to prove yourself is because of my ties to your mother. But by now she has been dead for far too long, and I have been far too patient with you."

Nitri brushed the long lock of hair out of his face and let us stew in silence. Feel the impact of his words. Only after Iniq relaxed back into her seat did he wave his hand and her jaw became unlocked.

"Do you not care about the deaths of your people?" she asked, the smile gone from her face and was now replaced with a scowl.

"*Your people*," he corrected. " It is *your people* who are dying. It is *your people* who you have continuously let down for six hundred years. *Your people* who died by the thousands while you frolicked around wasting time with Baecos."

"He kept me captive," Iniq hissed. Her hands gripped tightly at the chair that she was sitting on, her knuckles turning white under the pressure.

"You *let him* keep you. It was *your weakness* that allowed that. Tell me," Nitri leaned forward his chin resting on his open palm, goading Iniq, "when you released your power right before you entered this world, how did it feel?"

Iniq opened her mouth but Nitri waved her off again and continued.

"You don't have to tell me, I know. That power was always there, you could have left at any time but some part of you deep inside chose not to. What was that part? Hm, Iniq? It was the weakness. The weakness that has been following you around your entire existence."

Nitri got up from his chair and walked towards the entrance of the dining hall we were in. His own slaves followed closely behind.

"You are not worthy to be a king. You never were. *That* is why I refuse to teach you."

Without another look back, Nitri left the hall.

"Don't go back on your promise!" she yelled after him. The words were no use though. Nitri was not a man who cared about others, he had proven as much. He would take what he wanted, regardless of what it cost others.

I put my hand back on her slim shoulder and squeezed once more.

You are the strongest person I have ever met, Iniq, I told her in my mind and prayed she heard me. Heard my truth. There was never a day where I thought differently. From the moment I saw her for the first time until the moment I saw her in the fountain, I knew that she would be the change and that no one, not even Nitri, would have survived the way she had. She was so strong that she took her own life over and over again, not knowing if each time would be the last. So strong that she spent two years locked up by that *bastard.* And even when she finally was able to leave, she did not stop fighting until she stepped into this world and literally fell into my arms.

You deserve more than the crown, I told her. *You deserve the world. You deserve a happy life. You are strong.*

Iniq stood up abruptly and I let my hand fall to my side. She turned to me, her still green eyes flashing with an emotion I had seen far too many times in that dungeon. She turned back and walked towards the entrance.

I let a sad smile grace my lips and I followed behind her. Even if it meant being her slave, I would follow in her footsteps until the day where I wasn't pulled from my resting place. I didn't care if her soul was still scattered in a million pieces across the cosmos—the person she was now was enough for me.

Iniq's fingers were as light as feathers as they trailed over the rose's blood red petals. Her smile never came back onto her face. Instead, like most times when we visited her mother's garden, she would be deep in thought.

I had yet to see the smile that I had loved so much since she had entered this world. And as much as I hated to watch her with Nitri, it was at least some type of emotion. I would take anger or frustration over silence, over the nothingness. Sometimes it felt that no matter how hard I tried to reach out to her I would hit a blank wall, or she would rush off to some other place. I wanted more than anything to be there for her but it would seem that even after all this time, we were not ready for each other.

As much as Nitri liked to say Iniq was unworthy to follow in her mother's footsteps, he had still chosen to give her old room to Iniq, which had an exit to a garden still growing after the six hundred years of her absence. Faelin and Kneku were still kind regardless of the King who oversaw them, it was not hard to guess that they had to be the ones taking care of the garden. That much was certain when they made their stance. I had only wished there was another way.

Even though Nitri had stated she would get an audience

when she learned dark, I doubted Nitri would even care as much to follow through.

"Do you remember?" Iniq asked me as she plucked a rose off the stem and walked towards me with it in her open hand. I held out my hand for her and she plopped the quickly dying rose in my hand. I felt the magic leave it almost immediately. My heart clenched in my chest when I remembered the way she looked in the clearing when I had taken her to in the Light Kingdom. She was healthier back then and unburdened by the drama that hid in her memories. An evil part of me was secretly glad she didn't have to remember Baecos the first time around. There would be no way she could ascend to the throne with those memories weighing on her.

The red moon reflected in her sad eyes as they looked up to me. I hated that look. If she would allow me to, I would kiss away all her tears, but I didn't want to overstep more than I already had.

"I remember," I told her, my voice feeling hoarse. "I remember every interaction we have ever had."

She gave me a small smile. "I wish I could say the same." She replied and ran her hand across the other blood red roses that littered the area. There was a weight to her words that made me feel bad about my feelings of her locked memories.

"Nitri is wrong, you know." A wistful voice came from behind me. Even before looking I could tell by the voice and the magical signature that Kneku had joined us in the garden. He was quiet at first, and only spoke when really needed to due to Nitri's order. It was a surprise to see him here yet again. I didn't know what Nitri had threatened him and Faelin with but it had to be severe if Faelin avoided us like the plague.

I turned to greet him with a bow. His chin length silver hair hung limp on either side of his face, his horns were decorated much like Nitri had been, and he wore the customary black robes. Kneku held both water and fire powers within him but he was far from either of their kings. He almost never showed any emotion and when he spoke it seemed like he was just coming out of a dream.

"Nitri cannot be wrong," Iniq said with a sigh. She looked up at the full moon and the blood red rose was crushed under her hand.

"He is as flawed as any other being in this world," Kneku spoke, his thin fingers reaching out to run along the rose's thorns. "Do you know how we came to be in this world?"

"Nitri fell in love with Yara." She answered, her eyes flickering to mine. My heart soared. It was nothing to be excited about but it was enough to start my heart.

"And then was betrayed. His trust was broken so completely that we were forced to resign from the magical world to never set foot there again. That itself is a flaw big enough to have permanent consequences," he said and looked back up into the red moon. "I still dream of the blue sky."

"Did you fall in love before, Kneku?" she asked, her voice but a whisper.

"We left everything like that behind when we came to this world." He explained. "We broke our mating bonds. Every one of us."

At the mention of mating bonds Cruor's snarling face made its way into my mind. Jealously rose in me faster than I liked. She was a world away, I had nothing to worry about... or so I thought. It wasn't long until I heard Iniq say Cruor's name in her sleep, the first time it broke my heart, it became more bearable after the tenth and boring at the twentieth.

"Does he expect you not to have offspring?" I asked to Kneku. A smile tugged at his lips.

"My mate is a male, Spiris." He explained. "I have a few offspring out there but they feel no need to stick around, nor did I want them to. This position is my burden and my burden alone."

"Did it hurt? The bond breaking?" Iniq asked and wrapped her arms around her. She wore a human looking sweater she found in her mother's closet and a pair of leather pants.

"I wish it did," he said wistfully. "It would have made moving on easier, instead I just felt... empty."

"How did you do it?" she asked. Another bit of hope shot through me.

"You'll know when it comes," Kneku said. "It happened in an instant. Time pauses, the world is silent, and it is just you and the bond in that moment. That's when you need to do it. It will show itself to you when it's ready, until then the bond will fight. Fight to keep you together. Fight to pull you together if it gets even a whiff of a chance."

"It sounds like it has a mind of its own," Iniq murmured.

"It has one purpose in life, to bring you and your mate together," he said. "If it cannot continue one, it's asking you to end its' existence."

Iniq sighed and looked at her hands.

"Giving up your life when there is no other way forward is not a weakness," he continued, no longer speaking about the bond. "You never knew which time would be your last, Iniq. That alone takes a strength that none of us dare possess. Instead, we are but cowards hiding in a prison we built ourselves."

There was a pause between the group. Iniq mulled over his words.

"You are not weak, Iniq," Kneku said again. "That's what I came to say. And to implore you to get some rest."

Iniq gave him a forced smile and he left without a goodbye. I bowed once more as he left.

CHAPTER THREE
INIQ

*M*y dreams were never safe in this realm. I should have known as soon at Nitri's disgusting gaze met mine. There was no rest for me, one monster would be replaced for another as I closed my eyes to sleep. Instead of Nitri's gold eyes I would find purple ones waiting for me.

He would be standing over me when I opened my dream eyes. Just like every other night. I would be back in a dark dungeon and my arms and legs would be fastened to the cold slab of stone. Sometimes I felt that these were my previous memories instead of dreams, the pain always felt too real. The way his laugh reverberated around the room; the way I would feel my heart beat slower. It didn't help that Spiris would be dead in each and every one of my dreams. It wasn't explicitly stated, but I would feel the ache in my chest. I would feel the emptiness inside me and I knew that there was no hope for him coming back to save me. I was never saved from these dreams. Not Cruor, nor Fluvis, not even the door came to my rescue.

No one cared to.

Even in my dreams I could feel the bond. It happened when Spiris' hand first brushed across mine in the castle hallway, the bond would tug me back. It had never been so forceful until now, and even in my dreams when I thought of no one coming to save me, it would tug. She would never come though, even in my dreams she had turned her back on me, forgotten me. The person she stated to love. The person she grew up with. Her eyes would haunt me in the depth of the darkness and yet even in my dreams she left me, alone.

"We missed you, Iniq," Baecos would purr. He would always be so ecstatic when we met, like he really had waited forever for the moment. Like a lover yearning to touch his beloved after years apart. It was disgusting. "It was silly of you to think you could escape."

The tip of a dagger ran itself across my cheek. Cool metal would make my breath hitch. It was so real, every touch, every look, even the smell of the damp cold space infiltrated my sense carrying the metallic scent of drying blood.

Vitos appeared by my side like he always did in the dreams. It was a painful reminder that Spiris was dead in this reality. There were times were I truly believed the dreams, if not memories, had to be the reality where I did not escape Baecos. He would wait for me in every one. Was there not a reality where this monster had been killed?

"Cruor is not coming this time," Vitos taunted with a smile. "She handed you over to us."

"She acted like she wasn't listening as I told her all the things I wanted to do to you. But she was, Iniq, I saw the way her eyes would turn to me when I told her how I ravished your body," Baecos said and licked the blood the flowed off the cut in my cheek. "You know what she said, Iniq?"

"Don't touch me," I hissed at them, though it was no use by now.

"She said *good*," he finished with a laugh. "I have been waiting for this for so long Iniq, The gods really doomed you when they left you on his realm with me. I'll let you in on a little secret."

He leaned towards my ear. I tried to headbutt him but Vitos grabbed my hair roughly and slammed my skull against the hard rock.

"They did it on purpose. They knew that I would take you one day, when no one was expecting. All of this was predestined, and they stood there and watched it happen with smiles on their faces."

He raised the knife and implied it into my chest with one swing.

"Iniq!" A shout awoke me from my nightmare and a pair of strong hands shook me almost violently. I regained consciousness with a loud gasp, the dark crown molding of my mother's room coming into view just beyond Spiris's worried face. He relaxed significantly when his eyes made contact with mine but soon his face was blurred by the tears that welled up. I threw myself into his chest and he whispered to me as I sobbed.

This was a normal routine for us, a secret we kept. One we would refuse to talk about the next day. I do not know if it was the bond or my own cowardice, but I wouldn't dare bring it up the next day. Not my weakness, and certainly not the way I melted in his arms as he rocked me back and forth. Not the way his scent wrapped around me like a security blanket. I didn't even dare think about the way his hands felt as they rubbed soothing circles in my back.

Because of his relation to me, he occupied the room that was connected to my mother's. A servant's quarters that was small but at least decent enough for his basic needs. It came in handy when the nightmares dragged me down where even my screams were muffled. He would always hear them, somehow. I would be awoken the same way, in his arms. I felt bad that Spiris was never able to get a restful night's sleep. He had insured me that as a demon he would not need as much as someone like me but it didn't make me feel any better. I had promised myself that I would be stronger, that I would be able to stand on my own two feet. But night after night, his soft words and caresses broke me down even further until I was a complete and utter mess in his arms.

It was an embarrassment. As someone who should have been a ruler in this world to have fallen so far. A disgrace. A weakness.

"I'm sorry," I choked out against him.

"You have nothing to apologize for," he murmured against my damp hair. I hated the way I sunk into him, hated the way this made me felt, hated the way his king had let him down. "Lay back down."

I let him lay me softly back down on the bed. He slipped under the covers with me, facing me as he did so. The red of his eyes that barely showed in the daytime due to his black expanded pupils were now easier to pick out as they glowed lightly in the dark. I couldn't tear my eyes away from his face. The shock of his death was almost too much, every night I was convinced that if I had to relive it over again that I would go insane, but every night without fail when I opened my eyes to his face over mine, I was given a new strength. I buried myself in his chest and let out a deep sigh, unable to continue holding this stare.

"Thank you," I spoke into his chest.

"Sleep now," he said and brushed his lips over the top of my head, a ghost of a kiss. "I'll be here."

Sleep came easier in his arms; the nightmare didn't dare haunt me when he was here. But there was one thing that still breached the walls of his embrace. Glowing red eyes continued to haunt me even in the deepest of slumbers. Sometimes they were angry, other times they were sad. I had rarely seen them happy but that didn't bother me so much as the way the eyes tugged at my heart each and every time even as I lay against Spiris.

There were many things in the castle that seemed to radiate the same loneliness I had felt while being stranded here. A broken and crumbling fountain that was hidden behind a mountain of overgrown roses, an outdoor hallway made of stone that had long since lost its luster even though the realm that we were in had no changes in the weather. The one that had drawn me in since almost the moment I had arrived was an empty ballroom. It was as abandoned as any place else in the castle, but this place felt especially worn as if Nitri's forgetfulness of this place had a direct impact on the atmosphere in here.

I dubbed it as my new training center ever since Nitri had refused to teach me. While I might have been ashamed of myself, I held on to the vow I made myself and it only got stronger the longer Nitri refused to train me. I knew in my heart his words had weight, they hurt as they were slapped in my face repeatedly, but I couldn't give up here, not now. Not when I was so close to answers.

I sat crisscrossed in the middle of the room making sure there was enough space between me and Spiris, sweat pouring down my face as I pushed my magic to its limit over and over again. I had shrugged off the human looking cardigan that I had found in my mom's closest long ago leaving me in my leather pants and a loose tunic. My mother seemed to have a closet filled with human clothes that posed more questions than it answered, but if she was anything like me, I would have to assume during her rebellion against Nitri she had made more than a few pitstops to the realm that housed me for more than a hundred years.

Spiris gazing on me was always a heavy weight that itched my skin the longer it stayed.

No matter how long I had decided to stay in the ballroom he would stay perched near the wall, watching over me. Even as lonely as Nitri made me feel, Spiris would always be there to prove them wrong. After being here for the last few months it was clear that the Kings lived a life even lonelier than I was plagued with. The staff of demons that waited on them were the only other living things here that could talk. There were lives outside these walls, but I had never dared to test Nitri's wrath that far. Demons, offspring, they had to live outside of the confines of this castle, but not one King ever left this fortress that they had built. Kneku had described it as a prison. It proved that no matter the actions of Nitri, it seemed he had only built a bigger hole for himself and the other Kings around him. Not like he cared for their wellbeing.

Even though there was no magical signature in this space, it was crystal clean. The intricate gold patterns on the stark white floor sparkled under the hundreds if not thousands of glass chandeliers. The large windows gave way to the black sky and red moon outside giving the feeling that the ballroom stood on a separate pane. From the white floors to the white walls and glass chandeliers, it didn't match any of the other rooms or scenery of this world. The kings loved black and red and other deep jewel tones so to find something so *pure* looking was almost impossible.

I became as restless here as I had in the other realms, the magic itched under my skin, begging to be flexed. I took a deep breath and focused once more on my magic trying to visualize the darkness within me. My magic had always mixed together so seamlessly that trying to sort out the darkness from the light was like wandering through a maze in complete darkness. I could feel the walls of it, I had some sense of where I was going but I couldn't see the bigger picture, I became lost. I didn't know if in my past life I was able to separate it, but from what I could remember I only knew about slipping into others mind and calling forth the darkness ... I didn't know what else I could do with this power and the more I strained to call upon it, the more I strained to call my memories, the more painful it became.

Soon my head started to feel like it was cracking open. There was a pounding that drowned out even my own heartbeat. I couldn't even feel the darkness, the only thing that I had managed to do was create a shield around myself that was dark as night, but I had little control over it and it was gone in an instant.

I tried to recall how it felt when I used it the night I escaped. I tried to visualize the tendrils that wrapped around Claire, tried to call them forward... but when her dead face came into mind my concentration dropped and I felt my stomach sour.

Was this guilt?

As soon as I had come face to face with Nitri and the wait staff on the day I arrived, all the magic that was lashing out in my veins recoiled back inside me. It was when I could finally see clearly what I had done to Claire, to Callum. Sometimes in my dreams, Claire would show up looking like she had clawed her way out of the dirt just to come haunt me.

Sometimes I let her.

"No one has used this in at least a century," Kneku's wistful voice echoed in the large ballroom. My eyes snapped to his voice and even through my eyes had blurred I could see his petite form make its way over to where I was seated. He wore the customary black kings' robes with loose pants underneath. Robes that Nitri had conveniently taken out of my mother's closet after disobeying him one too many times.

Kneku in my eyes was the best of the Kings. He had risked Nitri's anger every day that he came to seek me out. Faelin hadn't even dared so far as to come within a mile of me but

Kneku consistently sought me out, providing information I didn't even think to ask for.

"Well, I highly doubt Nitri is throwing a party anytime soon," I commented, letting a tired smile tug at my lips. It always took far too much effort to smile anymore. Kneku stopped in front of me, pushed back the flaps of his robe, and mirrored my position. The move, as casual as it may have been, made my heart skip a beat. Here an all-powerful being had resigned themselves to sit on the dirty ground with me. Baecos words rang through my head.

As a king I will only kneel for you.

The stark difference between him and the real king in front of me made my headache throb even harder.

"Nor has he, since he brought us here," Kneku commented, his lips pursed before speaking. "You are looking at your powers in the wrong way."

I raised my eyebrow at him.

"I'll bite," I told him. He smiled at my words.

"What a unique phrase, I like it," he said.

"A mortal phrase," I explained. "Learned it throughout the years."

"They are resilient that bunch." He cocked his head to the side and spread his palm towards the ceiling. A sparkling orb of blue appeared in his hand. "Your magic is intertwined, there is no separating them."

The orb elongated into a staff, blue still the main color but there was an unmistakable red hue that seemed to glare in the hard light. Just like his words said, the staff became the perfect picture of mix magic. The unmistakable water magic was there but the red held its own as if it refused to be overshadowed.

"I separated them once, I just don't remember how to again," I told him with a pout and conjured a small dagger in my hand. It was black as night with a same iridescent hue, except mine was golden like the sun in the other worlds.

"You will never separate them," he explained and his staff exploded into a million small glittering pieces. "The point is not to separate them. Like your strengths and weaknesses, they must feed off of each other to keep them strong. You will never find a person with only strengths; a weakness will be there no matter how small. Just focus on the strength the darkness provides instead of trying to pry your magic apart from the seams."

I tried to close my eyes and visualize the power in a way that he described, but I still could not tap into it like I had wanted. I expected once I was here all my memories would come back and I would know exactly how to control the darkness inside me, but I really had no clue what dark magic could even do.

"I regret to inform you that you may need a teacher," Kneku said. I opened my eyes and gave him a half serious glare. "At least someone to explain what the darkness can do."

I hated the way the Kings were able to know everything as if they could see through all of us. I had embarrassed myself enough in front of King Faelin and I couldn't even bare to think about the stream of thoughts that they had overheard from me before.

"You and Faelin have done that before. Is mind reading a Kings power?" I feigning annoyance. I would drink up any information he could give me about what might possibly lie ahead of me. Kneku smiled softly and reached his hand out to me, palm open once more. I put my hand in his cold one and felt a jolt go through me.

"Kings are connected to the universe in a way no mere magician could be. While we are not all seeing nor all-powerful the intentions, surface thoughts, feelings of others and even bits of the future can be within our grasp within seconds if we so wish it," he explained.

My headache was gone in a moment my mind expanded tenfold, bringing a new light to the power of the Kings. All the information passed through my head at a hundred miles an hour. I could see the history of the ballroom. The staff that would dance in here during a time where they thought no one could see them, the slaves that would come here for solstice after punishment. I could feel their feelings, hear bits of their thoughts. A wish for a better life, a joke passing through the lips of another that they suddenly remembered. All the information should have been overwhelming, should have made my head explode, but instead it was easy to collect the small bits of information and store them in my brain. It felt like my mind was limitless.

Kneku retreated his hand and with it, the expanded view of the world. The sereneness vanished and the throbbing headache snapped back like a rubber band.

"That was an example of what I felt in the past," he said. "I like to turn it down when I can, but that is a small preview of what it feels like to be intertwined in the universe."

"It's a lot," I resounded, trying to find the words to describe what I felt in the moments he had shown me, but I found none.

"Yes, it is." He mused.

"If Nitri can see the future, why does he refuse me to ascend so badly?" I asked. Kneku cocked his head, his silver hair bouncing with his movement. He painted a perfect picture of innocence but the strength of the magic that flowed through his veins was unmistakable.

"The universe... has its own agenda," Kneku explained. "I still do not have an understanding of what exactly is controlling our powers or brings forth the future."

"Is there a pattern to what it shows you?" Spiris asked and came to stand behind me, his knee brushing against my back. It ignited a spark that shot thought me and made my skin tingle, it was just a brush of a body part but there was rarely a time where I would allow us to touch outside the privacy of the bedroom.

I liked it. I realized. *Touch.*

"Yes," he said but did not elaborate, instead he just looked at me expectantly. I swallowed thickly.

"I've been meaning to ask," I said and leaned back into Spiris' touch for strength. "Why are the kings positioned the way they are, isn't it enough to have someone like Nitri rule over the worlds?"

It had bothered me the more I learned about this world. The court was even, coming in at four kings meaning there would always be a draw, that is if Nitri believed them to be on the same level as him. That was obviously not the case given the way he forced their hand. And even so if he wanted such a tight control over anything and everything, what was the use of people like Kneku, Faelin, and myself?

"I cannot begin to understand the motives behind an existence that I cannot see or hear, but I had assumed it was for the balancing act. The three kings would rule over their kingdoms and if there was any issue in the courts or the world, that's where Nitri would come in," he answered, his voice was still as wistful as ever but his facial expression tightened slightly.

"He doesn't trust his own kings," I summarized.

"Why is that?" Spiris asked from behind me.

"Your questions will get you in trouble one day, Spiris," Kneku deadpanned. His sharp gaze turned back to me and in the moment, I felt the world stop. "Iniq, tell me… what do you want?"

I floundered at his question. My mouth opened to respond but no words came out. I had many things I wanted though it had changed since I first came to this world.

I was a lost girl that had been outcast by a home that was never even her real home. I wanted to find a place where I was excited to *be*. Be someone that mattered. Back then the pull of power pushed me forward... but now?

I wanted to show the world that I was worthy of the throne

and the power that had been handed to me. There were times where I hated it before, times where I wished to go back to the little mortal home that I had grown up in, but those times were over. I now had an entire kingdom that was suffering because of an empty seat that *I* was supposed to fill. But even through all that, the fears that had hidden themselves deep in my mind came forward once more.

You are weak.

You are a coward.

You will never be good enough for the throne.

"I don't know," I answered truthfully. There were many things I wanted... but were they even possible? He nodded like he expected my answer.

"So, becoming King then?" he asked but without my response he continued. "Is it because it's what you were born to do? Is it because it's your only option? Tell me Iniq, did you ever think about beyond what you can see right now?"

I cast my eyes downward to look at my lap. This time it was shame that filled me. I hadn't, even as I thought about ascending to the throne, I had no idea what a future for me looked like afterwards. Would I be stuck here for the rest of my existence? Watching as my offspring left the castle and I stayed behind to watch over the Kingdom? The stark realization of the possibility that I might never see the blue sky again weighed on me heavily.

"This will be your downfall, Iniq," he said earnestly. "Kings are supposed to be in their position because they love their people and want to do right by them. It is not for power. It is not to show the people that you can. You should do this because you offer a chance to build this world anew."

His words overwhelmed me. The Light Kingdom was perishing, and I was sitting here in a ballroom for hours on end while they died. It may have hit me hard when I saw the poor children in the Light Kingdom for the first time... but now the fears of my worthlessness overshadowed everything else.

I didn't even know if it was possible for *someone like me* to build such change.

"High King Kneku," Spiris spoked from behind me. "Was this what the universe asked of you?"

Kneku sent him a smile. "I hope Iniq, that when you are finally king you can set forth motions that will change the way we think about our duties as Kings, but you need to find the way to do that. I am here to tell you that practicing alone in an abandoned ballroom it not the way."

He gave me a hard look and then got up to leave.

"Then what is the way, Kneku?" I yelled after him.

He paused and turned to give me a smile. "If you cannot figure this out yourself, then maybe you are as weak as Nitri seems to believe," he paused. "But I doubt that's the case."

His eyes widened, then he looked forward once more.

"On an unrelated note. Aselia is coming back to us if you are curious about Nitri's offspring I suggest you go to the throne room before you miss her."

Without another word he was gone.

"It's totally not on an unrelated note," I huffed to Spiris as we jogged to the throne room. He had helped me skip toward the end of the hall for us not to attract too much attention from Nitri, but the end of the hall seemed to stretch on for miles and by halfway I was panting.

Once I got to the open doors of the throne room I paused and took a deep breath to try and calm my over worked heart, then stepped in. The throne room never failed to take my breath away. I had once thought the mansions that Baecos owned were the fanciest things I had come across, but the throne room of the castle made those mansions look like doll houses.

The pitch-black chairs had iron like vines for backings that twisted grotesquely together and flowed behind the kings who sat in them like dark tentacles. The black marble floors had only small whisps of white in them contrasting the red chandeliers hanging from the ceiling. They were together in bunches and left a sinister feeling to the throne room, as if there was blood dripping from above us ready to drop down any moment,

Nitri looked like the king he tried to portray himself as, sitting on top of the black throne in his black robe. He rested his face on one hand while his legs were crossed, giving of an air of boredom. His long blond hair fell over the sides of the throne giving him a regal look, but the cat like golden eyes cut through the charade. Inside him was the same person that had greeted me in such a disgusting way when I first came to this realm. He was vile and I couldn't help but pity the offspring that came from him as they were no doubt conceived in the same way he had used on that poor maid.

For the first time, there was a figure other than the Kings that occupied the throne room. She seemed to be a similar stature and build as I, but that was where the similarities stopped. She turned at my intrusion, her silky long black hair that was pulled into a tight ponytail on the top of her head whipping around her as she did. She had pointed ears and small neat black horns that curled on the top of her head. Her golden eyes narrowed in my direction and her full pink lips quickly twisted into a frown.

"Well, aren't you going to introduce yourself?" she snapped at me. The white long-sleeved shirt pulled against her form as her arms crossed and she jutted her hip out causing her black baggy pants to sway.

Damn. I felt a prick of irritation play at my senses. All the pity I had felt for her up until this moment quickly dried up.

"My name is Iniq," I responded. "The next Light and Dark King."

She paused for only a moment and then let out a harsh laugh that bounced around the empty space of the room. My neck became hot and I had to clench my fists tightly in order to calm myself. I wanted nothing more than to fight her right now. It was different when Nitri had called me weak and berated me, but someone like her who was in a position so similar to mine should know better.

"Aselia." Nitri scolded half-heartedly. The twist at the left side of his mouth showed me he did not mind her actions one bit.

"Sorry Father, I just assumed she figured it out by now," she replied with a smirk. Her gold eyes twinkled with amusement. I ground my teeth together and fisted my hand.

"Figured what, *Aselia*," I hissed at her. Spiris' hand came to rest on my shoulder, but it did the opposite of the grounding I knew it was meant to. It made me want to lunge at her. Aselia's eyes flickered to it and her smile widened.

"Father would never let a half blood like you onto the throne. No, half-blood isn't even correct anymore. You are barely a magician in that body. How you even crossed into this world is beyond me," Aselia said with a laugh and covered her face with her hand in attempt at mock modesty. I do not know where she got the nerve to treat others like she was, but it made me pray that Nitri never conceived a child ever again. I would not be able to handle multiples of these *brats*.

"It is my birth right," I told her. "There is no one else to take the position and the world is crumbling as you stand there laughing."

I felt my magic rise within me as if it was as angry as I was.

"You were never the only choice, Iniq." Nitri said. I met his gaze and the smile had widened now, showing the edges of his fangs.

This was *my right*. This was my only calling in this pitiful life and now he wanted to take the rug out right from under my feet? He was a sadistic bastard that was just stringing me along, dangling the prize of the throne in front of me when he knew damn well he would cut the string as soon as I was close.

"If you had other choices why call me here? Why not fill the throne as soon as possible? Why let millions die?" I asked, my voice raising with each word.

I may have not known what I wanted but there was no way a King could sit by and watch as all those people die. Kneku had said so himself, this was the *sole purpose* of a king and they both just laughed it off?

"Because *I* was off training," Aselia said with a sly smile. She strutted her long legs over to me and leaned in close to my ear as if to tell me a secret. "And that position *will* go to me once I complete my darkness training."

I was so shocked at her words I couldn't even move. How dare Nitri give the throne to his own flesh and blood? This was *my* birth right and I was the only one with both Light and Dark, why on earth would Nitri's offspring take that?

"Ah, I see," I said, an easier smile forming on my own face. I let out a giggle. Aselia's spine snapped back into position, and she stepped away from me. I held onto the way it caused a flutter of excitement to fan in my chest. "It's because *High King Nitri* never plans to give up his throne so he planned to put his biggest threat in a position that would ensure that she would never fight back... isn't that right, Nitri?"

I didn't have to read his mind to know I was right. He glowered at me from his position on the throne. His hands were gripping the edge of the arm rests so hard I could hear it cracking. His chest puffed with anger and I had the distinct image of a dragon glaring down at me ready to burn my body to a crisp.

"It is because you are weak. Being halfblooded is a disgrace for a king, yes, but even that could have been overlooked if you were powerful." He reposted his tone cool. "Millions of deaths or not, I will not put *just anyone* on the throne."

"It has nothing to do with power!" as I yelled, a stream of magic burst through me and hit the chandelier, causing it to rain blood like glass "You are a manipulative controlling King that cannot trust even the people who have been at your side for a millennium!" Spiris's hand became a death grip on my shoulder. "Regardless of me or Aselia do you really think that will change, Nitri? Seeing how you treat your servants I can only guess what you did to your own flesh."

There was a pause between the four of us as they digested my words.

Nitri is going to kill me. I groaned internally.

"You should have stayed dead," Aselia said, breaking the silence between us. Her eyes were hard but I didn't miss the way they widened when I raised my voice. She turned to her Father once more, "I will leave in three days' time." He nodded and waved to dismiss her.

She hit my shoulder as she passed me.

"Don't confuse the door with me, child." Nitri warned. He rested his cheek on his hand as if bored with the display. "I did not call you here. If there is one bit of honesty you deserve it is this: I never wanted you here and hoped that when Baecos had killed you last, like the words of my daughter, you should have stayed dead. This is your last warning before I end you myself."

I turned and left before I blew up the entire room.

The magic that I unleashed earlier in the day continued to course through me, causing me to seek out the solace of the garden. It was a different one than the one attached to my mother's room.

For the first time, I didn't want Spiris watching over me. I

left him in his quarters as he prepared for bed. It was the combi-
nation of guilt and shame that pushed me to leave him so
suddenly. Pushing Nitri like that was stupid, it not only endan-
gered myself but him as well. For someone who was still
haunted by his death in my dreams, it was just plain stupid for
me to go up against Nitri like this.

When I reached the entrance to the gardens, I was shocked to
see the once fierce looking Aselia starting up at the red moon with
an expression that resembled sadness. The girl who had wished
me to die was gone, and in her place was someone so looked to be
just as trapped and hopeless as anyone else in the castle.

"Came to fight me for your throne? Maybe slit my throat in
the middle of the night when no one was looking? They'd knew
it was you in minutes," she said with a deadpan look as her eyes
lazily made contact with mine. I could not tell if she was joking.

"I just wanted to come for a walk," I said. "It's hard being
cooped up in the castle."

She snorted. "You have been here what, a few months?" She
asked. "Imagine being here for nine hundred years."

"You were not here when I came to this world," I noted. I
brushed my hand over a deep blue rose, enjoying the feeling of
its' magic on my fingertips. I was beyond angry at her but something in her face told me that there was more to what I had seen
in the throne room.

I let my magic reach out to her, trying to make it as delicate
as possible. Her thoughts rushed through me. Images I recognized from lifetimes ago. Another castle, but this time in the
magical world. The rolling hills were filled with bright green
grass and only interrupted by various kinds of flowers all the
color of a burning flame. Then a person appeared in her
thoughts. A person I knew too well. Cruor sat on her own
golden throne as Aselia stood in front of her, there was a frown
on her face. I snapped my magic back to me, unable to look at

Cruor's face any longer without feeling the bond lash out widely.

"I was training," she said and plucked a blue rose off its stem. She lit it on fire. "Such a useless power. Kneku pushed me to learn from a king but it was otherwise a worthless trip." Why did I bristle at her words? I didn't like my body's reaction to someone insulting Cruor, even if it wasn't direct. "You were right, you know."

"I was?" I couldn't stop the shocked words from falling out of my mouth. She gave me a smile like we were sharing a joke.

"It has never been about your weakness," she said. "Control is his thing. I wasn't around yet for our entrance into this world but I can guess it started around then."

"The mistrust," I said.

"The fear," she corrected. The way the darkness danced behind her eyes caused my chest to constrict.

"Did you learn light yet?" I asked, trying to ease the panic that clawed at my throat. My words came out thick.

"Some," she admitted and sent me a smile. "Your mom was a delight to work with. I am sorry to say her child turned out so pathetic."

And there the fire was again. I had thought the Aselia I saw with her father was gone. She didn't realize how much fire magic suited her.

"I didn't know someone so old could be so petty," I commented and enjoyed the way she scowled at me.

"Your first form was good for a while though," she admitted. "I hoped that you would hold on to that. Even from so far my heart sped up when your name was mentioned."

"The power?" I asked not fully getting her words.

"The blood lust," she said her eyes narrowing dangerously at me.

I paused remembering the way Claire's neck snapped. I

would be thankful to never lose myself again like that if possible.

"Where are you going in three days?" I asked her and picked off my own rose. The magic seeped out of it in waves as it died in my hands.

"Father is pushing me to learn Dark magic from the Dark King," she said. "I guess he really doesn't want you on the throne, not that I could blame him though."

I tried not to fall into her coaxing.

"Why does he let you leave but not the other kings?" I asked.

She turned and walked towards me, this time she did not brush against my shoulder. She paused when we were shoulder to shoulder, her gold eyes meeting mine.

"He does not care if I die in the magical world," she said. "He may harp on you being a weak half breed, but he does not look over the danger of Baecos still living in the magical world. If I were to die, he can create another child. If you were to die, the light and dark bloodline would die with you."

I stilled and she used that to leave me standing in the middle of the garden alone.

CHAPTER FOUR
SPIRIS

I thought I was over the panic. Over the gut-wrenching terror I felt under the reign of Baecos. I thought that once we left that damned disgusting place that the ice cold fear would leave my veins, but instead it never left. It was in hiding and only poked its' head out in times like this.

I sat in the dark on Iniq's cold bed not knowing what to do. She left me while I was in the shower and when I came to say goodnight to her, she was nowhere to be seen. I had half a mind to run out of this room and through the decrepit hallways to try and find her, but instead I tried to work through calming steps in my mind.

Nitri had threatened her for the last time. However much Iniq tried to push him, she must have realized he was serious, right? Would he dare take her so boldly?

I wanted to believe the universe would have given a sign to one of the kings if he were to try something. After all this time and fighting it couldn't end here, right? I ran my hands through my wet hair, yanking at it to try and focus on anything but the thought of Iniq showing up dead once more under my watch.

I had only set out to do one thing as I was reborn into this world. Protect Iniq. All I wanted was to make sure she could live the life she deserved. My own selfish thoughts told me to steal her from here and take her to a place where no one would find us. We could live out our lives in peace not having to worry about Nitri, or Baecos, or even Cruor.

But I knew she would not settle for that. She continued to run headfirst into danger like it was her longtime friend, and now I only hoped she was not paying the consequences of those actions.

I decided in my mind that I would give her another few minutes and if she still did not return, I would seek her out. I would tear this castle from inside out and scream down the hallways if I had to. I would challenge Nitri head on, even though the promised outcome was certain death.

As if the universe heard my prayers Iniq's head popped through the door. She gave me a surprised look. Her bright green eyes were still in her skull, her milky skin had no wounds or blood seeping from it, the only thing wrong seemed to be her permanent dark circles.

"Spiris? Were you waiting for me?" she asked and shut the door as she entered. She gave me a small unassuming smile and sat next to me. I wanted nothing more than to pull her close, just like I had after her nightmares, only then would my fears be calmed.

"Just wanted to wish you goodnight," I told her.

I looked to her lips, remembering the time before I was forced into my current body. Would it be so bad to bridge the gap that had been created between us? She had pushed me away from her previously every time I had tried to feel my skin against hers, but today she allowed it. I prayed it was a sign that she was open to more than just the late-night secret cuddles but didn't want to get my hopes up especially when the demon king himself had warned me about my status.

"You are a slave here, Spiris. As lowly as they come. Even if Iniq is unworthy of becoming a King do not forget your status and hers. She is birthed from one of us and for some reason the universe decided to give you a second chance." His words cut deep even if they were spoken as if he was just discussing the weather.

He leaned close to my ear.

"If it was my choice, I would have left you dead. At least that would leave Iniq room to grow a bit of courage."

She gave me a small smile and this time without my prompting she reached for my hand, her delicate fingers curling around mine softly. My heart soared.

"Goodnight, Spiris," she said. I gave her a small smile in return and pulled my hand out of hers to go to my own quarters. I rushed past my ajar door and shut it as softly as I could. Only once I heard her light footsteps move across the room did I let out an exhale.

Even though she was obviously safe in the next room my heart did not cease its' sprint in my chest. All of the situations of her getting hurt or killed ran through me head repeatedly. Why didn't she tell me where she went? Was there something she didn't want me to know? I had gotten so caught up in the way she held my hand that I lost myself for a moment.

I swallowed thickly.

Why didn't I ask? This isn't back in the light kingdom. Even if Nitri was sour about my presence here, why should I still act this way?

I took a deep breath and sunk to the ground, my back to the door. I leaned my head back and looked at the decorative ceiling in the slave room they gave me. I wasn't sure if such extravagant rooms were normal for slaves or if Iniq's mom just loved her slave more than the other kings but the room was barely smaller than the one I had in the light kingdom. There was a fourposter bed, two nightstands, a dresser, and an adjoining bathroom. Everything was dressed in blacks and reds. I saw a hint of gold in the trimmings of some of the furniture but besides that the atmosphere was the same as the rest of the godforsaken castle.

"Safe," I whispered to no one in particular. I tried to focus on the way the molding in the ceiling swirled, hoping to calm my racing mind. "We are safe and we are free."

I left Iniq to her training alone the next day. There were only a few times where I felt she needed space and after much more rational thinking in the morning, I assumed her absence was a sign she needed it.

I walked the maze-like corridors searching for the library I had passed a handful of times since arriving. My curiosity peaked when I was first able to peer inside the dusty room. It was as big as the ballroom and had hundreds of shelves of books. I couldn't get it out of my mind, what would gods need with books? The thought seemed absurd but made it all the more enticing. The library was all but calling me in to take a look.

I opened the door slowly, the scent of aging books filling my sense immediately. I wandered in between the aisles looking for something interesting, but it was all in a language I couldn't understand. As I was reaching for a book, a voice startled me.

"Surprised to see you away from your loved one." Kneku's voice said, his form appearing at the end of the aisle. He was not holding any books and he stood with his arms crossed, his golden eyes seeming to glint from the dim lights above.

He had long since deduced my feelings for Iniq and had called me on it whenever he had the chance. He rarely did it in front of Iniq any longer, but it didn't stop the heat from raising to my skin. It felt like a father or a mentor teasing you about a crush you had, even if the love I felt for Iniq was much stronger than that.

"Some separation is good," I told him. "I didn't know kings read," I gestured to the books. "Don't you just know all this already?

Kneku gave me a small smile. "Books are useless to us," he held up a suspiciously modern looking version of a playing card deck. "We do enjoy a good game though."

I let myself smile at his offer and followed him over to a seating area at the other end of the library. The chairs were leather and I had to wipe a bit of dust off the chair before sitting. Kneku did the same and started to deal cards. Like many areas of the castle, the library seemed to be abandoned for a long time. While places like the ballroom kept their shine, the dust attached itself to every surface in here made my hypersensitive nose itch.

"Let's start simple," he said. "Highest card takes the other," he lifted up a card that signified the trump card, on it was an elaborate jet-black painted demon with red glowing eyes on a white background. The other side of the decks were just as black but if you looked closely, you could make out the swirls of grey hidden among the shadows. "High or low?"

"High," I responded. He nodded, shuffled the remaining cards, then put them into two equal piles. He pushed one towards me.

"Cards remain in the deck, you pick from the top when it's your turn," he explained. "Winning pile goes on the opposite side and we can reshuffle it once we finish the game... question?"

"Can't you cheat?" I asked and traced my finger alongside the figure of the supposed queen. She looked sad in this deck.

"I turned it off when I heard your incessant swooning over your loved one," I gaped at him then dropped my gaze to my cards. The next time I looked up Kneku was giving me a wide smile. "I'm sure one day she will appreciate your obsession but do think of yourself once in a while. I'll go first," he flipped the card over onto the table and the dust scattered.

The number six.

I did the same.

It was a number five.

He smiled and took my cards to put it in his pile.

I went again. A King.

He went and put down a two.

I took his cards.

The slaps of the cards on the table got faster as we acclimated to each other's rhythm. It was nice to lose yourself in the game, not thinking too hard about any one thing. I was enjoying the silence until Kneku spoke again.

"Did you two ever reach Aselia on time?" he asked as he slapped down a demon. I threw my card down allowing him to take it.

"Yes, she was less than pleasant," I told him.

"She has had a difficult upbringing," he said.

"What makes it so hard about being Nitri's daughter? He could give her the world, literally," I said with a scoff.

"Nitri once had many offspring," Kneku explained. He paused for a moment, his golden eyes searching over my face. "None of them he would dare lift a finger for, much less an entire world."

"We have only heard of Aselia," I told him.

"Yes. She is the last one left."

I didn't care for Aselia, but the way Kneku spoke about her siblings make the air in the room freeze. There was only one meaning to his words.

"Who would dare kill a kings' offspring? And Nitri's nonetheless?" I asked in a hushed whisper as if that would help anything,

"I have had a loose tongue as of late," he said, putting an end to the conversation.

I nodded and tried a different probe.

"Why does Nitri insist on giving her the throne?"

Kneku paused a moment, his petite fingers running the length of his deck of cards before he spoke.

"I believe your little king hit the nail on the head yesterday. I do not dare say more than that." He slapped down a three.

I placed a two softly on the table. I thought about Iniq's words yesterday.

It's because High King Nitri never plans to give up his throne so he planned to put his biggest threat in a position that would ensure that she would never fight back... isn't that right Nitri?

I ran out of cards in my pile and reached for my winning pile. Kneku did the same. I noticed his pile was much bigger than mine, he was sure to win.

I turned over the first card and a jolt went through me when I came face to face with the grotesque demon. I met his eyes and Kneku gave a small smile.

"Don't forget who you are, Spiris. Love is a beautiful thing but *obsession* can be dangerous," he said, his voice soft and wistful. "You will have a very long journey ahead of you."

He pushed forward his deck of cards and got up to stretch his neck, his silver head bouncing lightly around his head.

"I believe your king is waiting for you," he said and without another word he disappeared behind a bookshelf, his black robe flowing as he walked.

I cleaned up the cards and placed them in the middle of the table. My hand paused on the demon card. Before I thought too much about it, I slipped it into my pocket.

Aselia was waiting outside the door to the ballroom, peering in and watching Iniq as she pushed magic dark as night around her. Her hair was tied up high in a ponytail and she wore the customary black robe that the other kings had donned. Her eyebrows were pushed together and she had a small pout.

"Sizing up the competition?" I asked her. She jumped at the sound of my voice. Satisfaction unfurled in me when I saw her reaction. *So much for a king.*

"Don't speak so informally to me, slave," she spit out, but her eyes didn't hold the same anger as her words may have seemed to carry.

"Kings should treat their people with kindness, slave or not," I told her and let my eyes wander back to Iniq. She had yet to notice us and a semi-circle of dark magic began to grow around her. My chest caught. The last time this had happened was when she remembered something terrible and as if on instinct the dark magic shot out to wrap her in an impenetrable cocoon.

"Kindness makes kings weak," she mumbled.

Slowly the dark magic began to cover Iniq. My heart sped up and panic set in as it did but I tried to hold myself in place. Tried to trust that Iniq had a handle on it.

After not even a second the darkness disappeared and Iniq's wide green eyes met mine. There was a smile on her lips, I couldn't help but return it.

"I beg to differ," I responded and entered the ballroom to meet Iniq. She was dripping in sweat and her hair was a mess around her head but she was happier than I had seen her in weeks.

"I remember seeing you at a party in the fire kingdom," Iniq said jumping up to grasp at my hands when I was close enough. "We were children, we didn't talk but I remember your frown from anywhere."

I racked my brain to try and pull the memory up from the depths of my mind, but I couldn't find it. There had been many times I had caught a glimpse of Iniq before at the Light Kingdom but once Baecos had taken over as ruler I did not remember another time that I had seen Iniq when we were still young.

Iniq's smile dropped slightly.

"I'm sorry Iniq, I don't remember that time," I said, feeling bad about not being able to connect with one of the only memories she had gotten while in this realm.

"It's okay," she assured. "I saw you only by chance, nothing important to remember."

Her hand brushed the side of my jaw, startling me and stopping my breathing in its' tracks. I leaned into her hand, unsure anymore if what I was witnessing was real life or another one of those dreams that left my knees weak.

I am such a lovesick puppy and bend at the smallest things, but how could I ever get over these touches?

"So, this is the *kindness* you talk about slave. Disgusting for a king to act like that," Aselia said from behind me. Iniq's smile faltered even further and she peered behind me.

"Aselia," Iniq greeted. I stepped aside, hating the way her hand dropped and turned to face the interruption. I was sure she would have left by now but I guessed beggars could not be choosers.

"What do you need?" I asked her. She glared at me but answered anyways.

"You know some dark magic, and I would like to not look like such a fool when I meet the Dark King," she explained.

"Why would I teach my direct competitor?" Iniq crossed her arms over her chest.

Aselia shifted on her feet and her scowl deepened. It was as if she expected Iniq to say yes with no questions asked. Nitri seemed to have coddled her more than Kneku let on.

"Think of it as a way to build our relationship. We will need each other regardless of who sits on the throne at the end."

Iniq rolled her eyes. "Take me with you, when you go training next."

My gaze snapped to Iniq, she sent me a smile that did not calm the new panic that raised inside me.

"Nitri will be mad."

"You have a death wish?"

Aselia and I asked at the same time. I sent her a small glare which she returned.

"I don't care," Iniq said. "I need to learn darkness and this may be the last time I can see that world again. You know how he refuses to let his kings leave."

A part of me, the insecure part, had a feeling that there was also a person that Iniq wanted to see in the other magical realm but I pushed that away. I saw how Cruor treated her at the very end, she wouldn't even look twice at her.

"We can make it a competition," Aselia said after I was sure her silence indicated a refusal. "Whoever learns the fastest gets the throne. It's your death wish, Nitri isn't the only threat if you do this."

My blood turned to ice in my veins and my stomach sank to the floor.

No, how could I forget?

Baecos would feel us as soon as we entered. How could he not? Even someone as powerful as Aselia standing here unscathed was a miracle. He had to have felt the power shift in the world when someone like a King's offspring stepped out of that door.

What would happen if he cornered us? Would both of them and myself be enough to survive? Iniq's powers were still partially sealed and it would put us at a severe disadvantage if she tried to battle. Not to mention my brother would be there as well. He was ruthless.

My heart stopped when I watched as the smile I hated so much slowly made its way across her face.

No, Iniq. I begged in my mind hoping she could hear. *Please think this through. The throne is not worth Baecos. I can take you anywhere but there, we can be happy without the throne.*

She didn't even look at me when she answered.

"You have yourself a deal."

CHAPTER FIVE
CRUOR

I slammed my fist against the table, splintering the wood and sending it flying towards the shocked faces around me. The officers surrounding the table jumped but my court standing behind me were used to my outbursts and didn't even flinch. I ground my teeth together trying to hold in all the curses that wanted to spill out of my mouth.

They were all useless. Every last one of them. They had *one* job: Get Callum to confess every one of his interactions with Baecos. Get him to tell us why he would have attempted something so stupid.

"What do you mean he refuses to talk?" I growled at the men in front of me slowly meeting each of their eyes. The way they cowardly stared at my gaze gave me a small bit of satisfaction, but it paled in comparison to the anger that I felt. "We have been at this for months and you still have nothing to give me?"

We had taken over a cozy conference room on the west side of the castle. There a dark wood table that I had just damaged due to my punches, the wall to floor windows gave us a clear view of the green hills outside and a beautiful orange setting sun. If this was a better conversation I would have loved to relax in here as the sun set, but that was not the reason we chose this room. We chose this room because it was the closest to our dungeon. Closest to where Callum was being held for questioning since *that* incident. Once we had run Baecos and Vitos away from the water kingdom, Callum almost collapsed into tears over his sister's dead body and confessed to partnering with Baecos.

I couldn't believe my ears when he confessed. I couldn't understand how the hound that I had taken in as a pup, and raised the best way I knew how, could have turned on me so easily. I stayed up with him during the night when he had bad dreams, I fed him, clothed him, gave them status, hell even when Iniq was here they looked at her like a mother. Yet he partnered with the one person that was trying to kill her.

I didn't fully forgive Iniq for killing Claire, but I did understand it now. Claire as much as Callum had been the pups of the kingdom and grew up under our watch. It was hard to realize that the one I was fated to mate would kill Claire in cold blood... but the same went for those pups. Iniq had been there for every step until she had been captured, and they still turned on her.

I just needed to know why.

"My lord," spoke a water magician from the third seat to my right. "We have tried everything you have *allowed* us to."

"Which is not much. He is more comfortable than any of the other traitors we have taken in the last hundred years." piped in a fire demon. I glared at him. "At least let us cause some permanent damage. Pulling out an eye had been a sure-fire technique. I can have the information to you in less than a few hours."

"Have you heard of the earth bugs?" a fire magician spoke from the end of the table. "Centipedes, I think? Those would be fun."

I felt my magic explode around me. My chest was heaving as I tried to reel it in. This was the council I entrusted to get rid of the crime in my kingdom, they also got information out of spies, but it had been years since we had gotten one and the newest one just so happened to be Callum. I couldn't bear to think of them inflicting such pain on the poor boy, he may have messed up but his crying face was enough to send shudders throughout my entire body.

Ash's hand found it's home on my shoulder.

"You will obey what our King has laid out for you," he spoke in the hardest tone I have ever heard him utter. "Do not make this harder than it is. We pay you to do a job, and from what it looks like you have been doing a whole lot of nothing."

"Budget cuts may be in order." Felix said from behind me in a deadpan voice.

I was surprised Felix stuck around after the death of his longtime lover, Claire. It had taken me awhile to forgive her even with the bond in place, I was sure that Felix may never forgive her for as long as he lived. I didn't tell him that I had caught him in the garden outside of Claire's old room almost every night. Nor did I tell him I saw the tears when he thought no one was looking.

The men in front of me paled considerably at his threat.

I pushed the chair over and stalked out of the room. I tried to take deep breaths as I led myself down the familiar winding staircase to the dungeon where Callum was being held. I visited him at least once a week since he had been put down here just to make sure that the old bastards didn't get trigger happy.

"Cruor," Ash called after me.

I only heard one pair of footsteps so I was guessing Felix could not handle seeing Callum just yet. He had not been as keen to visiting him as I had been. We had spoken about Callum's influence on Claire before and refused to talk about it since. Even though they both would have been guilty, Callum was no doubt the one who guided his sister to make her mistakes. It had been like that since they were young, pushing Claire to sneak out of the fire kingdoms' barriers to explore the woods at night when no one was looking, throwing food at the elders in the dining hall.

I entered the damp dungeon and headed straight to cell number five. There were no other prisoners at the time, but in my anger, I asked that he be put in the darkest cell leading him to be permanently tied to cell five where the sun was sure to never shine. It was the cruelest I could have been at the time despite my anger. He had been fitted with special chains that locked any magical power that he had and forced him to stop shifting all together.

"You little shit," I called as I rounded the corner to cell five.

When the cell finally came into view my feet rooted in their place and my magic was extinguished like there had been a bucket of water thrown on my head. My heart and breathing felt like it stopped in sync. Ash stopped besides me and I heard him curse.

"Call the guards *now*," I hissed, unable to take my eyes off the cell. "Check the vaults, check my office, get them to reinforce the barriers, and for the fucks sake fire those goddamn guards that allowed this to happen!"

My voice vibrated off the stone walls. Ash trailed away from me, leaving me alone with the disaster.

Before me was the same cell that I had seen hundreds of times before. The thick blanket I had given him was covered in dark blood, the tray of food from the kitchen had been broken clean in half and even the metal bed was dented. Callum was no longer in the cell, instead the chains that had held him before had been unlocked and now laid on the ground with the key still stuck inside them and on the wall was a message written in blood:

Nice try.

I reached out with my magic to see if I could still decipher the magical signature and bile rose up in my throat so fast, I had to clutch my mouth and scramble back, away from the blood. My back hit the cold iron bars behind me.

It was Baecos blood, but the unmistakable thrum of Iniq's magic was still deeply intertwined with it. Baecos had come into *my* kingdom, stolen *my* prisoner, and even stopped to write a note in his own blood to taunt me.

"Cruor." Felix's voice called from the entrance to the dungeon.

"Get the army. Baecos could still be here." the words came out panicked.

"He already left." Felix said. My gaze snapped towards him and I was met with Claire's severed head. "And he handed me a present as he did so."

Felix cradled her head as if it was a baby and this time, he did not try to hide his tears.

"He defiled her grave." my voice cracked as I spoke.

Felix could no longer speak. The normally collected man fell to his knees and began sobbing just like the day that she had died.

"I'm going after that fucker," I croaked and left Felix on the cold stone ground hunched over Claire's head.

CHAPTER SIX
INIQ

*I*t had been awhile since I had seen Spiris so anxious. He paced the length of my room and pulled at the ends of his curly hair. It had been over an hour since he had started this and with every attempt to pull him back to me he would just stare at me with those jet-black eyes and continue to pace.

"Spiris, talk to me," I begged from my place at the end of the bed. I had long since changed into a sleep robe and when I had come back into the room from the bathroom he was still pacing.

He paused and walked over to my place at the end of the bed. My knees brushed his, I had to lean back on my hands so I could hold his stare.

"Why would you agree?" he asked, his voice held none of the anxiety his body was showing. I cocked my head to the side.

Why was this even a question?

"So, I can become king," I told him.

"Do you really think at half your power you can learn faster than Aselia? Not to mention you have to persuade the Dark King to teach you," Spiris said.

I looked away from him, unable to hold his gaze any longer.

"I can do it," I muttered.

His strong hand gripped at my chin and forced me to meet his eyes once more. I couldn't deny the way the forceful nature of his action made my stomach twist. The angry look on his handsome face made my heart speed up and I knew that if this reaction was guaranteed every time I had done something he didn't like, there would be no stopping me from going against him more often.

"The Dark King hasn't accepted visitors in centuries," he growled. "Why do you think your past self's dark power was so unknown? Because even the old Iniq didn't know how to *fully* use her power."

Old Iniq. The words kind of stung.

"I am different," I huffed and felt strongly like a two-year-old going against their mother but I wanted to see how far I could push him. Spiris let go of my chin and pushed me back down into the bed, I spread my legs to allow him closer access. He leaned over me, his face close to mine. My heart began to pick up at the position we were in, and my back arched without me thinking about it. We shared a bed but we had never been in such a situation before. The tension skyrocketed and the hardness in his eyes that I took as anger festered into something else.

My body was so willing to lean into his touch, wanted so badly to close the less than an inch space between our chests. His thighs brushed across the inside of mine and I lost my train of thought with him so close. Why was I so adamant about pushing *this* away? All the excuses flitted away from my mind as his curly hair tickled my cheek.

"Why must you run headfirst into danger?" he asked. "Can't you just stay safe? Stay here, with me?" I licked my dry lips. I was all too aware that the position left my robe in disarray showing more skin than I had anticipated. Even though the flaps of my robe were flipped over my thighs and the chest of my robe was open showing an indecent amount of skin, his eyes never wandered from mine. "We could rest here. Be happy. You need not fight for a responsibility that you do not desire."

His hand came up to cup my flaming face, I leaned into it. The desire to run my hand through his curls and pull his face to mine was overwhelming.

"I do want it," I said, my voice hoarse. "I want to be King."

He paused, then let his hand trail from my face to my neck, then to my collar bone. His fingers were light as they played with the edge of my robe, like he was considering the meaning of the stupid fabric.

"Why?" he asked, his voice barely above a whisper. His face was so close to mine now, just one more breath and I could close the gap.

"My life has been shit because the universe decided to give me the powers that I have," I spoke honestly. "The least I could do is demand the power that is rightfully mine. And it is not fair that so many suffer when the problem can be easily fixed."

"And what will you do with that power?" he asked as his fingers played at the hem of my robe.

"Destroy Baecos and create peace in the magical world," I vowed to him. His fingers snapped back like they'd been burned. He stood up abruptly and held me to his chest. Inhaled deeply and buried my head into his dark shirt.

He played with my hair lightly and did not speak for a few moments.

"Are you sure you do not just want to live out your life here *with me?*"

My heart pounded in my chest. I knew his question had a million meanings to it so instead I looked up to him and gave him a smile.

"I want you to come with me and reclaim the Light Kingdom. After we take care of what we need to I can promise you that no one will separate us."

Spiris gave me a toothy grin that showed his new fangs.

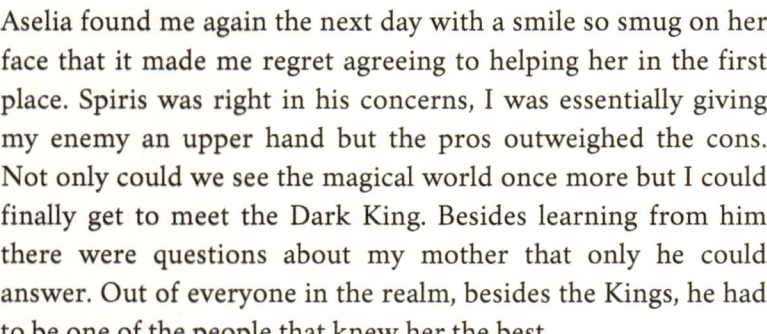

Aselia found me again the next day with a smile so smug on her face that it made me regret agreeing to helping her in the first place. Spiris was right in his concerns, I was essentially giving my enemy an upper hand but the pros outweighed the cons. Not only could we see the magical world once more but I could finally get to meet the Dark King. Besides learning from him there were questions about my mother that only he could answer. Out of everyone in the realm, besides the Kings, he had to be one of the people that knew her the best.

"Alright, where do we start?" Aselia asked and sat down in front of me much like Kneku had the other day. Her long hair was down and spilled over her shoulders, she placed a stand behind her ear showcasing its' pointed tip. She was dressed in the same kings robe that reminded me how Nitri had stolen my mother's robes from her closet.

Aselia was everything I was being denied. She was a full demon, had her father's support in taking over the kingdom, she could come and go as she pleased. As much as it angered me, I still couldn't get the image of her staring up solemnly at the moon out of my mind.

"Reach your magic out to me but make it discreet, invisible," I told her, trying to channel my inner Spiris. How a light magician could teach me dark tricks while only having one power was beyond me, but it just proved how talented he was in the first place.

She raised her eyebrow at me and reached out her magic slowly. It started at my feet then slowly made its way up my body. Her magic excited my skin and caused my own magic to react violently, tugging and pulling at me to consume some. Each person had their own signature with their own elemental attributes but hers... I could almost feel how well rounded it was and distinctly make out the different types of magic that swirled within her.

But that's where it stopped.

Even as her magic covered my head, something felt off.

Can you hear this? I asked in my head. She gave no response.

I reached my own magic out to her not trying to hide the intent behind it, I wanted her to feel what it was like for someone to invade her mind so she could replicate it. I felt her shock when she felt it and her mind was trying to piece together what was happening, but she couldn't locate the source of the intrusion.

Can you feel when I enter your mind? I asked inside her head.

Yes. She answered back hesitantly.

Try to do the same to me. I told her.

I felt her magic change slightly, becoming harsher but I could not tell if she had breached my mind yet. I pulled my own magic back from her to give her some time. Her magic tries to prove at my mind, but it never fully sunk in.

"Spiris," I called. He was by my side in an instant and sitting next to on the cold ground. His leg brushed cross mine as he did, bringing back memories of the night before. "I don't understand what is different. She cannot get in."

Spiris's eyes washed over Aselia, she met him back with a pout.

"She may have an intent issue." He explained. "Learning dark last may hinder her as she is probably using that part of her powers the same as she would fire or air."

"You don't even have dark, what would you know?" she snapped at him.

"Respect him or this is over," I growled back at her. She met my eyes as if she wanted to fight but backed down after a hard stare. "I have not known the dark power for long, but what I do know is that it is malleable."

"So is light," she muttered.

"Which is why his words have weight," I reminded her. "Intent behind darkness is different." I refused to breach the subject of controlling the darkness within someone's mind. While I might pity her, I did not trust her. "Darkness is all around us even in the brightest of lights. It is cunning, sneaky, and will hit you when you least expect it. You must harness that type of feeling, that type of intent for it to work."

The words flowed out with ease. I must have said them a thousand times in my past lives because even though I had never once uttered the words in this one, there was a comforting truth to them.

Spiris's hand brushed against my lower back.

Aselia sighed and tried to brush her magic against my head again. This time she sunk a bit deeper but I could feel her just brushing the surface of my mind. As if she was pushing against a rubber ball, almost puncturing it but not quite.

"Let me," I said and plunged my magic back into her head.

She was beyond frustrated. She hated that she did not excel at the power and that even someone as weak as me could do it better than her. She thought about the face Nitri would make when she had done anything less than perfect, it was the same one that I had seen so many times. It was disgust. She replayed his hard words to her.

Useless.

Never take a throne.

Disgrace that she was the one to live.

She tried to shut down those thoughts, but the more she tried the harder they came to the surface.

Don't you dare utter this to anyone. she growled at me.

I won't if you teach me how to skip. I told her.

Whatever, tell if you want. she grumbled and crossed her arms over her chest.

"Aselia has some really interesting thoughts over there, Spiris," I commented and watched as her eyes widened.

You wouldn't. she growled.

Your daddy issues are no secret to anyone, Aselia. I replied snidely.

"I am not sure if I would be surprised at what you told me," Spiris said playing along. He leaned in close to my side as he spoke, his breath tickling the nape of my neck. The distraction almost made me forget our ploy.

"Well looks like Nitri—" I was cut off by Aselia pouncing forward and covering my mouth with her hands. Her golden eyes were narrowed, and the decorative chains wrapped around her horns clanged together at the sudden movement. Spiris's hand was firm against my back and kept me from falling backwards. His other hand shot out and grabbed her wrist. They were in a deadly stare off until she let out a small growl.

"Alright," she hissed and removed herself from me. Spiris let go of her wrist as she did.

"Happy we can come to an agreement," I said with a smile.

"Get on with it," she mumbled, not looking at me. Her arms crossed back over her chest.

I entered her mind again, paying close attention to how it felt to slip through the cracks.

It is like you are finding an opening. I relayed to her. *I didn't think much of it before but it is like the darkness is a type of slime and it sinks lower and lower through the cracks in your... mind? Magic? I am unsure.*

She visualized it in her own head and I shuddered at the picture of black sludge she conjured. She closed her eyes and focused on the feeling of my mind. It was surreal to talk to someone like this. It was like we were frozen in time, the information sharing was immediate, and it didn't even feel like we were two people. I felt it when she sunk deeper, but I could also visualize it because she was. It was like a never-ending mirror, you didn't know where it really started and the information gathering never ended.

It's too intimate. The words were floating around my head, and I heard them as they echoed in hers as well.

Her magic had finally reached a comfortable point in my mind where she could see all she needed to. She was panting now, trying to get a handle on her intentions and controlling the very new feeling of darkness.

I did not like having my mind and soul bared to her in such a way. I didn't like how much of me she could see. It made my insides twitch and ice-cold panic played at the back of my neck. There were too many things that I didn't want her to see. What happened with Baecos, Cruor, my own weakness. The fear of her finally seeing how weak I actually was, how this whole part of me that stood up to Nitri and her was façade that ran on a mixture of my own shame and the excitement that I felt when faced with a dangerous situation.

Was this what everyone else felt? Before I knew what I was doing my magic reacted and somehow pushed her darkness out of my mind so hard that it recoiled into her and she had to brace her arms behind her to catch herself from falling to the ground.

"What was that?" she gasped. There was no anger in her voice nor her mind, Instead there was just shock.

"I don't..." I trailed off and Spiris's hand rubbed circles on my back.

"What happened?" he asked in a soothing tone.

"She pushed me out," Aselia said with a scoff. She couldn't believe it, neither could I if I was being honest. I pulled back from her mind, her thoughts becoming too overwhelming,

"I didn't know you could do that," he muttered.

"I have also never been around another dark magician," I told him.

I dove into his mind.

I panicked. I told him. *I am not sure how I did it, but I really did keep her out.*

Do you think you can do that with the king's power's as well? Their sight? He asked.

I have no clue. I mused and pulled out of his mind.

The level of the King's power was nothing compared to the child's play that we were doing with the dark magic, but it was worth it to try if it offered even a small chance at protecting my mind from Nitri.

I left without learning how to skip that day. Aselia was pleasantly surprised and happy that she could rest before the journey tomorrow and I used that to my advantage saying that I didn't want to waste too much magic in case we had to fight.

Once she left, I told Spiris my plan to test the magic on a King but would need to seek out the only one we could trust, but I had never been able to seek Kneku out, he always came to me.

"I think I have an idea of where he may be," Spiris said and guided me out of the ballroom hand in hand. I tried to swallow the feelings it called forth in me knowing that we had much bigger things to deal with.

It was a long walk to another forgotten place of the castle but when we arrived at a double wooden door, he pushed it forward with a hesitant smile.

"In another life, I think you would have enjoyed this place," he said. I looked around him into the dim room and my jaw dropped at the sight of the shelves of books that hid inside the otherwise unassuming room. If I had known this was here, I would have never gone to the ballroom, I would have spent all my time here reading the universes oldest books. The air was dusting, and the smell of the aging pages filled my senses but there was just a small enough bit of magic that it made the hair on the back of my neck stand at attention.

Spiris pushed me forward past the shelves and we came face to face with Kneku sitting in a leather chair. He had a book set out in front of him on the table, his eyes scanning over it.

"I assume you are not here to play cards," he commented as he looked over us. He closed the book without marking his place and motioned for me to sit in the seat in front of him.

"I thought books were useless to you," Spiris commented in a playful tone.

"Just here to pass the time," Kneku responded.

I sat down in front of him and kept my voice low as I spoke. The library was by no means a place that would shield us from the most powerful being in this universe but I would rather be overly cautious than careless and have to pay for it.

"I can push people out of my mind with darkness. I want to test if that works on a king too," I said.

His lips turned down at the sides. "You can try but I have never heard of it working, even with your mother."

"Kings can see other kings in the way kings see people?" I asked. He shook his head.

"But Nitri can *see* all of us," he said. I nodded and sat back again my chair and closed my eyes. I tried to visualize something akin to an impenetrable ball of black magic around my mind.

"Nothing is happening," he muttered.

"Wait for it," Spiris said. His hand found my shoulder and gave it an encouraging squeeze.

I tried to harden it, not wanting Kneku to hear my thoughts about having Spiris' sturdy hand on my shoulder. It was more out of embarrassment than shame at wanting his touch, but nonetheless it was private and I wanted to keep it that way.

"Wait," Kneku said. "It's a bit fuzzy now." He leaned forward and closed his eyes. "I can hear your thoughts but... it's muffled and your emotions are less sharp."

I let out an exhale and dropped the shield, unsure if I could keep it up much longer. Even though I had used energy saving as a farce, I would need to be careful when we entered that realm.

"Thank you," I said. His golden eyes met mine and he cocked his head to the side.

"Nitri will be angry you left," he warned.

"His daughter is leaving too," I pointed out.

"Yes, well... he has never held much regard for his offspring," Kneku said with a frown.

"Or the rest of the world," Spiris commented.

Kneku's eyes became narrowed.

"Be careful with that tone, Spiris," he warned. "It is okay when we are in company but if Nitri hears a *slave* question his kingdom so blatantly, you may lose a horn."

Spiris's hand came up to touch the tip of his black horn that was almost hidden by the mess of curls he had grown of late. He winced slightly.

"That would be, unpleasant," he muttered.

"More than unpleasant," Kneku shot back. "Like when a limb is cut off you will feel phantom pains, and those cannot be healed by your light magic."

I swallowed thickly.

"Will keep that in mind," I said and got up to leave.

"Iniq?" Kneku called as we were about to exit the library.

"Yes?" I asked and turned back to face him. His face was serious and his voice had lost all of its' wistfulness.

"Good kings have their people in mind when ruling. *All of their people.* Remember that if the throne is *really* the path you have chosen." his words echoed through me and I couldn't help but feel like they were poking at the darkest part of myself. There were definitely some of the people that I would like to see dead in my kingdom.

"Are you such king?" I whispered to him.

"Maybe one day," he said his wistful tone back. "When the

kingdom is destroyed and we can once again rule over the lands we were created to rule over."

I nodded and left the room.

When the day came for us to leave with Aselia, my anxiety seemed to be at an all-time high. Every shift or creak of the castle made me jump, I was scared that Nitri had found out and stopped me from leaving the castle. I had gotten up only after a few hours of sleep and began searching for her with Spiris, but she was nowhere to be seen after hours of searching.

My mind raced. Did she leave without me? I had spent the entire day yesterday training with her and then she just took what I told her and left? She may not have been able to get far on her training, but she at least had more information than she had before and that was more than enough to give her a one up.

I searched the library but there was no one there besides millions of dusty books. I raced down the hallway, Spiris hot on my heels, until we got to the garden that I had met Aselia in on the first night she was here.

She was once more staring at the red moon. This time she was in a white long sleeve shirt and leather pants. Same thing that I had worn a million times during my time in the magical world. Looking at Aselia like this made me think back to how similar our situations could have been. If my mother was still alive and we lived in this world, what would our relationship be like? Would I be here just like Aselia trying my hardest to leave the place even though I knew the dangers the outside held?

I had chosen clothes similar to hers in preparation for any possible battle, the only difference was my shirt was black. Spiris had taken a different route with an all-black turtleneck that hugged his figure and leather pants, since arriving here he had changed his style to match the darker theme of the place. I preferred his clothing that way, it fit him better than those disgusting light clothes. I met his eyes and he gave me a stiff nod.

"We are ready," I told Aselia.

She looked over at us, assessing our outfits. She walked over to us with a hand on her hips and a slight frown.

"From what I have heard, the Dark King doesn't let anyone near his kingdom so we will have to exit the door outside the range of his protection and try to force ourselves in," she said and pulled at the end of my ponytail. "I am not sure how long it will take; the Fire and Water kingdom are relatively close so we will have to play it by ear."

"Should we pack supplies?" Spiris asked from behind me.

"Silly slave," Aselia spoke. "Demons can live for weeks without food."

"For Iniq," he corrected.

"She will starve or hunt," she responded coolly.

"Is there no other way to get in?" I asked and Aselia's golden eyes snapped to mine.

"Already unable to handle the journey?" she jabbed while tugged at my hair.

I frowned and smacked her hand away. She gave me a smirk.

"Let's go," I told her. She rolled her eyes and in an instant the door revealed itself behind her.

It looked the same as when I had called upon it back in the magical world but there seemed to be no creature inside it, no one coaxing me to join them on the other side. It towered over us and was so black that it took in any of the light around us. It was the only thing that connected this world to the magical one. The only thing that protected me from the people who wanted me dead.

I looked towards Spiris to check if he could also see the door now with the change of his body. His eyes were wide and took in the sight of the huge door that towered over us.

"It's something, isn't it?" I asked him with a small smile. I had rarely been able to see Spiris so in awe of something, it was usually I who was the one in awe by what he was teaching me. His wide eyes ran the length of the door before meeting mine.

"I just missed it when you came into this world," he explained. "I didn't know I would be able to see it when I turned into a demon."

"There are many perks to being a full-blooded demon," Aselia muttered. "Hold on to your slave." She shot Spiris a look. "He is not who this door is designed for, who know what the souls will want to do with him."

I raised an eyebrow at her.

"The souls?" I asked.

She sent me a grin. "You went through this door and still don't understand what is inside?"

"Get to the point," I hissed at her.

"It's the souls of the universe," she explained. "The most powerful, to be exact. The ones that can reincarnated but choose not to. This is how the universe chose to deal with them."

I gulped.

"How did you know those are the souls in there?" Spiris asked.

She stepped forward, her foot getting swallowed up by darkness.

"The old king is in here somewhere. I would be surprised if you didn't feel her when you entered," she said and her form disappeared into the inky abyss. "I've felt her once."

My heart pounded. Old king. *My mother.*

I grabbed Spiris' hand and with a smile I pulled us into the door with an erratically beating heart.

∼

This time no souls dared to hold onto me like when I had entered the door. I couldn't help the giddy feeling that spread throughout my body... was that really the old king? Was that the figure who had held onto me last time? I distinctly remembered how warm the embrace felt, I even considered staying in the door because of how good it felt to be held by it.

Aselia's golden eyes stood out against the swirling darkness. As soon as we were fully in the door shut behind us and Spiris' hand squeezed mine.

"Let's go, children," Aselia commented and turned to continue walking in the darkness. The realm was quiet, and her voice floated around us.

The darkness felt eerily like the graveyards back in the mortal realm. I had visited more than my fair share when I was still living as Vien. First her parents' death had caused me to go to the cemetery every week for three years. I stopped my visits after I was faced with Addies' death and the town began to hate me. Cemeteries had this feeling to them, like a vibration under the soil. It may have been quiet but there was an unmistakable thrum of activity that vibrated the ground near your feet. At times it was comforting but once the towns people figured out where I was spending my weekends, they would meet me there when they thought no one was watching and harass me until I left. They had a right to, it was my powers that had caused the death of the girl that ruled the town with her smile and happy go lucky attitude.

I shook the dark thoughts out of my head. That life was no longer mine and I should be grateful for that, but I would be lying if I said that there weren't times where my body craved the mortal world. Even though *Iniq* is who I was now, those memories stayed largely hidden from me so all that I had left to remember were my times in the human world as a girl who had lesser problems than saving the world and running from crazy kings. It was the simplicity I missed most of all, but as Spiris hand squeezed mine I couldn't think of anything I wanted to exchange for losing him once more.

"How do you know where it will spit us out?" I asked as I shook away the bad thoughts from my head. We had to start jogging to keep up to her large strides. She was confident in the way she walked and her tied hair swung with each step, she had done this so many times that it made me almost jealous at how easily she could navigate a world that was still relatively unknown to me in many ways.

"I just do," she explained and her footsteps stopped. In front of her the exit opened and moonlight streamed in. "Fuck."

She jumped out and I ran after her with the irrational fear that the door would close behind us. I gripped Spiris hand tightly as we crossed the threshold. We entered the familiar forest of mangled dead trees that I had once raced through to escape from Baecos. I swallowed thickly, fear starting to claw at my throat. It felt like the dreams had come to life. Spiris squeezed my hand. I gave him a small smile but refused to remove my hand from his. I hoped he did not feel me shaking.

I was supposed to be his King, but it felt like it was him who was guiding me and pushing me forward.

"What's wrong?" I asked Aselia as she paced around the area.

"Well for starters I didn't realize it was night here," she grumbled. "And we are in-between the fire and water kingdom, meaning that we are much further than I thought."

Trying to remember the map Fluvis had once showed me made me realize that we were very far away from the light kingdom and I couldn't help but feel relieved. The mention of the fire kingdom also ignited something in me that it shouldn't have. I should have been pissed at the idea of being near the people that so easily gave me away to Baecos... but all I could think of was Cruor.

"How do you know where we are?" Spiris asked. Aselia looked at him then our intertwined hands.

"Reach out your magic, you will feel their barriers," she scoffed and began walking the opposite direction. I pulled Spiris along after her but tried to stretch my magic as far as it would go. There was a small vibration towards my right when I extended it almost as far as I could, the barrier. It was the same as when I felt it the first time in the water kingdom.

I wondered if Fluvis would still accept me after what I had done? He had to know it was self-defense, right? His warm smile and red eyes flashed across my face. Maybe it was what missing someone felt like. I met Spiris's dark eyes, I missed him too once.

We walked in silence with the only sound being our feet crushing the branches underneath. It was dark but I tried not to let it scare me. Instead, I tried to look at the moon and the dark blue sky. I wished that Kneku could be here to see this. It was such a refreshing sight. Instead of feeling like we were under a moon filled with blood, the open sky with millions of stars had lifted an invisible weight off my chest. I hadn't realized how trapped I felt in that world.

There were spoiled apples on the ground that smushed under our feet as we walked and wafted a foul odor in the air. What was the story they had told me about this forest again? As I racked my brain for the memory, I felt Aselia prod at my mind.

Do not talk, keep moving. Pull your magic into you. Aselia's voice yelled in my mind. I startled but did what she said. The panic in her voice set me off more than the fact that she had mastered plunging into someone's mind. *Tell Spiris.*

I did as she said and Spiris gave a reassuring squeeze. We continued forward in silence. Aselia picked up her pace. I followed her lead, my heart pumping wildly as we did. I couldn't feel what she could, and it was making me anxious.

Maybe it was a creature?

With a breath for courage, I unfiltered my magic ever so slightly, inching it around us trying to fill it with as much intent to be discreet as possible. It moved over the branches like slim fingers as we moved, feeling nothing. I almost let out a sigh of relief until I felt something that made my magical signature spike.

My magic wrapped around the very familiar body of Baecos, Vitos, and... Callum? How was that possible? Did they feel us enter this realm? There was not a word to describe how painful the panic was that pushed through my veins. Like my body contracted and forced icicles trough my blood vessels. Every hair stood on edge and my knees began to shake.

My breath caught and I stopped walking, Spiris running into my back. Aselia looked back at us with wide eyes then her head snapped to the right. I could feel her magic shoot out, taking catalog of how close our enemies were to us.

"You idiot!" she growled. "Run!"

Spiris pushed us forward and I ran at full speed after Aselia trying to force my knees not to lock up with fear. I pushed myself further even when I hear Baecos's booming laugh. I felt their footsteps following us. Even when I felt their magic try to reach out to us, I pushed forward.

"Go, go, go!" Spiris whispered through gasps of breath. He was trying to desperately push me forward and I could only think of what would happen if they got hold of him again. I couldn't think of it, I didn't want to allow myself to think about what life would be without him again.

Aselia stopped and turned to face our attackers that were still shrouded in darkness.

"Keep going!" she yelled and thrust both her arms forward. Air whirled around us and in front of her a dense wall of air appeared. She stepped back as Baecos was the first to show his face. His long blonde hair was shining in the moonlight, purple eyes widened with excitement and the same smirk that haunted my nightmares was plastered in his face. I shuddered when his magic reached out to us, mine was still intertwined with his. Did he keep my blood in jars or something?

He stood up straight as Vitos and Callum in his hound form showed up next to him.

"Spiris," Vitos breathed next to Baecos. His eyes were wide and he looked even worse that when I saw him last. His skin was pale and sagged as if barely hanging onto his bones. His black hair was greasy, the curls that him and his twin shared hung limply by his face. He had lost so much weight he looked like a third of himself.

Is it the guilt or Baecos that is slowly killing him? A voice whispered at the back of my head but I couldn't believe it. Vitos was just as much a monster as Baecos.

"What a surprise," Baecos said and let out a loud laugh as he tried to ram through the wind wall Aselia conjured. "Not only is our beloved Spiris back from the dead but it looks like he brought us our toy back." His eyes narrowed in Aselia. "I felt your magic once too, I'll enjoy making you bleed."

"Don't get ahead of yourself. You are nothing but vermin. Easily squashed," Aselia spit back at him.

"Iniq, come," Baecos's voice vibrated around us. I shrunk into Spiris and he wasted no time before he began pulling me in the opposite direction.

"Don't let him get in your head!" he yelled. I wasn't sure if it was to me or Aselia but regardless, it snapped me out of my trance and I pushed myself forward.

The night sky and trees around us became engulfed in a burning red light. *Flames.* I pushed my heels in the ground stopping Spiris from going any further.

"Cruor," I whispered, feeling the connection tug at my heart. I looked back behind us and saw Aselia in the same spot but on the other side of the wall of wind was another tower of thick burning fire. Even as far as we were the heat still licked at the edges of my toes and forest around us began to burn.

The flames left as soon as they came and behind the wall of wind now stood a singular person.

Cruor.

She hadn't changed much since I left but her face had lost every smile line that it once had and she was snarling as she pushed against the wall Aselia created. Just like when I first came into their world I was taken aback by her beauty. Her dark hair was still cropped and just brushing the top of her pointed ears. Her red eyes were intense, and her mouth was bared to us showing her fangs. It was dark so I could barely make out the tattoos that decorated her face but they were visible enough to cause her red eyes to stand out even more in the shadows. Her anger only added to her beauty, made everything more intense and took my breath away all the same.

"Where did they go?" Cruor demanded. My breath caught when I realized that Aselia had been training under Cruor. I wondered how close they had gotten? Did Aselia know about our bond?

Cruor's red eyes shifted behind her and dug into mine, the intensity made me shiver.

"I do not know," Aselia confessed. "They must have skipped."

"Why did you bring her?" she spat at her. My chest twisted painfully.

"You aren't happy to see your mate?" Aselia asked. "Not to mention Spiris being alive again? Oh, maybe you don't care about him much huh? I mean if my mate had a slave sharing their bed with them overnight, I would be pissed to."

My mouth dropped at Aselia's words. How did she even know that?

"Aselia," I hissed. "We have a plan and a goal. Let's go."

She looked back at me with a shit eating grin.

"Maybe I want to have a sleep over at the Fire Kingdom," she teased.

"Baecos could come back any second," Spiris growled, his chest vibrating behind me. "We need to take cover."

"Perfect. Cruor, take us to your kingdom," Aselia said and dropped the wind wall.

"No, we should head to the Dark Kingdom," I insisted, suddenly not wanting to risk what would happen if I got too close to Cruor. I reached out to Spiris with my magic.

What do we do? I asked him.

I know you may not like it but going to her kingdom will be safest for now. He replied.

I swallowed thickly, everyone's eyes were on my and heat fanned across my face. I straightened my shoulders and centered myself, at least trying to act like the King I was born to be.

"Alright," I said.

Cruor paused for a second then spoke, "You have to stop inviting yourself in, Aselia."

CHAPTER SEVEN
SPIRIS

We were not able to skip into the barrier, as Cruor and her people reinforced it around her kingdom so we were forced to follow her silently into the forest. No one dared to speak besides Aselia and her stupid singing. I couldn't recognize the song; it was in a different language but this was not a time to be calling attention to ourselves in the middle of the dead forest. The giddiness that radiated off her in waves shone in the way her eyes scanned the area and the annoying smiles she sent us. I could already tell that she was the type to push people's boundaries, and it had to be her biggest accomplishment yet. She had not one but three people who were silently fuming at her.

It was a logical step. *I knew that.* But that didn't help the feelings that festered inside me when I looked at Cruor.

I could deal if it was jealously, that was fine. What I couldn't deal with was the fact that I was staring at a person that if they had just listened to me in the first place, I would have been able to survive with Iniq in my first life. Because she doubted me and because she was too much of a coward to fight Baecos when she had the chance, I lost my life and Iniq spiraled into a type of trauma she might never recover from.

With each step the agitation I was feeling doubled and I could only hope that when the entire castle heard Iniq's nightmarish screams as she continued to fend off Baecos in her dreams, than they would really understand the severity of their mistakes.

Cruor stopped in front of the sparkling barrier separating the forest and her kingdom. It vibrated as we got neared and the magic tickled at my fingertips, sensing if I was friend or foe. Just beyond lay a field of blooming Spider Lilies much like we had seen in the Other World. In the distance stood a castle that I had seen too many times before. It was about the third a size of the High King's castle and was currently lit up.

"You can enter without assistance," Cruor grumbled to Aselia. Aselia gave her a smile and stepped through the threshold. The light of the barrier molded around her as she pushed through and bounced back into place after she broke through on the other side. Cruor's red eyes drifted over to us and looked at my hand intertwined with Iniq's. "I have to *touch* you two if you would like to enter."

"She goes first," I commanded and pushed Iniq's stiff body forward. Cruor's breath audibly caught and she rested her hand on Iniq's shoulder. Iniq was able to step through with ease just as Aselia had, but I didn't miss how Cruor's hand stayed a millisecond too long on her shoulder and the way Iniq's green eyes widened at her touch.

It was my turn next and I stepped forward casting my gaze downward to meet her eyes. Her lack of dark circles and worry lines only solidified my assumption. She was not effected by our departure from her world in the slightest.

"I am glad to see you are alive," she commented and then placed her hand on my arm and we entered the barrier together.

They were words of a king, polite words that sounded as flat as they felt.

I held my tongue, not trusting the words that played on the very tip of it.

Two hounds ran towards us from the castle. Ash and Felix, I recognized their fur colors immediately. Ash ran straight towards Iniq and as soon as he was close enough shifted and pounced on her. I ran to catch them both before she fell and gave Ash a warning growl. His black hair with a tuft of white streaked through it was puffed around his head and tickled my nose as he gripped on to Iniq. His tattoos wound around his neck and down his shoulders, and only when I caught his bare backside did I realize how naked he was.

Ash's eyes widened when he met mine and shifted position so his arms could circle around the both of us, pushing my front into Iniq's back. I cursed at the way my stomach twisted at the action of feeling her against me. It was different when we were in bed at night together, that was for her nightmares, but since I had pushed her down on the bed, her robe barely covering her body... It had been hard to control myself around her. My touches would linger, my thoughts at night would race, and this position was beginning to quickly become the bane of my existence.

"I never thought I would see you both again. I'm sorry Iniq I shouldn't have hesitated before you left to the other realm," Ash said in a watery voice. "Spiris, man, I cannot believe you are alive. The Kings must have favored you. They had to have known how important you are. To us. To Iniq."

I refused to let Nitri's words replay in my head but was ecstatic he spoke the words so loudly. Perfect for Cruor to hear. I would take my wins when they came. It would be difficult from now on. I never had a mate but I trusted Kneku's words and suspected that Cruor would make a move during our time here.

My eyes shifted over to Felix. He stayed in his hound form and refused to come closer to the group than was necessary. Cruor walked over to him, glancing at us once before her hand smoothed down the sliver tuft on the top of his head.

"Ash, let go," Iniq said in a small whine.

Ash did as she said but stayed standing fully naked in front of us. Iniq's eyes started to drift down and on instinct I reached out to cover her eyes and pulled her tightly against my front again.

"Shift back," I commanded towards Ash. He gave me an amused look that told me he had no intention of doing so.

I have seen a penis before, Spiris. Iniq chided in my head.

Please do not listen to my thoughts right now. I begged her.

I waited another few moments before letting the possessiveness that I felt take over my mind. I wouldn't let her see another's naked body until I was sure that I could keep her with me for the rest of our lives.

The air was thick with tension as we crowded around the dining hall in the Fire kingdom. Cruor had invited that we eat dinner and not a moment later was a feast sorted out in front of us by her wait staff. There was no one else in the hall as we ate, I was grateful for it. Even just dealing with the small group of people was a shock after Iniq and I being on our own for the last few months.

Cruor sat at the head of the table, her gaze periodically glancing over to Iniq and I. Aselia sat next to Iniq and Ash was across from her. Aselia would make snide comments here and there trying to fluster Iniq but Ash was more than happy to snapback at her playfully which left Cruor myself and Felix in a heavy silence. I was just happy that everyone was in their clothes now.

Iniq's hands stayed firmly planted in her lap, not even making a move to get any food even as the hounds made a mess of their plates. I tapped her hand and she met my eyes. Her magic tugged at my mind.

Are you not hungry? I asked her.

She looked down at her lap. *I feel uncomfortable.* She confessed. *And I have trouble picking food in this world. In the castle back in the other world I would do it t piss off Nitri but here...*

I ruffled her hair and with a smile I switched my plate with hers. I refilled my new empty plate with the same meats, salted vegetables, and bread that I had just given her. I could understand her hesitancy. She was still relatively new to this world even if others still wanted to treat her like the warrior she was in her past life. It was an unfair comparison.

Trust I have good taste. I told her. She lifted her head up and gave me a smile before hesitantly eating part of the meat.

What meat is this? she asks.

The fire kingdom has some forest but not many so I am assuming they got it from the mountains and it's the human equivalent to a goat.... Or a wendigo. I added on the last part as a joke but her face twisted in a disgusted horror that made my lips curl.

"I'm kidding," I whispered. She glared but began digging into her food.

The table had fallen quiet around us. Everyone's eyes were watching us. I met Cruor's and purposefully placed my hand in Iniq's lap and gave her own hand a squeeze. Cruor glared as I did so and the words I uttered so long ago seemed to weigh heavily between us.

I would be dammed if I didn't try.

And try I would because there was only one person here that had stuck through it all and had yet to betray her all those years ago and that sure as hell was not Cruor.

"So, last I checked Callum was begin chained to the dusty wall of the disgrace you called a dungeon... how did Baecos manage to get him?" Aselia asked, breaking the tension between me and Cruor.

"You imprisoned him?" Iniq asked, surprise filling her voice. I was also surprised; I didn't expect Cruor to put one of her own in the dungeon just because of Iniq. A person she was so willing to let Baecos get his dirt hands on.

"He was a traitor," Cruor said. "They deserved to be punished... just not by death." The words rang through the empty room. Iniq lowered her head as if ashamed by the words, from what she told me at night I knew that Claire still haunted her... but I think that she deserved her fate and they were too lenient on Callum.

"In the Other World a traitors' punishment is death," Aselia said and took a bite of the food on her plate, her eyes twinkling.

"The High Kings also fled this world long ago. I wouldn't say that they are the best judge of how to take care of things in this world." Felix shot back. His red eyes were set in a glare and his knuckles turned white and he gripped harshly onto his fork. If I remembered correctly, he was the one in the relationship with Claire.

"Baecos broke in," Ash hurried out trying to stop the fight that was about to break out between Aselia and Felix. Aselia's hand gripped tightly at the edge of the table as she glared at the scarred man. "We don't know how or why but he decided to break Callum out."

"Which is why you should have killed him," Aselia hissed at Cruor. "He is with an enemy that makes even the Kings weary of this world. You think that Baecos doesn't have a plan to strip him of all his knowledge to use against you?"

"I will get him back," Cruor vowed. "I will not let Baecos hurt him nor will I allow any harm to come to this Kingdom while under my watch."

I wondered what Kneku would think of this. From his relaxed personality I was not sure who he would side with. He had been lecturing Iniq on caring for all the people in their Kingdoms, would he be above killing someone who sought to do such harm? Particularly to a fellow King?

"Enough, Aselia," Iniq commanded. Aselia's eyes widened, but instead of fighting her like I had assumed she would she just slowly relaxed into her seat. "You have used a lot of magic opening the door, do not waste more time arguing. Save your strength for the journey ahead."

There was a shocked silence that went through the table. Iniq had been quiet until now while picking at her food but her tone was downright annoyed.

"Right uh... so the door, how did Spiris come through it? I thought it was only a High King thing," Ash said scrambling for a way to defuse the tension.

I met his eyes and gave him a small smile. Ash was not the issue here; he had tried his best so I wouldn't hold anything against him. If anything, we could use his nonchalant attitude to make our time here more bearable.

"I am a demon, with Iniq's help I can pass through easily," I explained.

Cruor scoffed. "Demons don't have horns."

"They do, actually," Aselia spoke for me this time. "Sorry to break it to you Cruor, but you are but a mere half breed."

Cruor's mouth dropped as she scrambled for words. Ash let out a booming laugh.

"The only full demon still on this plane is rumored to be the Dark King," I added on.

"What makes you so different than myself or Cruor? Some shiny horns?" Felix asked, bitterness clinging to his tone.

"Don't forget that I am a demon too, inbreed," Aselia snapped. "It's all about power and believe me when I tell you that any half demon or magician cannot hold a candle to a full-blooded demons rage."

"I wasn't picking a fight." Felix explained calmly, his scared face remained passive.

"Why are you here, Aselia?" Cruor interrupted. "I thought you were going back for good."

"Things changed," she responded with a shrug. I felt Iniq shift next to me.

"Iniq, why are you back?" Cruor asked changing her victim to one more likely to spill.

"Aselia and I are here to learn from the Dark King," she responded without looking up from her plate.

"There has been a vacancy since her mother died," Aselia explained. "No doubt that was causing the shift in magic and in order to stop that we need to have her ascend to that throne." When there was a pause, she continued. "I forget people of this world do not know much about the High Kings anymore."

"What did you tell Cruor when you came here?" I asked, not liking the suspicion that was gnawing at my gut.

"That I was a High Kings offspring, similar to Iniq," she said. I looked to Cruor with a raised brow.

"I didn't know Iniq was the High King's daughter until Aselia arrived," Cruor said defensively when she met my gaze.

"Did your parents know?" Iniq asks. "Fluvis?"

"I suspect they all knew," Cruor said without emotion. "They were around when your mother was still alive, but I was still young I do not remember her."

I tapped her hand.

What are you thinking about? I asked.

I am thinking about why Fire King took me and not the Dark one.

"I think it is time to retire for the night," Iniq said, leaving the room. I followed after her closely not bothering to bow to Cruor as I did.

❧

I had no idea where Iniq was bringing us but she seemed to know where she was going as she expertly weaved throughout the hallways. I didn't try to stop her, instead stayed closely behind and kept watch on her back.

She led us through a hallway with stone arches that looked out over a garden of Spider Lilies. Only then did she rest by leaning forward over the windowsill. Her eyes were wound shut and she took a deep breath as her fists balled against the stone.

"Are you okay?" I asked her and leaned against the stone letting it cool my face. The jog through the castle caused my blood to pump and I had already broken out into a light sweat. "Was there too much going on?"

"I don't want to be here," she confessed. "I thought I could handle it but I can't."

I reached my hand out and squeezed her shoulder lightly.

"Handle what? Cruor?" I asked.

"All of them. Their thoughts," she said and her watery green eyes met mine. I stiffened. "I read them, they still hate me for Claire."

"She was after you," I told her. "You did what you had to."

"But I didn't *need* to kill her, Spiris," she fought back, taking a deep breath before continuing. "I wanted to."

"You don't mean that," I told her, a chill running through me.

"I do," she said. "During that time, I wanted to so bad. I enjoyed the way it felt." I tried to speak, but she silenced me. "The feeling left after I had to deal with Nitri for the first time that's when I began seeing her face in my nightmares and suddenly, I couldn't believe what I did."

I didn't want her to be in pain or be hurt by the thoughts, but it did calm some of my worries. I never liked the way that smile would curl her lips and if she could feel this guilt, instead of being incited to continue to run into danger... I might just be getting the girl I loved back.

"Iniq." I pulled her into a hug. Her body relaxed against me and some tears fell from her eyes and onto my shirt.

"What's wrong with me, Spiris?" she asked.

I wasn't ready for the question. I smoothed her hair down, stalling. Thinking though my options.

"You went through a lot, Iniq," I told her. "With Baecos, with Cruor, your parents' death, Nitri." She stiffened with each word. "Nothing's wrong with you. You are healing. It's okay to feel like this after everything."

She gripped at my shirt tightly and I allowed my lips to brush her hair.

"It's weak," she told me through sniffles.

"These emotions are what makes you strong Iniq. No one in the three realms could have survived what you have." A light breeze passed around us and Cruor's magical signature tickled at my senses. Of course she would come and try to steal her away. "Let's go to the room, yes?"

She nodded in my chest. I felt Cruor come closer.

"Perfect timing," I told her and leaned my head back to meet her pinched expression. "Why don't you show us to our rooms?"

She said nothing but gestured for me to follow her up to the rooms. Iniq stayed silent by my side as we walked through the castle. Cruor stopped when we were on the fourth floor in the east wing.

"This is my room," Cruor said as she passed a double wood door. "Iniq across from mine," she pointed to the adjacent double doored room. I had a sickening feeling that this may have been Iniq's room in her first life.

"And mine?" I asked. A small smile played at her lips.

"Next to hers," she answered and pointed to the single door down the hall. It was as least forty feet away and there was no way I would be able to hear her cries before Cruor would. I gritted my teeth at her audacity.

"Will you be okay?" I asked Iniq and rested my hand on her elbow, more for show than anything else.

"I'll be fine," she said with a sad smile. "Maybe now you'll actually be able to get a good night's rest without me."

A smile played at my lips. What a perfect way to put it. I swear I could hear Cruor's teeth grinding against each other.

"Take some rest," I told her. She nodded and looked between Cruor and I before slipping into her room. I turned to Cruor and she had a frown on her face.

"She was crying," Cruor commented in a low voice.

"Yes," I said. "I hope you are not planning to disturb her now."

"Not tonight," Cruor said, and then sent me a smirk. "But don't be surprised if she finds her way into my bed in the middle of the night."

I gritted my teeth at her response, but before I could ruin our only chance at a safe shelter, I stalked my way down to the room that she provided for me.

I was pleasantly surprised to see it was actually a good-sized room, almost as big as the one that I stayed in in the Other World. Instead of the blacks and reds everything seemed to be in a warm brown shade from the bed frame to the cabinets next to it. The blankets were a cream color and I didn't realize how tired I was until my body moved itself over to the big bed and I fell face first into the soft mattress.

It was only then I let the images of my slowly dying brother fill my mind. I had tried to keep it on lock and focus only on the current issue, but they could not stay away forever.

My heart twisted when I saw what he had become, and I was sure that if my face was not buried in the blankets that I would have thrown up. Growing up with him, I would have never expected him to fall so far. I knew he had grown into something resembling a monster, but there was no way he deserved whatever Baecos was doing to him.

As we grew up alongside Baecos he had slowly changed from the protective older brother to someone who would bend at Baecos will and do almost anything for him. He had lost the light in his eyes and had fell into Baecos bad habits. It wasn't long until he started trying to take the magic from other magicians as well.

That was the first time I realized how alone I was in this world. I had followed him around our whole life and he left me in the dust like it was no problem. Someone who should have been the person to understand me the most was suddenly the person who I trusted the least. I had thought that I could talk him out of it but when Iniq came....

My stomach twisted painfully at the thought of what he did to Iniq. It was unforgivable, I knew that. And there was no way I could expect Iniq to forgive him for that but... whatever Baecos had to be doing to him must be enough retribution, right?

I finally pushed myself off the bed and searched the room for clothing to change into. The panic that had run through me when I had made eye contact with Baecos made me break out into a sweat and I wouldn't dare climb back into Iniq's bed smelling as bad as I did right now. Because that's what I planned, I didn't give a damn about her being right across from Cruor and I would make sure that I beat her to that room before she even had a chance.

I decided to shower quickly in the attached bathroom before changing into the strangely fitting male clothes that Cruor had left in the room. I wondered who had been staying here before me or if she had prepared the room long before my death was even in the equation. My chest warmed at the thought even under the warm water from the shower head. I wouldn't let the single act sway me though, mine *and* Iniq's blood still stained on her hands.

I dried my hair with a towel and begun dressing in the loose shirt and baggy black pants I found. Before leaving the room, I extended my magic towards Cruor's and Iniq's room. When I felt Iniq's familiar magical signature only a few feet away from my door my heart pounded in my chest and with a start I swung my door open.

Iniq jumped when the door opened abruptly and let out a small squeak. She was in a robe much like I had seen her wear in the Other World, her hair was slightly damp and there was nothing covering her bare feet.

"I decided to beat the nightmares before they came," she said and looked down at the ground. As if just noticing her state she hugged her arms around her body. I couldn't help the flash of heat that went through my body at the way the black robe fit her body. The sun on her chest poked through the valley of skin the robe showed and the rarely shown black feathers tattooed on her legs were bared to the world. She wasn't wearing under-garments from the way her nipples poked through the fabric and the robe barely reached her mid thighs. A stray water droplet fell from her hair to her neck and trailed down the strip of flesh between her breasts.

"Come in," I said with a hoarse voice. I didn't know what made me more excited, the way she was dressed or the fact that she had sought me out. Either way I strategically hid myself behind the door as I waved her in "I was just going to check on you."

She gave me a shy smile and walked past me and darted right into the bed. I got a flash of her underwear as she climbed into the too tall structure. I thanked the universe that she was at least wearing something under there because I was already holding on for dear life.

The tension between us the last few weeks had been unbear-able and when she had finally allowed my touches, she showed up *like that* in my room. She covered herself in the blankets and looked at me expectantly. I shut the door slowly trying to regain my composure as I did so. I walked to the side of the bed and jutted my chin out.

"Scoot over," I told her. She nodded and made room for me. I climbed in and winced at the painful swelling that was caused by the damned robe. "You aren't afraid that you will get sick?" I laid next to her, feeling the wetness from her hair.

"Because I am a half breed?" she teased.

"You are barely a magician in this body," I said. "But it does not matter if you are a mortal or a king, I would still worry."

She bit her lip and pulled the blankets close to her body. The room was showered with darkness but the perk about demon eyes was that I could see everything as clear as day. That included the way her eyes trailed down my exposed form. I lifted the blanket higher over me hoping she did not catch sight of the situation in my pants.

"Are you okay with me being in here?" she asked. "I know I told you I would let you get your rest but I didn't feel right being alone."

I swallowed at her confession. I reached out to touch the hand that still clutched the blanket slowly, unfurling her fingers and holding them in my own.

"I prefer it this way," I told her. "You could order me to sleep in your bed every night and I would gladly oblige."

Her eyes widened. "You don't mind?"

"What makes you think I ever minded?" I asked her and shifted closer to her. I tucked a piece of her hair behind her ear with my free hand.

"Just that it must not be pleasant to be awoken by screaming every night," she said, her voice catching.

I wanted so badly to breach the space between us, but this was hardly the time to do it, or the place. I could still feel Cruor's magic at the edge of my senses, no doubt waiting for her chance to sneak into Iniq's empty room.

"Don't worry about that," I told her. "Just sleep, okay? I'll wake you if you have a nightmare."

She nodded and pulled her hand from mine so she could turn around in the bed and face the other side where the windows overlooked the dead forest. I was grateful she did and tried to close my eyes and fall asleep. It was useless though; I couldn't get the image of her in the robe out of my mind and having her so close was distracting.

When her breathing turned deep, I wrapped my arm around her waist and pulled her against my chest. The type of robe should have been burned, it felt like there was barely anything between my fingers and her skin. I buried my head in her hair and inhaled deeply. I made sure to keep a space between my hardness and her, but I couldn't stop myself from at least holding her.

She shifted into me, pushing her back against my chest and brough her rear into my lap. I exhaled sharply into her hair to conceal my groan. My hand gripped her hip as she squirmed against me creating friction between us that hand me struggling to stay still.

This was going to be a long fucking night.

CHAPTER EIGHT
SPIRIS

*T*he next day was hell. I had hoped that with whatever sleep that I could get, I would be able to right myself by the morning but I woke up with my face still in Iniq's hair but instead of her back against me she had curled into my chest. This would have been fine if the stupid robe would have done its job but instead not only was the blanket somehow thrown off of us during the middle of the night her robe was also falling off her shoulders and her bare breasts were pushed up against my chest. My mouth watered at the sight of seeing them, they were so much more perfect than I had imagined all those lonely nights away from her, and they were out as if begging for me to take a hold of one.

I tried to pull myself away from her and fix her robe as I did, but that turned to be almost impossible with the way she was laying. Instead, I slowly detangled myself and put the blanket over her so she would not be left exposed. I almost ran into the bathroom and shut the door softly behind me, not wanting to wake her.

I turned on the shower and released myself from the clothing that had a chokehold on my body. My naked skin stood under the hot water and willed my now well-formed erection down.

"Now's not the time for this," I hissed at myself. "We have a fucking kingdom to save."

I tried to think of every gross thing that I could, but nothing willed the way of Iniq standing in the middle of my hallway, the way she felt against my erection, and certainly not the image of her breasts and the fantasy of the way they would feel in my mouth. I cursed and leaned my head against the cold shower, finally I let my hand find the length of my erection. I moaned at the way it felt, images of Iniq in the shower with me filled my mind without warning. Instead of my hand it was Iniq's as she slowly trailed her hand down my length. There was no hesitancy as she knelt naked in front of me. Her green eyes would watch mine as her tongue reached out to take me into her mouth. My hips snapped forward as if to bury myself in her mouth, she would take me without complaint. I imagined the way her hot mouth would feel around me. A groan made its way through my mouth echoing in the bathroom. I couldn't bring myself to care as the ministrations of Iniq in my mind brought me close to an orgasm.

In my mind I came over her face and watched as she licked up the residue that was left over my cock until she was satisfied, in reality I was left with a mess all over the shower and in my hand. A sense of disgust filled me. I couldn't believe I really came to the image of Iniq while she was asleep in the next room. It had never gotten this bad before.

I quickly cleaned myself up and stared at myself in the mirror while I dried off with a fluffy white towel. I sighed, trying to get over my embarrassment and wrapped the towel around my waist. A black card floated down toward the floor seemingly coming out of nowhere.

When I bent down to pick it up, my heart stopped when I realized that it was the same demon card that I had taken from

Kneku's deck. How did this get in here? I didn't even remember bringing it into this world.

"Kneku?" I whispered and I flipped the card over. There was no response. I let out a shaky breath and threw it into the trash can, covering it with the towel.

I redressed quickly, casting the card out of my mind so that I could go back into the room and see the angel in my sheets once more. Iniq was still asleep on the bed in almost the same position I had left her in. I swallowed thickly looking at her relaxed face as she slept. I moved to lean over her and moved the hair out of her face.

"Iniq, it is time to wake up," I told her softly.

Her eyes fluttered up slowly and she gave me a smile that made my heart flutter.

"Spiris, I didn't have any bad dreams," she said sleepily. "Maybe I should sleep with you more often."

She stretched, causing the blanket to almost fall off of her. I quickly grabbed the edge of it and covered her before she could expose herself.

"Be careful your, uh... robe is not great for sleeping," I told her while feeling my face flush. She awoke seriously now, her eyes widened and she sat up abruptly bringing the blankets with her.

"I'm sorry, I didn't realize," she blushed lightly.

"No need to apologize. I tried not to look as I covered you," I lied. I looked; I memorized the way her perky nipples looked enough to taste them in my sick daydreams of her. Even just remembering them now caused me to swell once more.

"I don't mind you seeing, I just didn't want to make you uncomfortable," she said with a shy smile.

"I would never be uncomfortable with your body, Iniq. It's beautiful." The words spilled out before I could stop them. I wanted to rip that damn cover off her and show her exactly what I thought of her body.

"Is that so?" she asked and I noticed a slight bit of confidence straighten her spine. "Then you wouldn't mind..."

Her voice trailed as she slowly loosened her grip on the blanket and began to pull it down her body showing more skin as she did so. I became rock hard at the action and my eyes were glued to the way the soft fabric slid down her body, the swells of her breasts appeared and she stopped the blanket right above her nipples.

"Iniq, I—" I reached forward ready to grab her neck and force her to me but I was interrupted by a knock at the door.

"Breakfast time." Cruor's voice called from the closed door. "You both are holding everyone up."

A sick twisted sense of accomplishment sprang through me when I realized Cruor knew we were both in here. Iniq didn't feel the same though because in a flash her robe was fixed and she went to open the door.

Cruor started at her wide eyed when she saw what she was wearing but Iniq didn't stay for long. Instead she brushed past her and ran down the hallway presumably to her own room to get dressed to meet the others.

"I didn't realize how hard the competition was," Cruor commented, her eyes taking in the position I was in. I turned towards her and crossed my arms over my chest.

"There is no competition. I just want whatever Iniq wants," I lied. It was a competition I planned on winning but I knew that even if Iniq went to Cruor I would have no choice but to fold. I loved Iniq too much to keep her from anything she truly wanted.

"Would you let her want me?" she asked with a smirk still plastered on her face. I hated how she still though she had done no wrong. Did she not realize that she had a hand in both of our deaths?

"As long as I can stay by Iniq's side, I don't care what she chooses," I told her and began undressing. She blanched and quickly left the open doorway.

I was really not looking forward to the rest of the day.

"I need to rest a bit longer before I lug you two up that mountain," Aselia said as she stuffed a bread roll in her mouth.

Iniq and I had joined not long ago and I was still irritated that Cruor had interrupted us. Iniq didn't act fazed at all, almost like nothing happened between us. She was playful like this back in the Light Kingdom once before, it gave me hope to see this type of attitude again. It could only mean that was healing, even if it was something as small as this.

"You seem fine to me." Felix said with a grumble from across her.

"Oh, don't be so fast to push them away, Felix," Ash joked with him and pushed at his shoulder. "We rarely ever have guests anymore and I want to make sure I can have time with Iniq and Spiris before they leave again."

I was surprised to hear my name lumped in with Iniq's. I didn't think Ash would care much about me; we were never friends. Even when we worked together, we never had a chance to bridge the gap between us. We were from enemy kingdoms and only brought together for one purpose: to keep Iniq far away from Baecos.

We both failed spectacularly.

"We can spar again," Iniq said a small smiling playing at her face. "I have been feeling restless recently."

"You and Spiris against me and Felix," Ash volunteered. I sat straight up when Iniq gave me a pleading look. It played on my guilt for what I did earlier in the shower.

"I'll sit out on this one." Felix said.

"You could always fight me," Aselia said with a dangerous

smile spreading across her face. "Or are you scared you will be beaten?"

His head cocked to the side. "Of course I am. You are literally the closest thing we have to a god. I like all my limbs attached, thank you."

Aselia stalled at his response before a smile spread across her face. "I like that kind of confidence in a man."

There was a pause before Ash burst out into laughter and Iniq giggled by my side. I couldn't help the smile that played at my own lips.

"How about let's actually preserve our magic and you guys can go stare at clouds or something," Cruor said with a grumble.

"I know the perfect place!" Ash said excitedly and tried to pull Iniq up with him to run off to god knows where but I gripped his wrist.

"Let her eat," I said with a light growl. Ash shot me a look but sat back down.

"Don't worry, I won't forget about you too Spiris," he teased.

"What about me?" Aselia asked with a small pout. She stabbed a piece of food with her fork without look at any of us.

"I can show you the garden if you'd like." Felix answered surprising all of us. Aselia raised her eyes to him and with a smile took a bite out of her bread.

"You have yourself a deal."

I had to admit cloud gazing, as childish as it may have seemed, was actually very relaxing. Ash had long since changed into his hound form and acted as a pillow for Iniq to lay on as we took our place onto the side of a grassy hill. It provided a perfect unobstructed view of the sky and Iniq quickly began picking out clouds that resembled earth animals.

"You mean to tell me there are animals in their ocean that

zap you with lightening?" I asked her disbelievingly. I had been to the mortal realm many a time to check on her while she grew up there but I had never heard of such a ridiculous notion. I wondered how the High Kings even filled that world with creatures, did they just put a few there and let them procreate? Did they ever add new ones for the fun of it? Nitri's narrowed gaze flashed across my mind, I doubt he did anything for the fun of it.

"Something like that," she said with a giggle. Her smile dropped in a moment and her tone turned serious. "Do you really think we can reach the Dark King?"

Ash shifted below her, he had been content to just lay there and sunbathe as we chatted but every so often, like the shift, he would give us an indication he was still awake and listening.

"We have to," I told her, even though I wanted nothing more than to live my days with her just like this in a faraway land where no one could bother us. "For the sake of the light Kingdom."

"I still don't know what to do about Baecos," she said in a whisper. Ash whined under her and she patted his paw lightly.

"We will figure it out once you sit on the throne. It can wait until then," I told her. Inside though, I was sure my brother would perish by then.

"I know I should hate Vitos," Iniq said as if we were in harmony. "But seeing him like that... made me feel bad for him."

"Me too," I told her and looked back up to a cloud that looked like nothing more than a blob. "I wished that there was a way to stop him back then, before he became so enamored with Baecos."

"Why does he follow him so?" she asked. "How are the two of you so different?"

I let out a sigh. This was my least favorite topic. Not my brother, but his decent into madness alongside Baecos. I bet that if Vitos had just a bit more courage... Iniq would have never died.

"He is his mate, or at least that is what I have determined. He never broached the subject with me," I told her. It was true he had never discussed the mating with me but the relationship between the two of them was obvious. It was horrible being around them in their teenage years, Vitos would wait for Baecos to come back home like a puppy and would pounce on him as soon as he arrived. Baecos forced him to calm himself when others were around and after a while barely took us out to any events, that was when I would hear Vitos complain. Those were the only times I felt like we were once again brothers, sharing things we wouldn't share with anyone else.

"I can't believe Baecos would do that to his mate," she said.

"Drain him? I asked her.

"Sleep with other people," she said. I wanted to correct her but I felt her gaze and she spoke before I had a chance to. "Would you feel comfortable doing that with the person you want to be with?"

Did we really have to do this in front of Ash? Even though he gave no indication he was listening I knew he was. It was too juicy of a topic not to.

"I wouldn't," I told her. "But if the person that I end up with," *you.* "wants multiple partners, I am okay with it if that's what they want."

She nodded and to my great relief she didn't bring up the subject again.

Dinner went by without an issue and before I knew it Cruor, Iniq, and I were walking back up to our rooms. I was tempted to drag Iniq back into my bedroom and finish what we started that morning but I didn't want to force her into anything she wasn't ready for so I let her choose where she wanted to sleep.

We stopped between Cruor's and Iniq's room. Iniq bid us a good night and rushed into her room, no doubt feeling the tension that radiated between us. My eyes trailed to Cruor who was still waiting and watching Iniq's door.

"Planning to sneak into her room tonight?" I asked her.

Her jaw twitched and her red eyes narrowed at me. "I want to apologize to her."

I raised my brow at her. "For not coming to her rescue for two years, or for handing her over to Baecos towards the end?" I let the venom seep through my voice.

"Both," she admitted. "I let my emotions get the better of me and now I plan to make it right."

I scoffed at her. "How do you plan to undo that?"

I couldn't believe her thinking. So idiotic. There was nothing she could do that would make up for what she did. And there was no telling what she would do in the future. Baecos could still very well take Iniq, and I didn't see Cruor wanting to help Iniq regain her throne.

"I will mate her," she said. My blood ran cold.

"After hundreds of years, Cruor? You are ridiculous." My magic flared and it took all I had in me not to tackle her to the ground.

"She was a magician then," she explained. "I didn't want the mating ritual to mess with her."

I rolled my eyes. The mating ritual involved sharing blood and magic, the mutual exchange for mated individuals would bond them together for eternity and they would not be able to be separated after that. There were some rumors demon blood would make magicians' magic react badly to it and lash out to harm the users own body. Many believed that it was because the magician and creature blood couldn't fuse but it was a stupid notion because if that was true why would half-bloods like Cruor even exist?

"Your own cowardice is the whole reason Baecos got her in the first place," I spat at her. "Don't blame it on the mating bond. You know what?" I gripped at her shirt and pulled her closer, growling in her face. "Your cowardice is the reason for all of this to happen. Her six deaths, everything Baecos has done to her, it's all you."

"Don't put that on me," she spat and pushed me away from her.

"What did you do while he was killing her, Cruor?" I asked my voice raising. "Raping her? Starving her? What were you doing?"

"What were *you* doing?" she hissed at me. "You were taking advantage of her right under his roof. I bet she ran right into your awaiting arms and you used her position to force yourself between her legs."

"I would never do that to her," I hissed. My magic lashed out wildly around me, begging to destroy something.

"Don't lie to yourself," she said with a mock laugh showing her fangs. "Then tell me Spiris, how did you help her? You could have run with her the very night she came back into this world."

Anger flooded my system and made me see red. What did I do? Is she blind?

"I died for her, Cruor," I hissed. "I died because you were *too much of a coward* to take her out while you had a chance. I was okay to die there! I begged you to take her and what did you do? You left!"

I slammed her against the wall ready to rip her throat out. My blood pumped loudly in my ears drowning out everything around me.

"You can't blame me for that," she rushed out. "Isn't this better now? You should be grateful for my actions because if it wasn't for me, you wouldn't be the demon you are now getting your dick wet by In—"

Cruor was cut off when I was thrown off her and a slap was delivered to her face. The slap echoed down the hallway leaving us all stunned. Iniq stood in front of her, still dressed in her clothing from before.

She had to have been listening to us the entire time.

Cruor's eyes were wide as she took in Iniq's face. I couldn't make out her expression as her hair covered her face like a curtain, but I could feel the way her magic rose sharply and poisoned the air like a dark cloud.

"I don't want your apologies," she muttered, her voice sounding hallow. "I would have maybe accepted them but not after those words. How dare you insinuate that Spiris just stood by? How dare you blame him for his own death?"

"Iniq, it's not like that," Cruor scrambled for words.

"You do realize that he is the only reason I can stand in front of you now, right? Tell me, do you know how it feel to die, Cruor?" she asked. There was a pause. "Do you?"

"...no," Cruor whispered.

"Take it from someone who has died over and over again. There is nothing worth death. Nothing," she pushed Cruor back harshly and grabbed my hand before slamming the door shut, leaving Cruor's stunned form still in the hallway.

CHAPTER NINE
INIQ

How dare she?
I was fuming. I couldn't believe Cruor. How dare she insinuate that Spiris did nothing when he had lost his life so that I could live? He had no guarantee that he would be reincarnated but he still did everything he could to get me out of that hell hole. Not to mention the days he spent with me, watching over me and making sure that I wasn't falling apart.

"Iniq," Spiris said and grabbed my shoulders. I met his gaze, his eyebrows were pushed together and a small scowl graced his lips. "Let's rest, don't mind her words. We will leave soon and you cannot afford to waste magic."

"How can I not?" I asked him, pulling at his shirt. "How could I sit by while she said that about you Spiris? How are you not angry?"

"I am," he said with a lopsided smile. "But seeing you slap her was one of the best things to happen tonight."

"That doesn't stop her words from hurting, Spiris. She doesn't know what you went through while you were there. She doesn't know that you are literally the only reason why I am still here." The words spilled out of me. "Without you Spiris I don't know what I would do. Seeing you die like that was the worst." I had to clear my throat. My eyes stung as the words left my mouth. I had thought it for so long but when had I ever said it? Did I ever tell Spiris how grateful I was for everything he had done for me?

"You don't want to ask what the best thing was?" he asked, startling me.

"What are you talking about? Nothing went well—" I was cut off by his lips coming down on mine. It was short and sweet; I couldn't even process it while it happened. He pulled away from me and a grin stretched across his face.

"A thank you. For fighting for me," he whispered. Blush tinted his cheeks almost immediately. "Uh... sorry Iniq, I just—"

It was my turn to cut him off by wrapping my arms around his shoulders and pulling his lips to mine. I tangled my hand in his soft curls and his arms wrapped around my waist pulling me closer to him.

"Don't be sorry," I whispered against his lips.

It had been coming for a long time, I felt it. From the touches and glances in the Other World to the way that he looked at me with hungry eyes last night. I knew that there was no way to push off this feeling for any longer. I didn't want to. Spiris made me comfortable, he was the one that understood everything, I wanted nothing more than to show him how much he meant to me.

Without Nitri here there was really no need to hide ourselves anymore. He had to know what was going on but he wouldn't dare reach out to us. And that just meant that I could be selfish. I could take the kisses I wanted, enjoy his company, be with him like I had always wanted to without worrying about a crazed High King threatening us.

"I've been wanting to do this since the first time I met you," he said. This time his lips left a ghost of a kiss on my forehead. I smiled and leaned into him.

"Let's prepare for bed," I said in an excited whisper. I pulled back to see a delicious looking smile grace Spiris's face.

"What does this mean for us?" I asked Spiris.

Once we had torn ourselves away from our heated kiss, we both washed and got ready for the night. I was giddy with excitement but the biggest feeling that crashed through me after the kiss was relief. Relief I wasn't alone in this. Relief that he chose me as I had chosen him. We no longer had to play the stupid game and there was no more wall between us.

Tonight, I had him join me in bed instead of him going to his room. I wore the same black robe that I wore the night before. It was satisfying and even a bit exciting to see the ways his eyes trailed my body. During my nightmares I could never think of the possibility of being touched by another, it terrified me, disgusted me. But if it was Spiris, if he wanted me as much as I wanted him... I trusted him intrinsically.

"Whatever you want it to mean," he replied and pulled me into his chest, his lips against my forehead. I sighed into it, pulling him even closer to me.

"Are you sure you want something like this with me?" I asked and looked up to meet his dark eyes. I wanted to give him a chance to pull away before I made the decision to change us completely. He smiled softly at me.

"I have never wanted it with anyone else," he answered. "Were you able to hear my last words to you?" He asked.

I love y—

"Yes," I breathed, my heart pounding in my chest. I wanted to hear them more than anything.

"Well, they stay true," he said. I pushed his back to the bed and climbed on top of him, straddling his lap. The black robe parted around my thighs and I could feel my already hard nipples poke against the fabric. His hand gripped my hips roughly.

"I felt you last night," I told him and ground my hips into him, enjoying the way his hardness felt against my thin underwear. "I was waiting for you to make your move."

"Iniq I—" Spiris started but I brought my finger down to his lips to stop him from talking.

"I wanted you to," I told him. "I wore this on purpose." I ground against him once more and let out a small whimper when I felt his length rub against my wet folds. "I don't want to deny this any longer."

Spiris's tongue shot out to teasingly lick the finger against his lips. Even just the small flick of his tongue made my insides melt.

"Say it. The thing you never got to," I commanded and leaned down so that I was only centimeters away from his lips. "Please."

"I love you, Iniq," he whispered. I captured his lips with mine again. I couldn't get enough of the way they felt against mine. They were perfect and so soft.

"Again," I whispered against his lips and bit them softly.

"I love you," he answered and groaned when I ground my hips into his. "Iniq, listen, we don't have to."

"I want to," I told him and sat straight up, undoing my robe. I was only wearing panties, and from the way his eyes widened, I knew he could see how wet they were. He sat up and gripped the back of my neck, forcing my mouth down to his. His tongue explored my mouth so expertly, it made heat coil in my stomach. He took control easily, and I felt myself melt against his touch.

He flipped us over so instead he was on top of me.

"I love you," he growled as he left wet kisses down the middle of my neck following the dagger. "I always have." His kisses went lower and I found myself gasping and arching into them his tongue lapped at my erect nipples. My hand pulled harshly at his curls and he sucked my nipple into his mouth in response.

"I wanted you to take me last night," I told him. "So badly. I didn't care where we were, I wanted to feel you inside me."

A hand pushed my legs opened and trailed the length of my thigh, leaving shivers in its wake. I opened my legs wider for him but he continued to teasingly brush his fingers against my thighs, getting closer to where I wanted him before pulling away. His mouth came to mine again.

"You can kiss me whenever," he told me. "I didn't know if you wanted this." His hand finally brushed the front of my wet panties. "I didn't know if *I was allowed* to be with you like this."

"Of course I wanted this," I moaned and arched into his touch. His hot tongue slid across the other nipple.

"Is this okay?" he asked as he tugged at the lace between my legs.

"More than okay," I responded. He slowly slid them down my legs leaving trailed kisses down my body as he did so. He looked up at me when he was level with my wetness.

"You tell me if you want me to stop," he said. I nodded then let out a gasp as his tongue lapped up my wetness. I gripped at his hair he sucked on my clit so hard I was sure I would come on the spot.

"Fuck, Spiris," I moaned. He continued to suck on my clit as one finger came to tease my entrance. I bucked into him, losing myself in the way his tongue would run down my slit then back up to suck on my clit. He inserted two fingers inside me slowly then began pumping into me.

He lifted my leg to rest over his shoulder, allowing his

fingers to sink deeper into me. My body tensed as I felt my orgasm come up on me faster than I was expecting. He must have felt it as well because his fingers pounded into me harder than before, and the pressure from him sucking on my clit became so powerful that I had to bite my hand to keep from screaming out.

His mouth left my clit to teasingly bite my nipple, then pressed a single kiss to my lips. I lifted his sleep shirt up and over his head, the fingers that were still pounding into me leaving me for just a moment. I paused as he hovered over me and his body was bared. I had forgotten about the tattoo on his chest, the one that matched my own. I traced it with my finger. I couldn't help the panic that clawed at my throat when memories of Baecos flashed through my mind. The space felt suffocating.

Spiris must have sensed what was going on because he leaned down, his forehead touching mine and exhaled slowly.

"Tell me what you need," he said, voice low.

"Tell me again."

"I love you, Iniq," he said with conviction. I exhaled slowly trying to get a grip on myself. I pushed him lightly over so he fell over on his back.

"Take them off."

He complied quickly and I was met with his hard erection. I teased his length slowly before straddling him. I grabbed his hardness pumping him once, twice, then I slowly rubbed the tip through my wetness. Spiris let out a moan, and by the way his eyes almost rolled into the back of his head, I could tell that the temptation was killing me as much as it was him.

The control was intoxicating, and I played with the idea of teasing him longer, but we could always leave the play time for later. This time I needed him. I slowly descended on him and groaned as he filled me. My head fell back when I felt the sheer size of him inside. His erection that was pushed up to my back last night didn't prepare me for his size. He gripped my hips lightly and thrust into me from below.

I gasped and grabbed his hands to rest them near his side. I placed my hands on his chest covering the sun from view and lifted up, only to slam my hips back into him. His hands grabbed the sheets below him tightly and a groan left his lips. I loved the sounds and swiveled my hips until I was rewarded with more.

With each movement I felt him reach deeper inside me than before and I couldn't keep my moans quiet. I looked him the eyes as I rode him feeling another orgasm rising fast. Even as the orgasm sent jolts through my body I didn't stop riding him until he came. Only then did I let his hand grips my hips as he continued to pump inside of me, filling me.

I rolled over onto the bed out of breath. Looking over to Spiris, I couldn't help but smile at him.

"Spiris, we need to go down to the dining hall," I said with a moan as he pushed my hips into the sink. His dark eyes met mine in the mirror and he had a deliciously devilish smile playing at his lips.

We had just gotten out of the shower, where he had insisted on eating his breakfast before going down to the dining hall. I couldn't complain, the way he worshiped me with his tongue was enough to send me reeling in a matter of minutes. Now he was behind me, pushing his erection into me. I didn't know how many times he was able to go but I couldn't deny him when he *looked like that.* His dark curls framed his face perfectly and gave me enough of a view to see the dark expression his eyes held. How could I have resisted him this long?

"Can you blame me?" he said and nipped at my ear. His hand lightly tugged at the towel that I was holding. I let it fall to the floor, exposing my naked body and allowing him better access to the parts that already ached for him. His eyes traced from the dagger tattoo on my throat to the sun. "You're so beautiful." His long fingers lightly arched my back and pulled my hips back. I bit my lip at the action feeling my stomach flutter.

I would never get tired of *this* Spiris. The commanding one. The one that knew what he wanted and would take it. This one I hoped would be mine and mine alone. I don't care what he showed the rest of the world but I wanted to keep this part of his self for me only.

I leaned my elbows on the counter and spread my legs for him, giving him a smirk in the mirror. He ran the tip of himself through my folds teasingly like I had done last night. I gripped harshly into the counter.

"Spiris," I called to him. He paused and met my eyes, his dark ones almost pleading for me to give him the signal. "I love you."

He stirred into action, entering me in one motion. His hands gripped the counter on either side of me and he trailed kisses across my shoulder and began to slowly thrust into me.

"Say it again," he growled, his teeth coming to tug my ear.

"I love you," I said and his hips snapped into me. "I love you," I was rewarded with another thrust. My hips were biting into the countertop, but I didn't mind so much, not when the way he filled me felt so right. A little pain was only adding onto the pleasure anyways.

His thrusts came faster now, his hips snapping into me. I arched further into him to allow him deeper access. I watched him through the mirror as continued his frenzied thrusts, teeth gritted and eyes hooded, small groans coming from his mouth. Seeing him like that only furthered my arousal.

I grabbed his hand as he pushed me harder against the counter, nails biting into flesh. I gritted my own teeth, the feeling of him moving inside me enough to send me reeling for a second time that morning.

His body shuddered against me as he came not long after I had. He didn't pull out until her had thoroughly kissed every spot on my neck.

"Hungry?" he asked with a shit eating grin.

After we finally tore ourselves off of each other we made our way downstairs They all looked at us as we entered. Aselia giving a knowing smile and Cruor had a scowl on her face. I had no doubt Cruor had heard me, but from the look on Aselia's face she had to have known as well.

I took my seat next to her.

"We are leaving today," I told her.

"Oh, that's no fun," she said with a pout. "We just started enjoying ourselves, no?"

"We have to stick with the plan," I growled. Spiris pushed a plate over to me and I gave him a smile. His grin stirred something in me.

"But the faster we go to the Dark King, the faster we have to go back home, and I don't know about you but I don't want to meet father again so soon," she threw a pink fruit in to her mouth and gave me a smirk.

"People are dying , Aselia," I reminded and took a mouthful of something that tasted eerily similar to cheese potatoes.

She gave a loud sigh. "Fine, after this we will leave while it is still early." She looked at Cruor. "Sorry can't stay that long this time."

"I wished you never came," she jabbed with a small smile.

"Ouch Cruor, I thought you liked me," Aselia said with a mock cry. "Felix, don't tell me you feel the same way? Ash?"

Felix gave her a deadpan look while Ash tried to speak through mouthfuls of food.

"Manners," I chided automatically. The table paused. I looked around at the eyes. "What?"

"You just... used to say that a lot," Ash mumbled and wiped

his lips. "We were baby mongrels when we came into the Fire Kingdom."

"You hated how dirty they were," Cruor commented from the head of the table. "I swear sometimes you sounded like Fluvis."

"Don't talk with your mouth full. Wear clothes in the dining hall. No fighting in the castle." Felix listed off. "But that Iniq wouldn't dare kill one of her own."

My heart clenched when he turned his scarred face towards mine. I deserved that.

"I couldn't imagine living in a castle with so many half breeds. They act like feral animals half the time," Aselia said with a snort.

"Aselia," I chided feeling anger prick at my skin. "You will be a king one day; you can't think like that."

"Don't tell me what to do," she growled at me. "You are worse than a half breed and you don't even half all your memories back. You are literally walking around with half a brain."

"Don't," Spiris growled from next to me. His hand gripped mine.

"Don't get me started on you," she said with a snort.

"Enough," Cruor said with a growl. "Eat and get out."

Not an hour later were we hiking through the woods once more. The sun was high over our heads and the dead gnarled tree branches around us didn't do anything to shield us from the rays causing my body to heat up as we walked. The Other World was devoid of this kind of heat, forcing us to always have to wear clunky clothing in order to keep warm. I am sure the full-blooded demons didn't have the same problem as I but then against that may have been the point. Nitri never wanted my kind to enter the world so why would he make it with them in mind?

Kneku and Faelin must have been going crazy after all those years. Or maybe at this point they were just used to it, void of all the emotions that once made them the least bit mortal. Kneku was different though, he was looking out for us and he provided a kind of comfort that I had thought the world could no longer provide me. At least while I was here, I could save the memory and show Kneku when I went back, maybe he would be able to feel the heat off it.

I didn't know how far we trekked through the bumpy terrain, but my irritation grew as we walked on. It seemed like there was no end to the trees around us, they started to blur together and I was no longer sure that we were not going in circles. I swear the trees looked the same. It didn't help that Aselia just had to sing as she walked, she did it on the way to the Fire Kingdom and now onto the Dark one. She acted as though it was her job to constantly find new ways to annoy us. She wasn't a bad singer per say, it was just that even though I couldn't understand the words I felt as though they were seared into my brain after hearing them repeated so often.

"How much longer?" I asked and stretched my magic out trying to feel for any type of barrier. There was none.

"No clue," Aselia said, continuing to walk without a care in the world.

I growled as my foot caught on dead branches. Spiris gripped the top of my arm, helping me steady myself. I sent him a smile. If he was as annoyed as I was by the way Aselia was acting he was an expert at hiding it.

"Are we even going the right way?" I asked as I jogged up to her.

"Yep," she said popping the "p". Her long dark hair swung with each step.

I sighed and tried to grab at her shirt but she slipped out of my grasp.

"Slow down!" I yelled at her and jumped forward to grab her shirt, but my hand went right through her as if she was a ghost. Aselia looked back at me with a bone chilling smile and then her body disappeared in cloud of black smoke.

"What the fuck?" I asked and looked back to Spiris and his wide-eyed stare met mine.

CHAPTER TEN
INIQ

I searched the forest around us. There was no sound other than our own pants as we frantically searched for Aselia.

She had definitely left with us, I distinctively remembered tripping into her multiple times as we climbed over the broken branches. She would turn back and sneer at me as I did. So, when did she go missing? How did she even go missing?

"It has to be dark magic," I concluded as Spiris came to join me by my side. We had both parted to search in the distance be remain in each other's view just in case. I intertwined his fingers with mine relieved that he was still solid.

"I didn't know dark magic could do that," he said. "Did you notice when she disappeared?"

I shook my head. "I was watching her most of the time, unless I was tripping, but that only took a second."

"Do you think the Dark King took her?" he asked and gripped my hand tightly.

"I don't know," I said truthfully. "Did you notice anything odd?"

Spiris shook his head and looked around the area, but I had

already checked. There was nothing around us that would give us any indication where she went.

"Aselia!" I yelled and pulled Spiris further. He pulled me back.

"Wait, let me try something," he said and used his fang to bite into his free hand. Blood swelled instantly and he swiped it against some of the dead trees. "So I can track our path." Even though this was a serious situation I could not help the way the sight of him biting into his hand caused my stomach to flutter.

I nodded and pulled him along, still yelling for Aselia. The ground before us seemed to get steeper and steeper as we walked causing me to have to stop multiple times to catch my breath. I looked around the area not noticing any type of incline or change around us. If I didn't feel the change in the steepness of the ground, I would have assumed that we were circling the same spot.

There was no doubt now that it was dark magic. We should have gotten somewhere.. It would have been impossible to walk as long as we did and not be able bump into any of the kingdoms.

There was silence between us as we both tried to catch our breath. I heard a light shuffle near us and then an ear-piercing scream somewhere beyond the tree line. My heart pounded in my chest and I felt my senses go on high alert, not unlike the times I was fighting against Vitos back in the Light Kingdom. There was a pause in the scream and then it picked up again causing the trees around us to shake.

This time I knew who it was. The scream was from Aselia.

I gripped Spiris's hand and ran towards the sound.

"Iniq?" Spiris asked, surprised. "Wait, what happened?" He dug his heels in the ground and pulled on my arm painfully. I looked back to him but there was someone else that held my hand in his place.

Instead of the horned curly haired man with a warm smile,

in his place stood a pale man with blonde hair and purple eyes. His lips showed that blood chilling smile that I had seen so many other times in my nightmare. Baecos had found me.

I instinctively tried to let go but his hand held tight.

"Don't let go!" he yelled. What was once Spiris's voice slowly morphed into Baecos.

"This can't be happening," I whispered.

"What do you mean, Iniq?" he asked his head cocking much like Spiris' would. I gulped and screwed my eyes shut, taking a deep breath.

"Spiris?" I whispered and used my other hand to feel the hand that was currently interlocked with mine. It felt like Spiris's warm one instead of Baecos's cold disgusting one. Spiris had much bigger hands than Baecos did. Baecos had one that showed his lack of work. It brought me comfort to know that this was some type of twisted dream and I was not really holding hands with my worst enemy.

"What are you seeing?" he asked.

"Baecos," I replied. "Did you hear the scream?"

"A scream?" he asked. "No."

"What do you see around you?" I asked.

"Uhh, trees still," he replied.

"Are we on a hill?" I asked and tried to feel around my surrounds. I made contact with a tree.

"Not a hill," he said. "We've been hiking up a mountain," I opened my eyes and was met with Baecos's purple ones once more. I quickly shut them feeling my stomach twist. I wanted to run from the sight so bad but I had to push the feeling down.

"I didn't know we were on a mountain," I told him. He tugged me closer and I deeply inhaled his familiar scent.

"Where did the sound come from?" he asked. "Point to it," I tried to point to the direction I was heading previously. He began slowly walking towards where I had previously heard the scream. After not even ten feet he sucked in a sharp breath of air. "Tell me what you see in front of you."

I opened my eyes and saw rows of trees and flat ground in front of us.

"Forest," I responded.

"I will lead us from now on," he said and pulled us in the opposite direction.

"What was there?" I asked and begrudgingly followed Baecos's form.

"Nothing," he replied hastily.

"What do you mean nothing?" I hissed. His eyes washed over me for only a second before continuing to lead me.

"I mean nothing. As in you were about to run off a cliff."

"Let's rest here for a moment," Spiris said while helping me to sit against the bark of a wrangled tree.

We had been walking for over an hour and still could not find our way to the Dark Kingdom. Every time that I reached out my magic it felt like we were further and further from any of the kingdoms. It didn't sit right with me because the map that I had once seen Fluvis and Cruor staring over showed that the Dark Kingdom, Water Kingdom, and Fire kingdom shouldn't be all that far from each other. The Dark Kingdom was North and slightly to the west while the Water Kingdom was straight north and the Fire Kingdom to the very west of this world. If that map was to be believed, how were we stuck in the triangle of forest that they created without feeling any magical barriers around us?

I peeked towards Spiris to check if the dark magic was still messing with his form. I had tried to keep my eyes closed or at least trained to the ground while we made our way back to a safe spot. I was pleasantly surprised to see his black eyes and tan skin looking back at me.

"Why do you think it is you can see through the magic and I cannot?" I asked and tangled my arm though his, allowing my head to rest on his shoulder.

"Maybe because of my power?" he mused.

"I have light too," I grumbled. "Maybe it's because you're a demon."

"Maybe."

"We have yet to pass the trees I marked earlier," he said after a moment.

"But it feels like we haven't gone far at all," I said.

"I know."

I let out a sigh and rubbed my sore ankle. I had rolled it more than once during our walk and it felt painfully swollen. I should have known that the Dark King pulled some shit when I tripped not once, not twice, but six times since we set out on our journey.

"Does it hurt?" Spiris asks and wrapped his long fingers around my ankle carefully. "Do you know how to heal it?"

"No," I confessed.

"It's about—"

"Intent, I know," I said and gave him a smile. He returned it softly and his hand glowed as he began to heal my ankle. Even as I saw the redness go down, I could not feel his magic clash with mine.

I sat straight up and grabbed his wrist.

"What's wrong?" he asked.

"Wait a minute," I murmured and focused on pouring magic into him. Black glittering smoke covered his wrist, but his body gave no reaction that he felt the magic. Usually when magic enters your body you would have no choice but to react. It was an intimate thing, pouring your life essence into another being, and to have no reaction was close to impossible. "He's blocking the signature."

Spiris's jaw tightened.

We were screwed. We were literally walking into this blind and deaf. The only person who could see though the tricks was Spiris, I was utterly useless. So far we had seen a fake Aselia, heard a scream, then the cliff, then Baecos, what else could this king do?

"At least I can see now," I mused and leaned back into the tree feeling at a loss.

"Maybe it's weaker in this area?" he asked and leaned back to look at the sky. I let myself drink in the view of him in the sunlight. We had been in the darkness of the other world for so long that I had forgotten how beautiful he looked in the sun. His warm skin drank in the sunlight and his black curls gleamed in the light.

I sighed and turned back to the blue sky. If it was weaker here that would mean we were probably further away from the kingdom than when we first started. How many more miles would we need to walk until we got to the kingdom?

Would the magic even let us in? So far, the magic we had encountered never took a solid form but I couldn't say what would happen when we finally made it closer to the base.

"We have to go back to the cliff," I told him. Spiris stayed silent, the only indication that he heard me was his hand squeezing mine. "The further away we are the less the magic right? So, if we *really* want to reach the kingdom we have to go where the magic is the most potent. He's probably using this as a way to guard his Kingdom without a standard barrier."

We stewed in the silence for a moment.

"Are you sure you want to keep doing this?" he asked. "We can go to the Water Kingdom. Fluvis will gladly accept us back."

"You don't know that," I said with a light laugh. I didn't expect Fluvis to hate me for what I did but there was a part of me that was still scared that I would meet his once warm eyes and they would be narrowed at me shining with hate.

"What I mean is we can give up the throne," he whispered. "We are here now, we don't have to go back to the Other World."

I thought over his words, it was tempting to say the least. Before the door had practically forced me back into the other world but now that I was here, and not as close to death, it hadn't even shown me so much as a whisper. It just left me alone with my thoughts giving me no indication what the right path was.

Did that mean that it gave up on me? Maybe it also found out that the weak emotions had gotten in my head.

I shook my head and stood up, pulling Spiris up with me. Running away from this would only prove how weak I was. Nitri's jabs would come true and he would be happy to prove that someone like me would never take over the throne. If it was not for myself, at least I could push myself just so that Nitri would forever live his existence knowing that he was wrong.

"When I entered that doorway, I promised myself that I would no longer let fate throw me around like a rag doll," I gave him a small smile and let my hand graze his cheek. He leaned into my touch. "This is the time that I need to make good on my promise. I can't give up so easily here."

"It's not giving up, Iniq," he fought back but his words had little power behind them. "It's choosing the easy life. Choosing a life you don't have to fight for."

"I am choosing a life that is rightfully mine," I told him. "You have seen how Nitri and Aselia think of the people in this world, it is unfair. People are dying left and right," The child from the market so long ago flashed across my mind. "Children, and they don't care. Imagine how many generations of families have been wiped out while I tried to figure out this mess?"

"If it's for the good of the world, I don't want to hear it," he said. "Can you at least do what you want for once?"

I gave him a sad smile. "This is what I want," I leaned forward and brushed my lips across his. "With you. I want to prove to everyone that they are wrong. I am not weak. I am the rightful heir to the throne and I will get there no matter the cost and change this world for the better."

He kissed me back.

"As long as I can stay with you all the while, I will follow you anywhere," he said.

I leaned back and pulled him forward.

"Let's get this thing done."

It was the visions that hit first. Spiris led me through the forest and with each step his form became increasingly like Baecos. First it was the eyes, then the hair, then the skin, and finally his face fully morphed into Baecos. The slow change was less jarring, it only really got to me when I could no longer hear Spiris' voice when he spoke. Then he started speaking on his own and would chuckle every now and then like he was giddy at the idea of capturing me once more. The likeness was too spot on and caused paranoia to creep up on me like an old friend.

"Do you remember when you tried to escape in the forest on you first night?" Baecos's form said with a laugh. His purple eyes met mine as he looked back at me. "That was so cute. You were so weak then, even weaker than you are now. I shouldn't have waited so long to drain you."

I let out a sigh and gripped Spiris' hand tightly.

"I've always wanted to drain a god's power," he continued. "Once the power was mine who was to say I could not become a god myself?"

I rolled my eyes. I wondered how much of the vision came from my own memory. I had never heard Baecos talk about why he even wanted the power so bad. Like yes, everyone wants to be powerful, but why *my* power? Especially when the dark king was right here? Baecos should have known he would never have been able to enter the Other World, right?

A breeze twirled around me and I felt a prick of magic in it. The first bit of magic I had felt since Aselia had disappeared from us. It was soft at first but quickly began to pick up paced. I gripped Spiris with both of my hands. His voice had disappeared a long time ago but I at least needed to tell him what was happening. Maybe it would point us in the right direction, or at least for me it would help me solidify my footing.

"Wind. Strong. Feels like magic," I told him. My body began shivering against the chill. Baecos's form still brought us forward with a smile on his lips. The likeness really was stunning. I wanted to feel proud of myself for being able to stand here and look at him, listen to his disgusting words but I couldn't when the fear of him sunk it's claws into my heart.

"So silly of you to think you could ever escape me," Baecos said. This time his form turned around to face me, stopping in his tracks completely. I froze.

"Spiris? Why are we stopping?"

There was no reply. Instead Baecos pulled me to his chest and tilted my chin, so I was looking into his eyes.

"Spiris is not here anymore," he answered. "I told you I'd come back for you, did I not?"

I screwed my eyes shut trying to force Baecos touch and voice out of my mind.

"Spiris?" I squeezed out and Baecos hand wrapped around my hair and gripped it harshly.

"He's not here, Iniq," Baecos cooed, and I felt his tongue lick the side of my face.

I pushed the form away harshly, unable to take the feeling of his hands on me any longer. When I did rain began pouring in the forest, soaking me to the bone in an instant.

Baecos looked up at the blue sky and laughed. I looked up as well. Was any of this real?

I know I shouldn't trust my eyes but there was no way Spiris would act like that. This couldn't be him. Did Baecos really find me all the way up in the mountains of the Dark Kingdom? The rational part of my brain told me it wasn't possible, but the one that was fearful of the monster that Baecos still was told me that this was *very real* and I should be running.

I turned to the closest tree feeling its' bark, checking if it was real and slowly sat down against it and brought my knees up to my chest. The bark felt wet and the rain quickly soaked my clothing. I tried to focus on my breathing, the same instinct that told me to run for my life pushed my heart to pound and caused me to breath in short pants.

Baecos knelt in front of me, hands on my knees. I tried to cover my eyes with my hands, but he forced them away. Just like before he didn't want me to hide from him. He wanted me to watch as he thoroughly destroyed my life.

"Face it, Iniq," he said. "It's just me and you out here." His hand trailed up the leg of my wet pants. They clung to me now and I swear I could actually feel whatever heat Baecos had sink through the fabric. "You can scream, you can fight, but no one will come get you. I wanted to take you in front of Cruor that night, do you remember? It will be all the sweeter when Spiris can watch."

My chest constricted. I tried to pool my magic in my hand to make a weapon, something, anything sharp but when I looked down at my shaking hands, my magic would not show itself.

"My magic," I whispered in horror. I tried again to conjure a dagger. Nothing showed. I met Baecos eyes slowly.

"You're stuck here," he said, a smile forming on his face.

I didn't want to believe it, I couldn't. But a part of me

believed him. Maybe I had never really left his dungeon at all. That thought alone was almost enough to send me spiraling.

I wanted to badly just to shut everything down. To close my eyes and cover my face until the nightmare was over but I promised myself. Promised the people of this world that I would take that throne at any cost.

This was that cost. No one said this would be easy. If anything, the world had consistently showed me that it would be the hardest thing I ever had to do.

I got up slowly, shaking violently as I did so. Baecos's form stood with me, he leaned close to my body with his breath tickling my neck. I tried to walk forward slowly trying to retrace my steps. Trying to figure out where the magic had changed.

"Where are you going, Iniq?" he said. "You are going to have to run faster than that if you want to escape."

"I'm not trying to escape," I said, gritting my teeth against the fear that was trying to lock my legs.

He's not real. He's not here. Spiris is here somewhere, he will help me.

I walked the path that I had with Spiris, feeling the bark of the twisted trees around me. I didn't know what his limit was but I had figure that I could still feel the scenery. From the mountain incline to tripping over branches, I could feel the real scenery around me. The only thing that still threw me off was the pouring rain.

"So pitiful," Baecos said as he came in front of me, blocking my path. His hands came to my sides hold my arms down. I tried to look away from him but he made sure to stay in my line of sight with that stupid grin and blond wet hair sticking to his face. I gritted my teeth and tried to fit my arms to his face. His eyebrows raised. "Coming around so soon?" I trailed my hand up through his long hair and then I tried to feel over the empty space on top of his head. "I stand corrected. You've gone crazy."

No horns. I gripped the empty air. This was a hundred

percent not Spiris. I tried to swallow my tears but my eyes stung at the realization that this really was a Baecos, or at least a version of Baecos that could touch me.

"Spiris?" I asked and tried to feel out around me for a sign that he was beyond the vison of my real-life nightmare. My hand came in contact with something soft and invisible. I tried to look over the area but I could only make out the trees beyond. I let out a sigh of relief.

I felt the invisible form and finally reached something akin to a hand. It wrapped around mine without question and I felt the figure lift it and place a small kiss on my hand.

Spiris. Thank god. The relief that crashed through me almost brought me to my knees.

I gripped the hand tightly and turned back to Baecos. He was watching with a smile. I walked around him dragging the invisible figure with me.

"You're going the wrong way," he called after me. "Go right!"

I continued my march. Did he really think I was that stupid?

"Don't you want to live?" he asked and jogged up to my side. His hand tugging at my hair. "Do you hear me?"

I winched and smacked his hand away from me, pushed through to the place he didn't want me to go. Invisible Spiris was still holding on. Baecos got angrier and anger as I walked on. Threatening to strap me to the table, to kill me for real, to kill Spiris again. I ignored it and kept on, until Baecos disappeared.

I looked back to Spiris and was met with something even more frightening than Baecos.

I was met with Claire. Her normally long grey hair was a mess around her head and covered in dripping blood, her neck was at a sharp ninety-degree angle and her eyes had frosted over.

Don't let go. I chanted to myself. I couldn't tear my eyes away from her.

She took a deep wheezing breath.

"You should have saved me," she said. "Not killed me."

"You're not real," I whispered and tried to walk back towards my path but she tugged me back.

"Did you ever think Baecos had treated me like you?" she asked. "Did you maybe think that I was trying to save myself?"

"Lies," I hissed. "You hated me from the beginning."

"You raised me, Iniq. You and Cruor were the closest things I had to parents, why would I hate you?" She asked.

I tore my tear-filled eyes away from her and grabbed the figure back towards the path.

"Do you know Cruor still blames you for my death? She was so ready to hand you over to Baecos," she said. "She wanted to see what he would do to you. Thought you deserved it."

I swallowed harshly.

Baecos's form appeared again near the trees in the distance.

"I would have given her the best show," he said and followed closely besides me as I passed. His hand brushed the hair off my shoulder and his face was close to my ear as he spoke. "You would have like it. I remember how much you wanted it. Practically begging me to fuck you."

"Shut up," I hissed. "I didn't know you then."

He asked and his hand rested on my chest, right over my heart.

"But you did. You always knew deep down who I was," he said. "It was just you were too gone to care."

I huffed and tried to continue on shaky legs. My head began to swim as I did and his touches started to burn.

"You know death does that to you," he whispered and pulled my hair harshly back causing me to stop. Claire's form bumped into my back.

No. I reminded myself. *It's Spiris. I never let go of his hand.*

"Dying does that to people," he said "Makes them go crazy, makes them loose the will to live. Even now," his hand gripped tightly at my throat. "Do you even know what you want? Do you even feel anything? For Spiris? For the people of this world? For yourself?"

"She enjoyed killing me," Claire said from behind me. The hand began crushing my throat, stopping my breath entirely. This was real. The way his hand gripped around my throat, the way my head started to swim. The vision may have been fake but this, it was real and it would kill me.

"You look so beautiful when you struggle," Baecos cooed.

My vision began to black out.

"Spiris," I choked out. I was going to lose consciousness. I couldn't hold on. And I didn't know what this magic would do to me once I was out. "I'm ... sorry."

Blackness enveloped me.

CHAPTER ELEVEN
SPIRIS

I caught Iniq's limp body before it could hit the rocky floor. We were too far into the mountain now and at such a steep incline she would surely roll to her death.

"It's okay," I murmured against her as I picked her top and tucked her body closer to mine. "You are okay."

I turned my gaze upward to glare at the overpowering figure in front of me.

He had horns three times as large as my own. His long black hair fell around him in waves stopping at his mid torso. They shrouded him much like shadows would but It was not to hide his form, instead they made it look more menacing. He had a bit of scruff on his face making him look older than anyone I had seen in our world. His red eyes were complemented by the black moon that sat in the middle of his forehead. He was wearing a robe similar to what I had seen the Kings wear but instead of all black his had intricate swirls of silver. The front of the robe was open showing intricate swirls of tattoos that did not belong to any elemental magician that I had seen before. His leather pants were peeking out through the robe slits as he stalked towards us.

The shadow figures that had been tormenting Iniq returned to his side like obedient dogs. I had watched uselessly as they abused and almost seriously injured Iniq. The Dark King waved his hand causing my magic to return to me and the surrounding flared to like at my side. The veil was lifted and my senses were attacked with the feeling of magic coming at me from all angles. I broke out into a sweat when I realized how powerful the demon in front of me was. His power rivaled Nitri, it stuck to everything in the area and created an impenetrable aura around us that made it hard to breathe.

"Why didn't you lay off when you saw me?" Aselia said coming up from behind me.

She had found us after our rest against the tree. She had explained that the Dark King had pulled them away from us and he continued to hide her from Iniq's view. He had stayed away from us until now and forced us to stand by helplessly as Iniq struggled. When Aselia had reached out to touch her, with a pained expression Iniq coiled away. Aselia didn't try after that, neither did I. I let Iniq come to me. It was painful for both of us to watch Iniq relive her worst traumas. I couldn't hear the shadow people as they surrounded her but seeing how she acted was enough for me to understand what had happened.

It had been a shock to see how riled up Aselia got after Iniq started crying. Even now she was still breathing heavily and the anger rolled off her in waves with her magic. She had not stopped screaming for the Dark King until he showed. I didn't know what the shadows would have done if she had not shown up when he did. I had tried to grab one as it was fighting Iniq but my hand slid right through it.

I didn't want to think of the way she called my name as she was almost dying. I couldn't help her, didn't know how to. My own eyes burned ad it repeated itself over and over in my head.

"I don't accept just anyone into the kingdom," his deep voice broke across the silence of the forest. "King's offspring or not, no one gets a pass."

"Why did you show up now?" I asked glaring at him. His eyes sized me up and narrowed in on Iniq.

"My shadows have never gotten as far as killing someone before," he admitted. "Many people just turn back when they are faced with what the shadows show them. They worm their way into your mind and pull out your darkest fears, no one can stand that for long. " He walked closer to me, his form towering over me. His hand reached out to trace Iniq's moon tattoo. "I was interested and wanted to test her, see if she really is what the rumors say. With you in the way you would no doubt hinder this experiment."

I pulled Iniq away from his grasp, glaring at him as I did. He raised an eyebrow at me like his power did not just try to kill her.

"Do you recognize her?" Aselia asked.

"I would recognize Neia's child anywhere," he answered.

"So she's a child and I'm an offspring?" she asked with a huff. The Dark King had a smile playing at his lips.

"Nitri is incapable of love. Don't think I do not know of the games he puts you through. So you are, by result, an offspring whose only use in the world is to wither and die unless Nitri will step down," he replied and reached out to Iniq this time, tugging at her hair. "Neia loved every soul out there and most of all, loved her child. I have never seen such a light until she came to me with a child growing in her belly."

"She came here to see you while pregnant?" I asked. "Do you know how she died?"

The Dark King didn't look at me, instead walked away and gestured for us to follow,

"That information is for her child to ask once she is ready."

The Dark Kingdom was located in the heart of the biggest mountain in this world, making it the safest and most impenetrable place. The entrance was at the top of the mountain and gave a birds eye view of the dark forest that surrounded the area. It was also easier for the Dark King to spot when someone had entered the barrier he had placed to scare people away.

As we walked up the mountain the Dark King waved his hand and a door as black as night appeared before us. He didn't look back at us as he opened the iron door and walked into his kingdom. I steeled myself and pulled Iniq closer to my body, she was still shivering.

As we walked inside, we were met with warm air and we came face to face with the throne the Dark King had claimed for himself. It was all black much like the ones the High Kings had, but instead of the twisted iron his had live shadows that hugged the area around the chair. They shivered as he came near as if they quivered in fear of their own King. He sat down in the chair and the shadow people who had been following behind him joined him at his side as if waiting for a command. They were faceless and see though and seemed to work on auto pilot.

Around us were no chairs or furniture of any kind. The floors were made of a black type of rock that shined under the warm lights that were attached to the sparkling ceiling. The ceiling made me distinctly feel like I was under the night sky as each sparkle seemed to shine with its own light. The walls were all made with rough rock, rock that seemed impenetrable and sharp. It felt like he carved a hole out of the mountain and made a kingdom for himself.

"Where are your people?" Aselia asked.

"Inside the mountain," he replied.

"Is the only entrance the one you conjured?" I asked looking around. There was no indication of another door that led away from this room. We were trapped inside with the deadliest king on this world.

"For outsiders," he replied simply. His rough hand lifted and with a flick of his wrist Iniq jerked against me, gasping.

I lowered her to the ground. Her eyes were wide and she was searching around us, no doubt for the shadows that had tormented her earlier. It didn't look like she even realized it was me holding her.

"Iniq," I called softly and place my hand gently on her cheek, trying to calm her.

"Spiris?" she asked. Her eyes shone with unshed tears. "What happened."

"You met my shadows," the Dark King said from his throne. In an instant her tears had dried, and her face went slack.

The change chilled me. All the progress she had made seemed to disappear in a moment's notice.

I helped her stand. She looked over at Aselia pausing before meeting the Dark King head on.

"They didn't look like shadows," she commented and I watched as her eyes shifted to the shadows at his side. "They still look like people to me."

"Because you are not in a demon's body," he said. "Demons can see through my shadow work if I so choose it. Magicians go not get the privilege."

"Why is that?" Aselia asks.

The Dark King ignored her and instead left his throne to stand right in front of Iniq. He glided across the stones, the shadows around him shifting with each step.

"Why are you hear, daughter of Neia?" He asked.

"To learn from you," she answered. "I want to take my rightful place on the throne, but Nitri refuses until I can learn Dark Magic."

The king paused, looking over her. I wanted to know so badly what he was thinking. This demon had to be as old as the kings, the secrets he held must be vast. He had seen it all, from creation to the downfall.

"You do not need me to learn," the Dark King said looking over her as if he was bored. "Someone of your rumored caliber should be able to do it yourself. Or are you not the warrior I was promised?"

"This body is weak," Iniq said. "I am not who I was before nor can I do this alone."

"You truly believe Nitri will let you ascend if you are able to learn?" he asked.

"I don't," she answered. My gut clenched. "But it better than sitting and doing nothing."

"And if he doesn't allow you to ascend?" he asks.

Iniq shifted on the balls of her feet. "I will take it. Forcibly."

It was Aselia that scoffed this time. Neither looked towards her, they were locked in stare. Were they talking in their minds?

"Wanna share with the rest of us?" Aselia said, calling them out on their private conversation.

"Nothing to share," the Dark King said and turned his back on Iniq. I gripped her and pulled her closer to my side. Only once seated did he speak again. "I refuse."

There was a silence.

"What about me?" Aselia asked.

The Dark King looked over like he was bored.

"You don't want the throne," he commented. "Nor would I want to aid you in getting it. Your mind is selfish, uncaring, a real king needs to protect their people and I imagine someone with such a selfish mind doing that."

She bristled but did not fight him. I knew that she was selfish, immature but I was under the assumption that she came her from only one reason: to ascend. My eyes narrowed at Aselia, what was her motive?

"Why?" Iniq asked.

"I care about my people, this information you are asking me to share with you is dangerous. With it comes all the secrets of my kingdom," he explained. His eyes dared her to fight back, they pinned me in place but it seemed to do the exact opposite for Iniq. Her body shook and her fists clenched at her shirt.

"But if I can learn this, magic will be restored," she pushed. "Isn't your kingdom also suffering?"

"No," he answered simply.

I chewed over this information. Hundreds of years ago the Light Kingdom was prosperous even after the death of Iniq's parents. I tried to pinpoint when the kingdom began falling apart but I couldn't pinpoint where things started to go awry. It was like it slowly crept up on us. Magical sickness effected one or two towns then the next year all towns in the Light Kingdom had taken a turn for the worse and graves began to overflow. I shuddered at the memories.

"That doesn't make sense," Iniq said. "Is it because Baecos started messing with peoples magic?"

"I cannot attempt to understand Neia's decision," the Dark King mused. "But I know that she would not risk innocents lives if not absolutely necessary."

"Don't you insult High King Neia like that," Aselia hissed at him. My head snapped to look at her clenched fists and bared teeth.

"It is the truth child, not an insult. Didn't your father teach you anything?" he said and stood once more. "The seat may be empty, may be weak, but the throne will follow the wishes of its previous master until another takes over. Neia taught me as such." He walked down the stairs once more. "She saw you, child. Coming to beg me to teach you."

He was talking to Iniq now. His magic responded to his anger and flared around him widely. The cave shook around us, threatening to collapse under the intense magic pressure.

"Do you know what she saw after that?" he asked. Iniq shrunk back into me. I glared at the Dark King. "Destruction and death. For every kingdom, not just Light and Dark."

"How is that possible?" Iniq whispered.

"She tried to stop it, and it led to her and your father's death," he spat at her. "So, *I refuse*. Refuse to start the cycle that caused Neia's death."

He stormed back to his throne, leaving us all in a state of shock.

"You can rest her for the night and then I will deliver you back outside the barrier for you to figure out the rest for yourself," he said. The shadows came at us, caroling us towards one of the walls where another door appeared out of thin air.

"Is this why you left me with the Fire Kingdom?" Iniq asked pushing against my arms and the shadow figure that pushed us forwards.

"Yes," the Dark King said darkly. We were pushed into the adjacent room and darkness fell over us.

"Don't you dare think to do anything freaky while I am here," Aselia hissed as she sat on the edge of the bed.

We were given a room with a similar cave feeling as the throne room, the only difference being the large bed that spanned across half the room. The *only bed*. And there was no frame or headboard, just a mattress that was placed directly on the ground with a mountain of pillows and blankets.

"Shut up Aselia," Iniq growled and sat on the other end of the bed. I followed her but opted to sit on the floor instead. "Why did you lie to us?"

Aselia crossed her arms and looked away from Iniq, Her hair swinging widely as she did. "I didn't lie."

"The Dark King said you didn't want the throne," I said. "The whole point we are here is to learn dark magic so one of you can take it over."

"I would have let Iniq win anyways," Aselia said with a pout.

Iniq shot up and tackled Aselia to the ground. She straddled her hips and gripped her shirt to pull her closer to her face. I didn't even attempt to pull her off. A smile found its way to my face, I liked that Iniq was showing some emotion. Anger. It felt like she was getting herself back after the horror the dark king put her through, And Aselia deserved it for lying so blatantly.

"That's cheap," Iniq hissed at her. "What was that you played with Nitri, huh? A half-blood like me not getting the throne? What was your plan?"

"Don't get testy, Iniq," Aselia growled, and I felt her magic rise. I began to stand to pull Iniq out of the way but I felt Iniq's magic rise sharply and a glittering cloud hung over the two, almost shielding them from view. "I never wanted this. Ever since I had won, I never wanted the stupid throne, all I wanted was to get father off my back."

Aselia was squirming under Iniq obviously distressed at the magic around her, and I watched as Aselia's skin began to sizzle. I pulled Iniq off of her by the collar, my skin burning as well when it breached the magic that surrounded them. I hissed and Iniq immediately pulled back the magic.

"Sorry," she muttered to me. I forced a smile, my hand beginning to heal itself. A useful demon quirk. "Won what?" she asked Aselia.

Aselia let out a bitter laugh. Her skin healed itself in an instant leaving her skin as smooth as before.

"Did you really think I was my father's only child?" Aselia shook her head. "From young he makes them battle until the strongest one shows themselves." Her eyes were cast downward now. "Many give up and just let the others win because they are so tired. The only one really to keep me going was your mother, Neia was a godsend. She would always tell me I was too important to give up, that I was needed. But she lied. After she died, I realized that I was never needed, that Nitri never planned to step down."

"Of course, he wouldn't step down," Iniq muttered.

"What happened when they lost? Did you kill them?" I asked her. Her eyes were trained on the floor. Was this the *games* the Dark King had mentioned? If so, Nitri was far crueler than I thought possible.

What happened to make him fall so far? It couldn't have been Yara's betrayal. We were missing something important.

"No," she said, her voice sounding hollow. She met our eyes finally her gold ones shining. "Nitri consumes them, stealing their magic and life force."

CHAPTER TWELVE
INIQ

"*He* what?" I asked not grasping what I was hearing. I marched up to Aselia and forced her eyes to meet mine. "A king can take another person's magic from them?"

On top of ignoring the death of millions of his people, he also forced himself on his staff and now I was hearing that he had been killing children? It almost made too much sense, how would a monster like him even care about the lives of his people if he was okay with killing his own children?

"The same thing the Baecos, attempted to do to you," she explained, a frown on her face. "Except when a High King does it, they can take the power for themselves. You forget that the High Kings are partially responsible for creating this universe, Iniq. This is their powerhouse. They can do anything they want."

The absolute horror that filled my veins was something I hadn't felt since being tied to Baecos's stone table. How could he just snuff out their life like that? My stomach felt like it was going to collapse in on itself.

I imagined Aselia as a little girl, her high ponytail swinging about. She won while she battled against countless others, her siblings. The only people who would understand her in this life and she was forced to determine their fate… how could a child live through that? She was the lucky one. Was she ever allowed a moment of happiness in her life? The image of little Aselia smiling in my mind was replaced with the terrifying image of the same girl watching as Nitri drained the magic out of her siblings and dropped their dead bodies in front of her like sacks.

No wonder she acted the way she did.

"No, they can't," I shook my head and marched back to the stone wall we had walked through. "Open up!" I pounded on the rock. My mind was decided. I would not let this continue to happen, I couldn't. Something pushed me forward, egged me on. Like a whisper in the back of my mind . I punched the wall, making sure to put my magic behind it.

You can stop this. The voice whispered. *Go, child. You know what to do.*

"Iniq, stop," Spiris said and pulled me away from the wall. "You will hurt yourself."

I called upon my magic at the command of the whisper in my mind. The information poured into me, and I knew exactly what I needed to do. I waved my hand across the space calling forth all that remained hidden.

The door appeared in front of me. Spiris's grip on me went slack.

"How did you do that?" Aselia asked pushing past me to inspect the door.

"No clue," I told her and gripped the door at the handle and swung it open. The Dark King was still on the throne where we had left him what seemed like moments before.

"No doubt you are Neia's child," the Dark King commented, his red eyes looking over me lazily.

"I demand you teach me," I stormed up to his throne. Even as he sat down, we remained the same height. My legs brushed across his. He raised his eyebrows at my actions. "If not for the light kingdom, then to throw it in Nitri's face."

"Why would I want to do that?" he said with a hum. "I am pretty comfortable living out the rest of my existence there.

"That is a lie," I pushed. "You have been pushed out of the kingdom. You are a full demon, but Nitri had exiled you here forcing you to be the only full demon left in this world."

The Dark king had a frown on his lips.

A mate. The voice whispered to me. I recognized it as the one that came out of the door so long ago. A smile played at my lips. *Of course* this was the reason Nitri wanted him here so badly. It would be the only way to separate him from his mate.

"You're a high king's mate," I summarized. He stiffened. "If you teach me, I can bring him here."

The Dark King straightened in his seat, his eyes narrowing.

"You are promising things you cannot keep, child. Do not test me," he said. "Your offer does not stop the fact that I refuse to participate in the destruction of this world."

"Kneku misses you," I said in a soft tone. His eyes widened at the name but he was not swayed.

"It is not worth the price," he said. "I trust Neia's vison."

I didn't like the idea that popped into my head but it was the only choice at this point. There was no other way to prove to him that I was not what he thought I was. I mean, if my mother could visit us right here and now, I was sure that he would drop it but *that* was unlikely. I swallowed my feelings of discomfort and pushed forward.

"I can show you that I will not lead the destruction of this world," the High King stood up, forcing me back. His large hand gripped the front of my shirt.

"I do not like *liars," he* growled.

"I am not," I told him. "There is a mirror that shows your future, if you promise me that you will be willing to teach me, I can bring it to you here in the matter of two weeks' time."

He paused, letting go of my shirt and plunging into my mind to check if I was lying.

I swear to you. It is real. Please, you are my only hope. I told him.

"If you can show me such a thing exists *and* it shows that you do not destroy this universe, I will teach you," he said.

I let out a breath and turned to Spiris and Aselia with a sheepish smile.

"I guess we have to go back to the Fire Kingdom."

"She will not help you," Aselia said with a scoff. "Not after you fucked your own slave under her roof."

I looked at her my mouth dropped. How did she know?

"I have to agree," Spiris said for once agreeing with Aselia. "She was bound to hear us, Iniq."

I felt my face heat as I led us down the mountain. The Dark King had told the shadows to avoid me and I was grateful because I didn't know if I could handle another trip with Baecos's smirk.

"How did you even do that back there?" Aselia asked jogging to keep up with my fast pace.

"The voices from the door told me," I answered honestly. Aselia stopped in her tracks. I shot her a look.

"They talk to you?" she asked incredulously.

"They don't talk to you?" I asked her. She shook her head.

"I could feel them, they even reached out to me before but never spoke," she said.

"Oh," I said and continued forward. "They told me how to use the power."

They did much more than that. They protected me even when I thought they were there to harm me. Without them I wouldn't have made it this far, I probably would still be stuck in Baecos's mansion... but I wouldn't tell her that.

"Are you sure it's the voices from the door?" Spiris asked intertwining his fingers through mine. His fingers tapped rhythmically against the back of my hand.

Taking the hint, I entered his mind.

Maybe it is how the universe has chosen to speak with you. Spiris said. *Remember how Kneku saw visions?*

Yes. I sent back. *My mother saw them too though.*

"Is that how you knew about his mate?" she asked. I hummed in response, not attempting to talk to both her and Spiris at the same time.

I am worried about Cruor taking us. I told Spiris. *She may not agree to it.*

What will you do if she refuses? He asked.

Maybe go to Fluvis? I guessed. *If not, we will just have to think of what she wants and give that to her.*

She wants you, Iniq. Spiris replied the bitterness coating his thoughts. I watched the conversation they had through his eyes.

I left his head after that not wanting to think about what Cruor will propose. I knew that he had some merit to his thoughts, but I didn't want to entertain it. I chose who I chose, and I didn't want a jealous demon to ruin that.

There had to be something else I could offer her.

The voice was quiet as we walked but it ignited something in me that I hadn't felt since I was first introduced into this world: excitement.

I remembered when my heart would pound when faced with the unknown, how much I wanted to learn about this world. Even if I acted like I didn't want anything to do with it I knew better inside.

I loved the power I was able to exude over the Dark King, and when he stood up to me, I couldn't help but smile. It was dangerous but I knew I would be fine coming out of it, it was exciting. I loved it. And now I couldn't wait to find that mirror and force his hand.

I was also excited to see what I could do with my newfound power. I flexed my hand as I weaved through the gnarled trees. I hoped I would be able to hold onto the feeling this time instead of it disappearing as soon as I had a moment to breathe.

"Have you thought about what you will say to your Fire King?" Aselia teased as we walked besides the barrier. It would take less than a minute for Cruor to come running to us. I had been preparing myself the entire walk rehearsing what I wanted to say over and over again but I knew something like this would have to be played by ear. Cruor, at her best, was unpredictable and impulsive.

"We will have to see what she asks for," I said and walked through the barrier hand in hand with Spiris.

It gave way without a fight, molding to our bodies as we passed, allowing us to enter into the field of spider lilies. The same stone path that was covered by darkness the other night now was visible and it lead straight to the castle. It was almost dark now and the journey had started to weigh on me. There was an ache in my calves and my legs threatened to give out on me any second. I put on a brave face not wanting to worry the others any more than I already had.

I also just felt plain embarrassed at what they had witnessed. Spiris would never hold it against me. I thought Aselia would make fun of me but she didn't mention it once on our way down the mountain. I was grateful because my pride couldn't take any more hits. I was a king, one that needed to act like it.

I prayed that Cruor would at least forgive us enough to give us some food. My stomach on cue gave a noisy rumble. Spiris gave me a pitiful look. Maybe Cruor would just deny us entry, if she did, I did not know if I would make the trek to the Water Kingdom.

As if my thoughts called her, I watched as her and her hounds appeared in front of us. Cruor stalked towards us with Felix and Ash at her heels. They both stayed in their hound forms allowing Cruor to take the lead and watching intently as she looked over our group. Spiris removed his hand that had been glued to mine for almost the entire trip.

"Am I to take this as a sign that you couldn't reach the Dark King?" she asked as she crossed her arms. Her red eyes glowed in the darkness, I felt them scrutinizing me from head to toe. I took a deep breath as my heart pounded in my chest. This time it was from nervousness, almost all of the excitement from showing up the Dark King left me when her eyes washed over me.

"We did but we need," I paused. "I *need* your help. Can we talk inside?"

Her eyes shifted to Spiris then back to mine. Without saying anything she waved her hand and in a flurry of dark shadows and in an instant, we were back inside the warmth of the castle. She had taken us right to the entrance and she didn't look back as she led us through the castle. Ash shifted and stood in between Aselia and I as we walked not caring about his sudden nakedness.

"Glad to see you made it out alive," he said and wrapped an arm around my shoulder. "How was he? As scary as the rumors say?"

"Terrifying," I answered with a small smile. I didn't want to admit that I missed his happy attitude.

"Yet Iniq though it would be good to get right in his face and demand that he teach us after he threw us in a literal dungeon," Aselia added on.

"You didn't," Cruor gave me a deadpan look pausing just long enough to cause me to flush.

"You're so cool," Ash cooed near my face.

"He said no," I said a smile still playing on my lips. "So not cool enough, I guess."

Cruor opened the doors to the dining hall and I felt myself shrink when I noticed that the entire castle seemed to have joined them for dinner tonight. Heads turned as we entered, and I tried to not let it affect my newfound courage. Obviously Ash didn't give two shits because he was just as naked as the day he was born.

I now understood when they told me how I nagged them about being naked in the dining room . I grimaced as Ash sat down fully naked on the table's bench. How many people sat there after him? I doubt hounds like him even took care of their hygiene as well as they should. I actually had a very distinct feeling telling me he did not shower as often as a normal person. He shot me a grin and dug into his half-finished plate.

"Eat first," Cruor said. "Since you so rudely interrupted our dinner, you might as well help yourself," she sat down with a huff and pushed her black hair out of her face before she dug into her plate. I felt the bond tug at my stomach harshly, begging me to touch her. It was such a menial thing, watching her eat, but right now it took all I had to plant myself to the ground.

My stomach grumbled as the smell of food hit me. Spiris sat down and began fixing our plates immediately. He was too good for me.

I dug into my plate and ate in silence with the rest of the group until Aselia spoke up.

"You were in the human world for a few years, right?" she asked me.

I looked over at her with a raised brow. "Yes," I answered hesitantly.

"How is the world ruled over there?" she asked, shoving an orange vegetable in her mouth.

"Why, are the High Kings too much for you?" Ash teased. Felix sat behind him still in hound form.

"No, just curious," she said with a shrug.

"There is one planet that I know of and have lived on," I told them. "Unlike here they have many countries, and each country has a ruler. They follow very strict rules and usually have many people helping them rule the country. It is flawed because they continuously fight wars for resources The world there is slowly dying because of mortals not taking care of what they have."

I reached out to Felix with my mind feeling uncomfortable that he refused to sit with us. I didn't want my presence here to be the one affecting his mealtime.

I hope you are not still in hound form because of me. I said.

Like you have influence over me. He shot back but I saw my past self fly across his mind, yelling at him for being naked in front of the entire castle.

Up to you. I told him and pulled out of his mind completely.

"They need some ruling," I told her. "If Nitri was any good he would be overseeing them instead of letting them rot."

The table froze at my words. Felix chose that time to shift and join Ash at the table. After seeing him shift I came face to face with just how scarred his body was. I thought it was just his face once, but the scars trailed down his torso as well. It was like he was attacked from another hell hound, there were three long claw like marks that trailed down his body. I averted my gaze.

"That is a losing battle," she said with a sigh. Her face was contemplative. I wanted to talk to her about her upbringing but that would have to wait until we were out of the woods with Cruor. Right now, that was the most important thing.

Spiris's ghost of a touch slid across my thigh. Even such a light touch sent a wave of desire through me. Between him and Cruor I might have very well just died in my own puddle.

Focus. I chided myself internally.

"Maybe not," I mused and poured myself a cup of water from the pitcher that was at the table.

"Is that what you came to talk to me about?" Cruor asked. She leaned forward on her elbows looking intently at me.

"Not entirely," I told her. "But like you said, it can wait until we are done eating. We *were* rude."

It was a double meaning—she knew that by the look on her face. My chest twisted at the obvious manipulation. It was a low blow and I was not sorry about the rudeness earlier. She sat back against the chair, her eyes not leaving mine.

"When you are done come find me to talk. I'll be in my room," she said.

I gritted my teeth and tried to calm my rising magic. I reached out to Spiris.

I don't like where this is going. I told him.

This was your idea. He said with an equal amount of frustration. A memory of him telling me *this is whatever you want it to be* ran through his head.

He regretted those words.

I'll go ask her what she wants. I told him, stealing another bite of the food and leaving the dining room and the eyes that followed behind me.

My body was too familiar with the castle because I found myself standing in front of Cruor's room in less time than I'd hoped. I really dreaded the conversation and all the confidence that I had from earlier felt like it went up in smoke for the second time that evening.

I didn't want to say that I regretted what Spiris and I had done but it would sure be a complication if Cruor was going to ask for what I thought she was going to ask.

I hesitantly knocked.

"Come," came Cruor's muffled voice. I swallowed thickly and entered the room.

The room was so familiar it jarred me. It was warm, with brown furniture, rugs, and blankets, The three large windows across from me showed the night sky and overlooked the glowing flowers from below.

Cruor leaned against the side of her bed waiting for me. She hadn't changed clothes, she had been waiting for me, and there was a glass in her hand that resembled human whiskey.

"What do you want, Iniq?" she asked. "You made it *very* clear last night that you wanted nothing to do with me while you fucked Spiris under my roof. Why are you here?"

I licked my dry lips.

"I need you to show me where the mirror is, the one that tells the future," I told her. "It was the only thing that the Dark King would accept in return for teaching me."

She scoffed. "You mean you and Aselia."

"No, just me," I told her. "He is convinced that teaching me darkness would ruin the world."

She let out a bitter laugh and downed her glass. She stalked over to my form, I tried not to back down as her face stopped centimeters away from mine.

The red eyes that have been haunting me seemed too surreal now, too angry. A part of me felt relieved that I was so close to her. A part of me wanted to reach out and touch her. *The bond.* I realized, but the rest of me remembered what she did. The rest of me knew who I chose. And the remainder was still angry at her comments from the night before.

The excited part though…. It pushed me to take the path of least residence. The one that was sure to end up with me tangled in her sheets even though I already had Spiris waiting for me.

"What if I refuse?" she asks. "What will you do then? Where will you go?"

Her voice was a whisper and the alcohol wafted across my face as she spoke.

"Then I will never forgive you for the two years you left me to rot," I told her simply. "Help me with this and I will no longer hold it against you."

She tilted her head back and laughed loud.

"It doesn't matter," she said. "Why would I want someone who doesn't want me to forgive me? Tell me what happens to me when you leave? Will I be left here to oversee my kingdom alone? Do you know how this stupid bond makes me feel when you are gone?"

"If it made you feel anything you wouldn't have done what you did," I told her.

"I thought you left me!" she yelled. "Please tell me the bond isn't only making me crazy." Her voice turned to begging. "Please, tell me you feel it too? Even when I am with others, I can still fucking see your face, feel your touch. I *hate it.* "

I swallowed thickly.

"It's not just you, but that problem could be easily solved," I told her. She gave me a dark look. "Bonds can be broken."

"Don't you pull that," she hissed and gripped my shoulder. "You would have never said that before, never even attempted it. What happened to you?"

I didn't want a repeat of my last night in her realm. How could she still not get that everything that happened up until now ensured that the Iniq she once knew was never coming back?

"Many things," I responded. "So will you help me or not?"

She pushed my shoulder harshly and walked over to a small cabinet in the corner of her room laughing as she did. She poured more alcohol in her cup, downed it, then refilled it.

"Mate me," she said turning to face me. "Mate me this time and I will take you right to the mirror."

"Nitri doesn't let Kings mate," I told her, a sweat breaking out on my skin. My bond rejoiced at the words. I felt the unfamiliar feeling of giddiness run through me. I knew that couldn't be my real feelings. I was still angry. I had Spiris. *God, Spiris.*

"Then a chance to be with you," she said. "Until you can do whatever you Kings do to get crowned or whatever."

"Ascend," I corrected.

"I don't care," she said and her burning gaze met me once more. "A chance. Let me show you that I can be the mate you want. You don't have to stop what you are doing with Spiris," she took another sip of her alcohol. "Just let me have a chance too. You can make your choice once you complete your goal."

"Should we have this talk when you are sober?" I asked her and backed away from her. Her hand shot out and cupped the back of my neck, pulling me closer. I could almost feel her lips brush mine.

"It will be the same," she said. "Say yes to this and I will help you."

"I should talk to—"

"This is your decision, not his," she said. "You make this decision and *you* tell him why you are doing this."

I thought over her words without needing to. I could still ask Fluvis but I didn't want to. I was enticed by her offer. The guilt that I felt when thinking of Spiris was minuscule to the feelings that were raging inside me in that moment. It should have been right, but it was so very wrong.

"For your courage," she said and pushed the glass to my lips and helped me drink a sip of the brown liquid. It was sweeter than human whiskey but tasted aged like it.

Without breaking our gaze, I lifted her hand and downed the glass. Her eyes widened.

"What if I don't want to choose?" I said. "Is both an option?" Her tongue shot out to lick her lips.

"Both *can be* an option," she confirmed.

"You have a deal. For a chance and me for the mirror," I told her. She threw the glass across the room shattering it against the wall and covered her lips with mine. They were just as soft as I remembered and without any hesitancy, I began kissing her back, our hot tongues dancing together perfectly. I couldn't believe I forgot how *good* it felt to kiss her. She pushed me against the door and hiked my legs up around her. My hands found themselves tangled in her hair. She trailed hot kisses down my neck and her hands dug into my thighs. The electricity between us was undeniable now. Just like the first night in the Water Kingdom, there was no way to stay sane with her touching me like this.

"This is more than a chance," I gasped to her.

"You kissed me back," she said and ran her hand across my ass.

"I need to talk to Spiris first," I told her. "He deserves to know about the deal."

"Afraid he will leave you?" she asked and nipped at the side of my neck. I stifled a gasp.

"No," I told her honestly. Her tongue licked the length of my neck. "But he deserves more than this."

She paused, and with a heavy sigh she put me back down on the ground.

"Go then and tell him tonight you will be in my bed," she ordered.

I gave her a hard look.

"Only if I choose to be," I told her. "Remember you get a chance, no promises."

I left her room and shut the door with a pounding heart.

This is fucked.

I took Spiris to the hallway overlooking the garden for the news my heart pounding the entire way. I knew my lips must have been puffy and my face flushed, he had to have known what happened. He had a stoic look on his face and refused to meet my eyes the entire way. The guilt intensified when his black eyes met mine, he was expecting bad news.

"You were right," I told him. He looked up to the stars tearing his gaze away from me. "She wanted me to mate her."

"And you said yes," he answered for me, his tone drawing my gaze back to him. His fists were clenched, and his neck tensed.

"I said no, told her Nitri doesn't allow it," I told him. His gaze snapped to mine he was a stride towards me when I put my hands out to stop him. "But, in return she just asks for a chance to prove herself as a suitable mate," I paused looking down at my feet. "And I let her kiss me but stopped it because I wanted to talk it through with you."

"But you said yes to the chance," he said as he walked towards me. His shoes reached my sight and his hands rested on my shoulders. " *Just* a chance."

"I did," I said and looked up at him. He let out a sigh and a small smile graced his lips. He leaned down and brushed a kiss across my lips. My eyes widened at his actions.

"Where else did she kiss you?" he asked with a growl. My knees became weak at his voice.

I pointed towards the side of my neck. His hand came to tilt my head gently and he began replacing her kisses with his. I shivered when his tongue came out to lick the spot she had bitten.

"Anywhere else?" he asked. I shook my head, but he still backed me to the wall and brought his lips to mine once more. His kisses were soft but they melted my entire body and made my belly warm as his tongue danced with mine.

"Spiris, why aren't you mad?" I asked him. His kisses went back down to my neck.

"I am furious," he said in between kisses. "That she thinks you'll choose her."

I gulped at his words. His hand ran up the side of my pants.

"But we kissed," I told him.

"I told you that you decide what we are." His hand moved to unbutton my pants. "But promise me one thing."

"What is it?" I asked him. He paused and pushed his middle and ring finger into my lips. I opened for him and sucked on his fingers lightly. He pulled them out and his wet fingers slowly slipped into my underwear and teased my folds. I did not realize how wet I already was until his finger easily slipped through me. I moaned against the feeling and spread my legs for him.

We were out in the open, anyone could walk in on us but that paired with his commanding attitude made the simmering tension all the better.

"You'll come back to me. Every time," he said. "You can give her a chance." He thrust his fingers inside me and I couldn't help but let out a moan. "You can kiss her." Another thrust. I bucked my hips against his hand. "Fuck her." He pushed his fingers in deeper grinding his hand against my clit. I covered my mouth with my hand to stifle the cry. "Whatever you want. But promise you'll come back to me. My arms, my bed, my life. *Forever.*"

His thrusts were frustratingly slow but it made the moment so much more intimate. He took each breath with me and his eyes never left mine. It was powerful, he knew he had the control here and who was I kidding? Of course, Spiris would always be there, he was the one to see me through everything, I could imagine my life without him. Many times I entertained the idea of dropping everything to be with him even though the fate of the Light Kingdom was in my hands.

"I promise," I gasped out. "You." His movements came faster and her curled his fingers inside me. "Always. You."

"Forever," he said.

I nodded. "Forever."

"Leg," he commanded and I helped him hook a single leg over his hip and pushed down my pants slightly so his hand better access. His fingers pounded into me and I arched against the stone wall and the heat rose in me becoming unwarily hot.

"Spiris," I moaned his name as his hand pounded into my clit. I was rewarded with a kiss.

"It'll always be you for me, Iniq," he said against my open mouth as moans slipped through. "Remember that. Always you. I don't care how that looks but I will never let you go again."

"Please don't," I moaned against him.

I felt my orgasm rise through me. He pulled away slightly and trained his eyes on my form as I shuddered though it. He didn't pull out of me until my orgasm had passed.

He put my leg down and kissed me as he pulled my pants back up.

I heard a sigh from the end of the hallway. Looking over, it was Cruor who was leaning against the wall watching us. Embarrassment flashed through me when I realized she heard and *saw* all of everything that just happened. I scolded myself for not paying better attention to the magical signatures around me.

"So, we have an agreement," she said with a shit eating grin.

CHAPTER THIRTEEN
INIQ

*T*he wind tickled my skin, leaving a cooling sensation that chased asway the heat across my flushed goosebumps. A sweat had broken out only five minutes into the exercise and my clothing now stuck to my body. It was uncomfortable the way the clothing moved with each inhale and would deter my focus, causing my magic to lash out wildly. I didn't know how long I had in this kingdom, so I wanted to take advantage of the free time and safe space while I had it. The sun shining down on my back after months in darkness was a nice touch even as it let me sweat.

The conversation with the Dark King yesterday still weighed heavily on my mind. Even as Spiris left hot kisses on my skin and whispered against my lips there was no forgetting what had happened. I wanted to enjoy this time with him, away from Nitri's kingdom but there were just too many questions that needed to be answered.

Why would my mother condemn the Light Kingdom to such a horrible fate? This couldn't have been the same person that everyone held in such high regard. She had been described as caring, selfless; she would have been the last person to have condemned all those people to death. The more I thought of the sheer amount of people that had died at the hands of my mother the more the weight on my chest seemed to intensify. Almost six-hundred years' worth of people in this realm had their lives stolen from them and no one even seemed to care about them.

There was something that had flickered in my dreams last night that I couldn't quite understand. It was Baecos's father. I don't recall any interaction with the man but his face had been seared in my memories with a disgusting smirk that almost turned my stress dreams into nightmares. I was able to strongly recall Baecos's fathers face, the blond hair and purple eyes that matched his son... though I couldn't remember his name. I hated him. I didn't know where it came from, it was a dark heavy hate that seemed to fester inside my core. A hate that was so potent it caused me to lose control of the magic that I had been gathering in my hands and explode the rock I was trying to conceal. It left a dust cloud in the air that invaded my senses.

A violent cough pushed through my lungs and I swung my arm in the air to clear the leftover residue. I sighed, looking at my now empty hand. The Dark Magic was harder than I had first believed it to be. I foolishly believed that because I had seen the Dark King use his magic, I would be able to replicate it but every time I tried, it used a significant portion of my magic. A magic that was still half of what it should have been because of the seal on my memories.

If I had been able to wrangle Nitri back in the Other World I would have tried to finesse him removing my seal but even just getting that demon to hear anything I had to say was a grueling process. I was convinced he did it on purpose, trying to slow down the inevitable. A world where he was no longer in control.

Part of me worried about what I would see when the rest of my memories were unlocked. The majority of things coming through were insignificant and I feared that the doors warnings about my weakness was different than the one Nitri focused on. The door—or the souls inside it—seemed to know more than it was letting on. Since the door had been trying to save me the entire time, I would put more faith in their words than I ever would Nitri's.

I had been at the exercise for only twenty minutes and the overwhelming feeling of disappointment was almost enough for me to call it quits. I had forced Spiris and Cruor to stay away and they only listened when I threatened to call off the deal and leave them both. There was only one thing that made them somewhat cooperative, otherwise they would be glaring daggers at each other the entire time and I didn't need that tension while I was training. I sighed again and ran my hand through my hair. My life was such a mess I didn't know how to keep up with it.

I reached into the grass around me until I found what I was looking for. My fingers found a smooth rock and I moved it around in both hands, memorizing its' shape. I twirled it around, looking for any cracks or deformities. I realized after the first time that the less I knew the object, the harder this was to manage.

After I was satisfied, I closed my eyes and nestled the rock between both hands. I called forth my magic and imagined it coating the rock fully, filling every crack and dip until it was completely shrouded in a magic that fit it like a second skin.

That was the easy part. Next was the hard part.

I imagined the rock becoming transparent. I imagined it slowly dissolving. This is where I had to pour more magic in though I was not sure how to manipulate it just yet. This is where I got it wrong every time and if I put too much force into it the rock would literally explode. The thought of that happening to a human almost distracted me enough to ruin this round.

I had been to a carnival once with Vein's mortal parents, I

remembered being so in awe at all the things I saw. It was that moment when I realized nothing was as it seemed. The magic was all tricks, everything was hidden by a mirror to make you think that you were looking at an empty box but in reality...

That's right, child. The door whispered in my head. *Dark magic is all about concealing what is there. Use it to fool your enemies.*

Memories that were not my own flooded through my head. A dark magician had was sitting in the grass much like I had been, I couldn't make out his face, it was blurred in the memories but I had a vague sense of recognition when I saw his dark hair. He plucked a bright yellow flower and held it up in the air. I watched as his magic covered the entire flower in a dark cloud. Slowly starting from the top of the flower to the bottom of the stem it started shimmering in the sun when the light finally let up there seemed to be nothing in his hand.

Reflect the environment around it. The door said.

The door was always watching, even if it had left me for a moment and I couldn't be more grateful because in that moment, something clicked.

I opened my eyes while I slowly peeled back my hands to check on my experiment. I could feel the smooth rock's weight still in my hand but from the naked eye it looked as though my palm was empty.

"Holy shit."

I turned it around in my hand, and the illusion stayed.

I tried to cut off my magic from feeding into it, praying that it would keep its shape. The image wavered slightly showing me the grey surface beneath, but it snapped back into place and I was able to hold it without feeding any more magic to it.

"Yes!' I yelled and begun searching the area around me for more rocks.

"Someone's happy today," Aselia said from behind me. I met her face with a smile and the sly grin she was wearing intensified. "I would be too if I got myself a harem of lovers."

"It's not a harem," I told her and placed three more rocks on my lap.

"Right sorry," she said and sat down next to me in the grass. "A harem is more than two. I'll join if you ask nicely."

I rolled my eyes at her.

"Open your hand," I told her. She raised an eyebrow at me but complied. I dropped the invisible rock in her hand.

"You didn't!" she said with a gasp and prodded at the invisible rock with her finger. "First the door and now these rocks? Is your memory coming back or something?"

"Nope," I said and tried to do the same thing with two rocks in my hand. I closed my eyes to concentrate. "I could never do this in my past life anyways."

This time it came faster, now that I knew how it felt there was something tangible that I could hold onto and it made visualizing my magic all the easier. There was a click and I cut off my magic before opening my hand to find it empty once more.

"So you are telling me you just woke up this morning and could do this?" she asked incredulously as I placed two more rocks in her hand.

I searched for more. I found a slightly bigger one this time and paired it with the other small rock. When I opened my hand next the biggest rock was still semitransparent while the smaller rock had become fully invisible. I frowned.

"It's all about intent," I recited Spiris's words back to her. "You just have to visualize it right? Feed your intent into it as you cover it with magic." This time I made the rock invisible with my eyes open. "Fuck yes."

"I feel like I am looking at a different person," Aselia muttered to herself.

I dropped the bigger rock in her hand. She scowled. "Try to take off the illusion."

"I told you I don't want to learn dark. Your throne is safe from me," she said, but I saw the way her eyebrows wrinkled.

Even though I felt sour about her lying to us I couldn't really say that I didn't understand her motives. I had been like that too when I first came to their world. There may have been a small part of me that pushed me towards the magic, pushed me towards the heart pounding hair raising excitement of becoming powerful, but I never wanted the responsibility that came with it. It would have been easier just to go back to my mortal life and have the world forget that I existed. But Aselia... I had felt her magic before, even thinking about it caused chills to run through me. She was as deserving as the throne as I was and after all the shit that Nitri had done, there was no way I would stand by his side for the rest of my existence. There had to be another way, but if Aselia did not even try to learn the last of her powers, then that road would be blocked off for good.

"Do it," I commanded. "You need this. A some point you will take over a throne, even if it is not mine."

"Don't insult father, he will be angry when he hears this," she said. I saw a small drip of sweat run down her face. I smiled.

"Close your eyes," I told her and lifted up her free hand to wave across the rocks. "Use your magic to command the rocks to show themselves."

"You don't command inanimate objects, Iniq," she growled.

"Trust me a little, okay?" I asked her and left her side to find more rocks about three feet away. When I had collected about ten more rocks, I heard her gasp.

I turned around and was met with the most innocently surprised face I had ever seen Aselia make and in her hand, was a small pile of rocks. She showed me the pile of rocks in her hands as I walked closer. I curled her fingers over the rock and gave her a small smile.

"Good job, Aselia. I knew you could do it." Her face turned bright red and a small scowl made its way to her face. I bet no one had uttered those words to her for a long time. In front of me, even though Aselia remained years older than me, I felt like

I could see the kid she never allowed herself to be. "I have an idea on how we can test these."

I pulled her up and led her back to the castle.

As luck would have it, there was an abandoned area right outside the castle that seemed to have been used for the brick work that littered the castle. It was a small dirt yard and there were various half-finished walls and arches that were crumbling with age. There were even some broken statues further into the yard partially hidden from view that would make great targets.

Perfect.

"Watch this," I told her with a smile and felt around in her arms for a small rock. I lifted up the invisible rock then wound up my arm. Right as I threw it, before it left my hand, I infused some more magic in it and watched with pure joy as the rock shot forward, tearing right through the already broken statue of a naked lady I had first spotted.

The lady cracked in half and the top fell to the ground with a thud.

I met Aselia's jaw dropped expression with a large smile. I couldn't help myself; a small laugh made its way through my throat. It felt good to let the magic out and it was even greater that I could make someone as strong as Aselia speechless.

"Do you want to try?" I asked. She nodded and rushed to hand the rocks to me. I grabbed the end of my tunic and lifted it out so I could hold the rocks without losing them.

She hesitantly grabbed a rock and threw it against a crumbling half-finished wall nearby. I had to shield my face from the debris that shot back at us.

"I didn't mean for it to be that powerful," she said with a twinkle in her eye, not looking regretful at all.

"Try another," I told her and grabbed a rock from my shirt. "I don't know about you but I have a few choice people that I am imagining being at the end of these rocks."

I threw one at an arch further away from where we were

standing but added a little bit more magic. The rock tore through the arch and embedded it into the stone pillar behind it, cutting them both clean in half.

Aselia grabbed another and threw it at the same spot animating the rest of the pillar. She came back for another, destroying a statue. Then another, and another, and another until there were no more rocks left. She looked around the ground and started picking up the scattered stone and throwing them at whatever was left standing. She didn't even attempt to make them visible nor did I try to stop her. I did not plan for this to be an anger release but by the look on Aselia's face, she would need to do this fifty times over if she were to get rid of all the anger that stayed guarded behind those golden eyes.

I felt the all too familiar itch on the back of my neck. It had been some time since I wanted to destroy something. Since I felt excited about the possibility of destruction... but the more I watched her the easier my breath caught and the further I was hoping she would go. I grit my teeth against the feeling and tried to calm my breathing. Luckily, Aselia had slowed before I decided that we needed to cause more havoc, spill innocent blood.

When she had finally done enough damage, she paused and looked over the area, not once looking back to me. The contagious smile that was once on her face was gone. Her chest rose and fell with violent pants and even from behind her I could see the sweat the clung to her skin. There was something unreadable in her eyes, but it didn't take a genius to know that she probably had never taken her anger out in such a way.

Becoming this close to Aselia was not something that I had set out to do. I wasn't prepared to hear about her horrendous childhood nor was I did I ever realize how lonely she must had been in that castle. It made me see myself in a different light. Before we came back, I thought we were almost opposites in the way that we had been brought up but I knew the look on her face far too well. Her hard attitude and sarcastic tone made painful sense now.

On a whim I walked slowly to her side and lightly wrapped my arms around her shoulder. She was shaking as I did so. Without hesitation she leaned into me and buried her face in the crook of my neck, her arms forming a death grip on my waist making it impossible to move. Not that I would though. Maybe we both needed this.

"You remind me of Neia," she whispered with a sigh. "I... miss her. The only reason I lived was due to her guidance, to her kindness."

I leaned my head against hers. Spiris smiling face flashed through my mind. While I may have not had someone like my mother here to guide me along, at least I was lucky enough to have Spiris with me.

"You've been through a lot," I told her. "It won't be like this for long, I promise you."

She nodded against me. "Your mom," she said and gripped me tighter. "She was exiled when she was pregnant with you. Nitri had turned a blind eye to her sneaking out to this realm but I assume that he had found out that she was with child. She always wanted to check in with the kings like she usually had but one day, she didn't come back."

"How?" I asked. I tried to pull her away so I could look at her but she didn't let go.

"I don't know. I think he closed the door."

"I thought it had a mind of its own?" I asked.

"To an extent. Listen carefully Iniq." Her voice was a whisper. "His power is waning. You and Spiris being able to enter is only proof of that. He doesn't want you there for reasons I am not sure of yet but I have a feeling it has to do with what the Dark King told us about."

"Why are you telling me this?" I asked her. She finally looked up at me unshed tears in her eyes.

"Because you were kind," she said.

I nodded and looked over the destruction of the area.

"That could come in handy when—"

"What the hell do you think you are doing?" Cruor's angry voice came from behind us.

I turned and saw her, Spiris, Felix, and Ash staring at us. Her hands were on her hips and she gave us a death glare that elicited an almost inappropriate reaction from my body. Spiris was slightly amused with a raised eyebrow and a poorly hidden smile. Ash's mouth was wide open in shock, and Felix of course looked as unamused as ever.

"Your rock graveyard needed some love," Aselia spoke with a smirk, all of the heavy emotions left her face, she gave me a look that warned me against saying anything.

I picked up a discarded brick that was about half as big as my head, showing the group. With a smile I used my magic to turn it invisible and the look on their faces were too satisfying. I decided to up it a notch and turned back to the area, there were barely any things left to destroy so I aimed the brick at the ground a few feet away.

Dirt flew everywhere on impact and Aselia used her wind power to make sure it didn't reach us by creating a protective barrier.

"You and your damn rocks," Spiris said, coming to my side and wrapping his arms around me. I met his small smile with my own. "How did you manage the dark magic so fast?"

"It's all about intent," Aselia answered for me and did the same thing with a stray piece of statue.

Spiris's smile widened.

"Learned it from the best," I told him.

CHAPTER FOURTEEN
INIQ

I was far from satisfied with the ability of my dark power. I knew the rocks were just the surface and the more I thought of Nitri waiting for me back in the Other World, the more panicked I became. I could imagine the look on his face when I met him back in his throne room, he would be waiting there of course to remind me who was *really* in charge. His golden eyes would probably twinkle with delight, he was waiting for a chance to expel me like he had my mother and now would be the perfect opportunity.

That was even if I was still allowed in the Other World. Maybe what Aselia had said about his power waning was a mistake. Maybe him consuming all the souls of his children would provide enough sustenance for him to keep the door on a tight leash.

"What are you thinking about?" Spiris asked me as he stood in front of my place on the bed. I hadn't even realized that he had finished his shower until he had spoken. His black curls now lay limp by his face and they left small water droplets on his night shirt.

"I need to up my practice," I told him and maneuvered him

so he was sitting on the edge of the bed instead and I had taken his place standing.

"You have done enough today," Spiris said in a low voice. His hand grabbed mine and he rested it against his soft cheek. "We have time, at least two weeks."

"It needs to be before that. Nitri is impatient," I argued and closed my eyes. I tried visualizing the magic I had earlier with the rocks.

"That old man has been alive longer than anyone else," Spiris said with a huff. "He won't notice a few weeks."

My concentration flickered at his words, and I felt a small smile force itself up through my anxiety to show on my face. I opened my eyes to give him a hard look before going back to trying to coat him with my magic. It was slow at first, I pushed it out and visualized it cloaking his skin, but not quite touching it. I felt him shiver against the feeling in my hold.

I opened my eyes to check my work and frowned when I realized that the magic barely covered his appearance. I could make out the blankets on the bed behind him but there was no way the illusion would fool anyone.

"If I cannot hide even one person how the hell am I going to learn how to hide four and two hounds?" I growled. My jaw was already sore by how much I had been grinding my teeth. I didn't even notice I was doing it until Spiris's hand brushed across my jaw.

"Tell me how I can help," Spiris said. He looked at me like he was in physical pain and it made guilt wash over me. It was my burden to carry, he shouldn't be the one worried.

"I don't know," I admitted. "It was easier with the rock. It was small and I could memorize it easily."

His eyes drifted towards his hands, then his arms.

"Is there a part of me that is less visible than others?" he asked. I wanted to give him another look getting tired of the questions, but it only took me a short second longer to realize that his face was slightly more invisible than the other parts of him. His horns and legs seemed to be the most visible.

"Your face," I muttered and moved his head to look at it from multiple angles, he smiled as I did so.

"Try it on yourself first," he said. I frowned, what would that even do? "Trust me."

I closed my eyes and tried the same thing. My magic cloaked me quicker than it had Spiris and I visualized the mirror trick. I was almost afraid to open my eyes until Spiris gave a noise of approval.

I looked down at my hands and the rest of my body and was surprised to see that even I could not see my body.

"I still do not understand how you know dark magic so well," I muttered acting slightly annoyed, but I was more than grateful to have Spiris by my side.

"I think it's like when you use light for healing," he explained. "You have to memorize the area so you can heal it correctly. I don't know if I should be hurt that you have not memorized me."

I waved my hand, dispelling the magic between us and leaned closer to him, my lips brushing across his.

"We can fix that," I whispered.

He leaned forward to kiss me but I pulled back just enough so that I was out of his reach. I moved to straddle him and moved my attention to his hair and horns. I ran my fingers through the still wet locks and raked my fingers against his scalp. He let out a small sigh and rested his face on my shoulder. I took advantage of the position and let my fingers trail up the horns that still seemed so new to his body. They were smooth to the touch and felt like hard leather, his hands gripped my hips as I ran the length of them and his hot breath exhaled onto my chest.

"It feels nice," he murmured. "To be touched like this."

I was tempted to dive into his mind to understand what he

was feeling but I left his thoughts alone for now wanting to give him the same privacy he awarded me. I trailed my hands down the back of his scalp feeling at the hair that now almost touched his shoulders. I gripped the back of his neck and ran my hands over his shoulders. I started to knead into the place where his neck met his shoulder trying to disperse the tension that was no doubt the consequence of years of anxiety under Baecos reign.

He let out a whine. A damn *whine* that sounded so sinful that I almost threw him down to the bed right then and there. If I had not been feeling the effects of him being so close already there was definitely no denying the things I wanted to do to him. I pushed my thumb harder against his shoulder and was rewarded with an even louder groan. He pushed my hips down so that I would be able to feel the hardness in his pants. I ran my hands down his back trying to memorize the feeling of each vertebrae as it passed under my fingertips.

"After I finish this," I told him and pushed him down onto the bed softly. I couldn't help but chuckle when I saw the small frown on his face. I continued to rub my hands down his arms and chest until I got to the edge of his sleep pants. There was no hiding was happening and by the look on his face he wanted me to know very well what his reaction was to me. I teasingly brushed my hand across the front of him and was rewarded with a hiss. I moved to kneel by his knees, pushing his legs open for me.

"You don't have—" he started but let out a yelp when I dug my nails into his thigh.

"I need to concentrate," I told him and ran my hands down his thighs. I let my hands linger between them and gave the inside of his thighs a teasing squeeze. He spread his legs wider as my hands rubbed circles down his thighs to his calves. I used the time to massage other knots that seem to lay deep in his lower leg muscles.

Slowly I closed my eyes and tried to cloak his skin once

more. I visualized it like they were following the path that my hands had taken. I opened my eyes to see nothing in front of me. I hesitantly tried to cut off the magic from myself. The image flickered much like the rock had but in a second it was gone and Spiris was invisible from sight. I stood back and looked over my handiwork, making sure that no part of him was shown. The only indication that he was there was the slight dip in the bed which shifted as he took, what I assumed to be a sitting position.

"I can't see myself," he said and I saw the indent disappear entirely. I could hear his feet shuffle against the wood floors.

"Something I will have to fix, and the noise," I told him. I felt his hand brush across my arm lightly, sending small shivers through me.

"Is it wrong for me to say that I think this power has a lot of potential?" he asks and his hand trailed up to the side of my neck.

"If I can get this right maybe even Nitri wouldn't be able to see through it," I murmured suddenly distracted by the way his hand buried themselves in my hair.

"That's not what I am talking about," Spiris replied with a breathy chuckle. I felt his lips brush across my forehead before he pulled at my hair causing my head to tilt back. Understanding and heat washed through me at the same time. It was odd to be at the mercy of someone you couldn't even see, and slightly erotic. It was vulnerable and comforting all at once. Comfortable because I trusted Spiris more than anything and vulnerable because I had no way to see what he was doing. "Why don't you go lay on the bed for me, hm?"

I swallowed thickly at his words. I could hear him move around me, giving me a path to the bed.

"I didn't know you were so adventurous," I teased. I felt myself shiver with excitement and I placed myself on the edge of the bed.

"Take your clothes off," he said but I did not feel him get close to me. I loved the commanding tone of his voice that only I would hear. No one would be able to see Spiris in such a way and it only fueled me forward. I slowly pulled my top over my head. Spiris was here obviously, but without being able to see him it felt like I was in the room alone and it added to the tension in my body. I slowly took my bra off. My nipples were already erect, and the act of stripping made my belly coil. I couldn't see his face but I hoped he was watching me intently. I unbuttoned my pants and pushed them off my hips leaving me in only my underwear. "Keep those on."

I raised my eyebrow at him. "What do you have planned?" I asked him and leaned back with my legs spread. I arched my back slightly and heard the small intake of breath that made a smile play at my lips. I felt the brush of his fingers start at the hollow of my throat and trail themselves down the middle of my body. It was my turn to take a sharp intake of breath at his actions. I felt him stand in between my legs. His hand grabbed mine and guided my hand to my breast, without his prompting I began rolling my nipple between my fingers.

"I want to see what you would look like if I wasn't here," he said his came from close to my ear and his breath teased my face. I stifled a moan at the feeling of him so near yet so far. "Show me how you would touch yourself."

His hand left mine to trail around the edge of my underwear.

"And if I want you to touch me?" I asked him but still trailed my hand down to rub my slit through my already wet underwear. His hand gripped my thigh causing me to jump at the sudden feeling.

"I will," he said. "But you have to make yourself come first."

I dipped my fingers into my underwear making contact with my throbbing clit. The moans slipped through my lips as I furiously abused my sensitive clit. I wanted nothing more than to feel Spiris inside me, and if there was only one thing standing between us, I was damned sure I wanted to get it done.

It was easy to lose myself in the comfort of his presence especially when his hand made soft patterns on my thighs. His ragged breath egged me on. I felt like I could really loose myself in the feeling. His hand tugged at my underwear and slowly separated the wet fabric from my skin. I let him achingly pull them down my legs.

"Spiris," I let out a breathy moan when his hands teased my inner thighs. I felt his fingers trail until he hit my wetness. The tips of his fingers played at my soaked entrance, I threw my head back and upped the pressure on my clit. He slowly entered two invisible fingers into me and curled them once they were fully sheathed. "Going against your own rules?"

I thought he was going to pull his fingers out but instead he just thrust me into them again. His kept his motions slow but deep and pushed them into me in a way that complemented my own strokes.

"I couldn't help myself," he said. "Look," I looked at where his fingers would have been entering me but instead, I just saw my own slit stretching around him. The sight made me come on the spot. I waved my hand to dispel the magic and crashed my lips to Spiris's as soon as they came into view. I pushed his pants down, not caring to fully undress him before taking his erection in my hand and guiding it to me.

His hands gripped my thighs and pulled them harshly into him, sheathing his length inside me. His hips snapped into me with no rest. His nails dug into my thighs but I did not care, if anything the pain aided me in losing myself in the feeling of him once more.

"I love you," I said with a groan against his lips. His hand left my thigh to tangle in my hair and pull my head backwards so that his fangs could tease the skin.

"You are the only thing I am willing to die for, Iniq," he said against my throat. "You are the sole reason that I can continue to go on. I love you more than life itself."

His kisses trailed up to my lips once more and I came around him violently. He continued to pound into me until my legs were shaking and on the brink of another orgasm. Even as he came inside of me his hand dove between my legs and carried me over once more.

"Don't doubt yourself just because it's takes you awhile to learn," he whispered against my sweaty forehead. "You have come farther than anyone had dreamed you could and you still shatter expectations."

Besides myself I began to tear up. Embarrassed I hid my face in his chest.

"Let's go shower." came my muffled voice. He let out a small chuckle.

~

Two hounds, two demons, and a half-demon stood in front of me in various stages of annoyance and anxiety. No one really wanted to be a test subject to some unknown type of Dark Magic.

Spiris had gotten a dose of my magic last night so he was no stranger to it but the way his eyes glided across the others showed me that he was none too happy about what we would be doing today.

Aselia was more eager than she had once shown herself to be. I had a plan for her today and every now and then she would shift uncomfortably in her place. When I told her that we were practicing again today she got a small light in her eyes, probably thinking that we could destroy some more of the castle, but that was not in the agenda.

Cruor gave me a lingering glook. I knew she wanted to talk. I had been avoiding her ever since I had agreed to give her a chance. It's not like I regretted my decision. I just knew that the minute we were alone again we would have trouble controlling ourselves and that was not what I needed in this moment. What I needed was to make sure that we were prepared in case Baecos found us on our journey to the mirror.

It was too unreasonable to pray that he would not come after us. He had been trying to chase me for over a hundred years by now and to think that he would stop now would only prove how stupid I was. I didn't know to what extent I could build upon my power, but I needed to make sure that at least myself *and* the group could escape the harm that undoubtedly awaited us beyond the barrier's protection.

Ash was a ball of nervous energy while Felix next to him looked like he wished to be anywhere but where he was. I had been careful not to enter anyone's mind since the first night, I was still worried about what I would hear in there and I wanted to keep the momentum. I just knew that if I heard them think about how much they hated me that I would feel the need to lock myself in my room for the rest of our time here.

"Aselia," I called. "I will work on trying to cloak them and you work on trying to hide their magical signature."

Aselia raised an eyebrow at me but nodded and came to my side anyways.

"Who volunteers to be the test subject?" Aselia asks with a devilish smirk, her eyes narrowed in on Felix. Before anyone could move, even Spiris, Cruor stepped forward with a sly smile.

"I'll go first," she said and came to stand in front of me. I was taken aback by how well she had put herself together today. She wore an open chested button down that had intricate embroidery on the seams. Her leather pants seemed to be a deep shade of brown that had an expensive looking sheen to it. Her hair was combed over showing the intricate lines that were tattooed around her face. She leaned close her voice but a whisper when she spoke. "If it's anything like what I heard last night I cannot wait."

My face had the audacity to heat at her words. Aselia let out a snort.

"I'll have to familiarize myself with your bodies for this to have a chance to work," I told everyone while meeting all their eyes slowly. Spiris gave me an encouraging smile when I met his gaze. "Apologies in advanced."

"Nothing to apologize for," Cruor said with a smug smile, her fangs popping out of her lips slightly. "I will thoroughly enjoy your touch."

"Stop with the mating call already," Aselia hissed.

I rolled my eyes and began trailing my hands from the top of Cruor's head to her shoulders. Small shocks seemed to play between us and I felt myself having a difficult time from keeping my hands in appropriate places. I trailed her back and circled her body, maneuvering myself downwards as I did so. I was kneeling in front of her when I met her eyes. From the looks of it her eyes never left mine and they now stared down at me hungrily. Her fists were balled, indicating that she was struggling as much as I was.

I closed my eyes after I felt a flare of heat run though me and tried to focus on cloaking her with magic. My control wavered and I felt her let out a small breathy exhale. I cursed internally and tried to reel in all of the emotions that were violently coursing through me. When I finally covered her entire body, I focused on the mirror trick.

"The pace you move is terrifyingly fast," Aselia muttered. "At this point we may not even need the Dark King."

I let out a sigh as I disconnected the magic from myself and stood to view my work. She was fully invisible.

"Try to make her signature disappear," I commanded Aselia.

"Don't act like you are in charge of me," she halfheartedly grumbled.

"When you are my King, you may command me," I told her. "Now concentrate."

She didn't fight back this time and I watched as her eyes closed. I could feel the spike in her magic as it moved like a cloud over the space that Cruor was once standing.

I entered her mind slowly. She could feel Cruor's magical signature, but she was at a loss on how to make it disappear.

Think of it like your own. I told her in her mind.

She visualized Cruor's magic much like a fog that surrounded her body. I closed my eyes to see through her mind. I could feel her magic play at the edges of Cruor's she surrounded it with her own and slowly started to flex it back into Cruor's body. Like smoke that became trapped in a jar it tried to weave around and find a place to escape, but there was none.

"Do you feel okay?" I asked Cruor my eyes still closed.

"I can feel her magic against my skin," she replied. "It's uncomfortable but nothing hurts."

I nodded. Aselia had finally pushed the signature back inside Cruor's body but even from where I was standing, I could still feel it. Sure, it was less but I could feel it nonetheless and even just a sliver of power would screw us.

"You continue with that," I told Aselia as I withdrew from her mind. "I will focus on the others."

She did not reply as I moved to meet the others. They met me in a semi-circle. Spiris had an easy smile on his face while Ash almost looked scared.

"I will try to connect us," I told them. "The Dark King was able to allow some people to see through the magic, I want to be able to do the same."

"Do you think you have enough magic to sustain the trip?" Felix asked. There was no malic in his voice, but it still felt like an attack.

"Maybe not," I replied honestly pushing the need to defend

myself down deep inside me. "Maybe we will leave you both behind."

"I wanted to go on an adventure with you," Ash said with a pout.

"It's not an adventure," Felix replied back dryly. "It's a death trap."

A smile tugged at my lips. I couldn't fully remember when I had seen them do this before but there was something very nostalgic about the way they bickered with each other.

"Now children," I chided and circled around them my hands brushing across their skin as I did so, cataloguing their shape in my mind. "We will bring you a souvenir, I promise."

"Wait you really aren't bringing us?" Ash asked. I could hear the frown in his voice even without looking at his face.

"Felix is right," I said with a sigh. "I don't know how much magic usage I can sustain throughout this trip and I don't want you two subjected to Baecos again. Leave that to us."

I closed my eyes once I got a feel for their bodies. With each time it became easier to mold my magic to them, but even after just these three people I felt my head become light. Instead of cutting off my magic I focused on creating a tether between us starting from Felix, then to Ash, then to myself and back to Felix.

Opening my eyes, I was disappointed to see that they were invisible.

"It didn't work," I muttered and closed my eyes again. I tried to visualize a strong tether connecting our eyes together but when I opened my eyes again, they were still invisible.

"See, you already ran out of magic, and you want to bring our king with you?" Felix asked. "You can't even cover two people with your magic."

"That's not the problem," I growled at him. "I want to make you see each other."

There was a silence between them and Ash let out a small chuckle.

"Felix, better check yourself before you speak so soon," Ash jabbed. "We can see each other just fine. We didn't realize we were invisible."

I felt a sense of relief crash through me. At least I could do this much. Aselia's cheer came from behind me. With just a quick check it seemed as though she was able to achieve her goal.

Spiris rested a hand on my shoulder.

"Good work guys," he said to us both but his eyes were firmly on mine.

My heart soared under his touch.

"So now that we know this is actually possible," Cruor said as she led us to a quiet sitting room. There were two large arched windows across from the entrances and the two other walls were filled with books. In the middle there was a large couch, a table, and two other love seats for guests. "I suggest we start planning to go get the mirror."

Just like a majority of the castle, I knew deep inside that I had been to this room many times before. I knew this place like the back of my hand it was just the memories wouldn't dare come. For example, I could point out a dent in the floor that was from the hounds wrestling as young ones, but I couldn't remember them actually fighting or the lecture that I had no doubt given them afterwards. I knew that the dark wooden table Cruor led us to was new even though it had long since lost its shine. A sense of longing and loss filled me all at once, but I couldn't sense why.

Cruor grabbed the roll of dark stained parchment paper and spread it out for us to see the intricate drawings it held. It was a map very similar to the one that I had seen back in the Water Kingdom but this one primarily focused on the east side of this world, specifically the Earth Kingdom. A rock formed in my stomach at the thought. I didn't anticipate having to sneak into a place that was so highly intertwined with the Light Kingdom. I remembered the way the Earth King laughed at me when he thought I was powerless.

"I thought the mirror was in the water kingdom," I hissed at her, leaning over to look at the map. The earth kingdom seemed huge, and it unsettled me that the area labeled "main castle" was so close to the edge of the kingdom. There would be no hiding us when we entered the barrier. Even though I did not know the ins and outs of how magic in this world worked and it was obvious that as soon as we entered, the King would be alerted of our presence much like Cruor and the Dark King had been.

"I never said such a thing," Cruor said from next to me. Her arm brushed mine sending sparks up my skin. I cursed the stupid bond that seemed so desperate to bring us together. It had already been hard enough to keep myself from jumping her in the field and now that we were in such close quarters it was impossible to ignore her.

"I met the Earth King. He seems vile," Aselia said with a huff. Her dark hair was sticking to her face and she was still slightly out of breath for the exercise we had conducted. "Where is the mirror?"

Cruor pointed to the outer edge of the earth kingdom, the one that shared a forest with the light kingdom.

"Are you trying to lead her to death?" Spiris hissed from my side. Cruor's eyes narrowed in his direction. The tension seemed to rise between them creating a thick air in the small room.

"She is the one that asked for this. Coming to me and begging that I take her. Don't blame me for her actions," Cruor said and took a deep calming breath before continuing. "It's in a

sea cave." Her finger ran along the very edge of the earth kingdom. "I bet if Iniq and Aselia can perfect that little dark trick of
theirs we can make it past no problem."

"It takes a lot of magic for both of us. If he does find us, we
would be at a severe disadvantage," I noted. There was an
anxiety that floated around the groups and suddenly I felt as
though were inexperienced kids trying to achieve something
that by all standards should be impossible.

"And Baecos will feel the magic," Aselia said from across the
table. "We would have to continuously block the magical signature." She shifted and cast her eyes downward. "I am not profi-
cient enough at dark magic to ensure we can remain hidden."

"You can learn it on the way," Cruor insisted. "Or stay here
and learn it, then we leave. Either way I won't complain." A
small grin played on her lips. "The longer you stay here the
easier it will be to convince me to never let you leave."

"Don't get cocky, there are bigger things waiting for us out
there than you," Spiris huffed and wrapped a hand around my
waist pulling me closer. "We also only have two weeks until we
need to be back in the Dark Kings' cave."

"The we better up the training," Aselia slapped Spiris's arm
before speaking. "Right, teach?"

My heart warmed at her words and from the surprised look
on Spiris's face I knew that this was a gesture that far exceeded
his expectation. I knew it was too soon to insinuate a friendship
between them but even this gave me hope that Spiris and I
could create something for ourselves. Maybe something akin to
a family.

"How long will the journey take?" I ask Cruor. There is a
frown on her face as she looks at Spiris arm.

"If we travel by foot, it will take five. If we do not rest, three,"
she said. "The hounds can get us there fast, but as we saw
earlier, I think that may be pushing it."

"Let's take a week," I told the group. "And then we will see how long we can keep up the magic before burning out. Then another day for rest, and then we leave."

There were nods all around.

"Now that that is taken care of," Cruor said as her hand brushed mine. "I would like to speak to Iniq alone if you do not mind."

I gave her a questioning look but she just met me with an unchanging expression.

"I min—" Spiris was interrupted by Aselia pulling on his arm harshly and tearing him away from my side.

"I'll take him to go practice a bit more," she said. "As much as I loathe to admit it, I think Spiris can help me with control."

I gave them both another forced smile as they left the room, shutting the door loudly behind them. I didn't want to be in a room alone with Cruor. I had been avoiding the inevitable since I had agreed to give her a chance. I knew Spiris was okay with whatever I chose to do with Cruor but a part of me still felt unsure about the relationship. I didn't like how the bond was reacting to us being so close and deep down I still felt hurt about what she had done in my past lives. I had been working to move on from them, but it was hard when the reminder was staring you right in the face.

"Have I done something to anger you?" Cruor asks as she leaned against the table. She made no move to reach out to me but her red orbs watched me like a hawk. Her words stirred something in me, a small bit of panic that tingled the back of my neck.

"No, not at all," I rushed out and looked up at her through my lashes. "I am thankful for all that you have done for us," I paused and swallowed, trying to find the right words. "You have put your kingdom in great danger while we stay here, that is not something I will forget."

"I do not mean to bring this up to make you feel bad, Iniq," Cruor said and moved to grab my hands in hers. As soon as her skin touched mine, I had to suck a sharp inhale of breath. The bond was pushing me closer to her, begging me to close the space between us. It was an odd feeling. I wanted it—I knew I did of course. Cruor was attractive and we had years of history together but that paired with the bond made me feel on edge with only one thing in mind.

"Either way it is a thank you that you deserve," I told her. "And I have been..."

"Ignoring me?" she supplied with a sad smile. "Destroying my castle? Torturing me every night?"

"Every night?" I asked her with a raised brow.

"You are right next to me Iniq, you must have known I could hear you," she said. "I really do not mind that you are with Spiris in such a way but only if you can divide your attention equally. Spiris has had many months with you and who knows how many months he will have with you in the future?" she let out a sigh and brushed her fingertips across the top of my cheek. "I just ask for your attention during the few weeks you are here. Can't I have that?"

I didn't know I could feel such guilt when it came to Cruor. I did promise a chance regardless of what I got out of it and here I was already breaking the promise.

"I just don't want this to be just a sexual relationship," I said. "If I am giving you a real chance at being a mate that would mean more than just sex and every time, I am near you I can't help but want to tear off your clothes."

Cruor threw her head back and let out a laugh that reverberated off the walls. I jumped at the volume but as she continued to struggle to stop laughing, I couldn't help but also find the situation just as funny.

"I'm glad to know you still find me attractive," Cruor said wiping a tear from her eye. "I propose your dinner times are mine, since you insist on staying with Spiris during the night."

A memory popped in my head that made my hear pound in my chest with excitement.

"Breakfast," I compromised. "I remember a bakery you took me to had delicious pastries."

Her smile grew tenfold, "Tomorrow morning before training, I will take you to your favorite place."

"Just us," I promised her. She lifted my knuckles to her mouth as if to give her thanks.

CHAPTER FIFTEEN
INIQ

*J*ust as I promised, I awaited down near the castle entrance for Cruor. Spiris surprisingly let me go with just a kiss and then went to go get himself some breakfast with the rest. They welcomed him with open arms and smiles. I felt slightly envious when I saw that even Felix's lips twitched at the sight of Spiris but it went away quickly when I thought about how much he deserved to have a group for himself that welcomed him so easily.

Spiris had lived a lonelier existence than I had. I always had him looking out for me but he never once had anyone to watch over him. I would have assumed that his brother was better before they joined Baecos but I didn't know too much about their childhood and by the way that he easily gave Spiris up in the end, I am assuming there was much to be desired when it came to their relationship.

Cruor's slim form entered my vison and distracted me from my thoughts. My mouth dried at her outfit; it was what I would have assumed a king of her caliber would wear. She had a similar button up as yesterday and paired with leather pants the outfit had already been jaw dropping with the way it stood out against her skin and hugged her form but paired with the jacket that she wore... she looked utterly royal. It was an all-black jacket with gold intricate designs that seemed to shine against the morning like that surrounded the castle. Her hair was slicked back showing the face she often kept hidden from sight. She even had golden rings that decked her fingers. She met my shocked gaze with a grin.

I felt almost self-conscious as she approached. I was dressed in a long sleeve top with sleeves that flowed around my arms allowing for a cool breeze to brush across my skin when I moved. I had my normal leather pants paired with the only pair of boots that I owned. Compared to her I looked utterly ordinary.

"Sorry," I said quickly feeling a heat flash across my face. "I didn't know we were dressing up."

She gave me a smile and ruffled the top of my hair. I was grateful I let it fall around me in waves that day or else she would have just ruined my hard work.

"I am the King of this land. I have to dress nice when leaving the castle," she explained. "The other times you have seen me in this life I had never the occasion to dress in my formal wear."

"I hope I don't ruin your reputation," I teased.

"Nonsense," she said and linked my arm in hers. "No one will be looking at me when I have you by my side."

I didn't have time to react to her comment because shadows engulfed us immediately. My stomach twisted as we traveled but Cruor's eyes stayed on mine the entire time. The journey ended in less than a minute and the next time he shadows dispersed I was met with a town more beautiful than the one in the water kingdom.

The town we were in had a similar feel to the water kingdom but instead of a river of water that flowed through the town there seemed to be a bonfire fit at every corner of the square we were in. The stone under us was a light grey that complemented the cobblestone paths and buildings that lined the area. Each building had a hand painted sign and what I assumed to be a shop keeper outside the store's door. They all turned to look at us when we made out appearance. I prepared myself for the crowd to rush us much like they had at the light kingdom but instead many just sent a smile our way and continued to yell out to the passerby's that walked the streets.

There was many more people than I was prepared to meet. Families and couples littered the area. They were eating food as they walked, children were screaming with delight, I even saw a few people riding horses through the town. I tried to push down the panic and anxiety that rushed through me, but it must have been too obvious on my face because Cruor's hand squeezed mine.

"I remember that look," she said with a small smile. "Pay attention to me. They will mind they own business."

"Aren't they happy to see their king?" I asked in a whisper as she pulled us through the square and down a narrow street.

"Do you see anyone angry with my presence?" she said with a teasing tone. "I come here often and hold monthly sessions where the towns folk can bring up any issues to me. They are just used to being in my presence."

I was surprised at her admission. I had never once seen Baecos do anything similar and it made me realize how much different the kingdoms were run. Maybe it was what I should be striving for. As she had promised, no one dared come up to us. There were a few waves and shouted greetings but besides that they all just went on with their day. It was almost surreal to be so noticed yet left alone so easily. I had been thrown through a whirlwind of being bombarded by Baecos and his court, to being thoroughly ignored in the Other World... and now being here I could feel a piece of my anxiety chip off with each step.

We stopped in front of a store front that was made almost entirely from glass. Inside I could see only three people and two of them were behind the wooden counter that separated the customers from the workers. It reminded me so distinctly of the modern cafes in the mortal realm that I almost forgot where I was. The two worlds blurred together just enough for me to stumble.

"Are you okay?" Cruor asked shooting me a worried look. I nodded and looked over the café. The painted sign above the door called it *Novis's little beginning's.*

"It just reminds me of the mortal world," I told her. She gave a huff.

"Maybe the mortal world reminded you of this and you just didn't realize until now," she supplied and opened the door for me to enter the café. "Remember, you have been in this world longer than the mortal realm. This is your home."

I nodded not trusting my words. I wanted to tell her that I didn't have a home. That I didn't belong here nor in the mortal realm, but I left it for now. I wanted to give her a chance even if it was just to be in the company of a friend for a few short hours.

The café was a bit chilly as we walked in and the air smelt faintly of brewing coffee. There were some tables and chairs scattered around the small café but only one person stayed in their seat, and they didn't even look up as we entered. There were thousands of pictures on the walls that covered almost every inch of the place. I couldn't make out all of them but there seemed to be the same person in the pictures I could make out and they were surrounded by what I assumed to be different customers. I glanced over to the workers, the person at the counter looked similar to the one in the photos that plastered the walls.

"Minnie?" The man asked as he made eye contact with me. He had long brown hair that was pulled back into a bun on the top of his head. His face and neck were covered in fire tattoos and markings of another hell hound. His red eyes were wide as he took in my form.

"Iniq, this is Fye. His father owned the café the last time you were here," Cruor supplied. "He moved on to the next realm not long after you left us."

I gritted my teeth against her words. It's not like I wanted to leave.

"Is it really her?" Fye asked Cruor. When Cruor nodded and Fye jumped over the counter and rushed towards me. I took a step back but Cruor stopped Fye before he got too close.

"She doesn't remember much from her past lives just yet," Cruor explained. "I'm hoping seeing you will help."

Fye looked between me and her. "Do you remember me, Minnie?" he asked and clutched at his shirt as if the act of me not remembering him physically hurt him. "I grew up with you here in the café almost every day. Even when everyone was at war, you would come back to check on Father and I at least once a month."

I floundered for the words. I couldn't remember him, there was something in the back of my mind telling me he was right but I couldn't remember what him or his father looked like back then. It felt horrible for a kid like him to be so excited to see someone he knew so well and only to be crushed because I couldn't remember anything.

"Let's get the regulars and you can talk through some memories with us," Cruor offered and her hand found my elbow. Fye gave her a small smile before leaving us. We sat down at a small table near the window. I had to take a deep breath to calm my pounding heart. "You were popular among a few places here."

"I had no idea they would even remember me," I told her. The idea of me having a life here unsettled me. It made me feel guilty to have just forgotten everything that I had once had with these people. Watching Fye I couldn't help but wonder how many memories we had together, it would never compare to

Cruor's though. Six-hundred years' worth of memories forgot-ten, yet she still pushed forward every day to rebuild a relation-ship that was all but nonexistent to me.

"Here we go." Fye said and brought a chair over to sit across from me. Cruor's hand brushed mine under the table. If I was any less anxious, I would have jumped at the feeling, but I couldn't help but just stare at the young man before me. "I am guessing you don't remember me at all?"

I shook my head.

"Don't worry she thought I was the enemy when I first saw her again," Cruor assured. Fye let a lopsided grin show on his face.

"Well, you did have your fair share of fights," he said. "I swear Minnie would stay extra-long on the days she didn't want to see you."

Cruor let out a small laugh. "I'd just come and get her anyways though."

"There was a time it was so late I was going to offer to build a bed for you right on the café floor but Cruor came in the nick of time." Fye said to me. "No one could stand up to her but you. The customers were more scared of you than her if we were honest."

"Lies," Cruor huffed and brought her ice coffee to her mouth. "Try it."

I took the iced coffee from Fye and hesitantly took a sip. I almost moaned at the taste. It was a sweet nuttiness that gave you the taste of coffee but also had a sugar coat to it. It was the best coffee I had ever tasted.

"I would ask you if you could taste the difference, but I am afraid you wouldn't be able to tell." Fye said with a sad smile. "It's okay though, it's a chance to wow you once more."

"It's delicious," I told him. "Best coffee I have ever tasted."

"It's gotten better since he took over," Cruor said and motioned to the rest of the store. "It may not look like it but his coffee is really popular in these parts. A once run-down café turned into a booming business."

"It was never run down." Fye pouted.

"Just needed some love?" I supplied with a small smile.

"Exactly, see Minnie gets it." Faye said with a defensive tone.

"Why do you call me that?" I asked him. His smile fell slightly before he responded.

"I could never pronounce your name when I was younger so I tried to get as close as I could, and that version just stuck." He held up his finger and left the seat to grab a frame off the wall. "This was when I finally learned your name, we wanted to commemorate it with a photo."

"I didn't know this realm had cameras..." my voice trailed off when he pushed the picture in front of me. The picture was in full color, I could see my golden eyes reflected back at me in the picture. I was smiling widely with what looked like a young Fye in my arms. Cruor had her arms over us and was smiling as well. I would have thought it was a heartwarming picture if not for the person on the far right of the frame. Baecos stood toward the right of the photo, he had a smile on his face but his eyes held something that sent shivers done my spine. "Why is he there?"

"Baecos?" Fye asked. "You would bring him here sometimes as well. You guys were good friends and would sit here for hours sometimes. But he hasn't come by since your disappearance, must have messed him up."

Cruor shifted in her seat but made no move to remove the photo from my hand. I knew that I had known Baecos in my past life, but I never could figure out the extent of our relationship. It seemed weird to think that I would hang out so closely to my would-be murderer.

"What changed?" I asked.

"I don't know when the shift happened," Cruor said. "There was never an indication of his true intentions. We were all friends. He would come here often and then just one day... you were gone."

"And then you felt my magic on his," I said connecting the dots. This whole time I had thought that Baecos was some sort of a villain that was watching slowly from the sidelines and came to grab me from my old life, but from the more I learned it turned out I was the one who let him into my life to begin with. I was the one who had started the downward cycle that we were in, even my past self couldn't see through his true intentions.

"Did something happen with Baecos?" Fye asked given me an odd look. I forced a smile on my face.

"Nothing you need to worry about," I told him. "Now, tell me more about these pictures."

Fye smiled widely at me and jumped into a flurry of conversation. Cruor eyed me from the side of the table but I kept my eyes planted on Fye and nodded as he spoke rapidly.

I tried my best to push the questions out of my head until I could see Spiris. He would have answers, he always did.

We left the café after an hour of speaking with Fye. He was disappointed to see us leave but I promised him that I would be back at some point. It wasn't a total lie. I would be back at some point but I just didn't know when I would have the chance.

As soon as we got back, I told Cruor I would be changing for the training and ran to the room. I felt Spiris's magic from the room before I even reached the floor and let out a sigh of relief when I saw him waiting on the bed for me. Without a break I pushed myself into his arms. His arms wrapped around me tightly.

"There is something wrong," he stated. I should have known he would have caught on right away.

"I learned that I was friends with Baecos," I told him. "For years. I brought him here. I just can't understand what happened. Why would he change into what he is now?"

Spiris rubbed circles in my back as I hit him with all the information I learned today. He didn't stop me even when I continued to repeat the same things over and over again. He would just listen and nod his head.

"I knew of you," Spiris said. "But I had rarely seen you in the light kingdom before you were taken. Baecos kept his relationship with you locked tight."

"Did you know when he was going to do it?" I asked against his curls. I inhaled his scent and a calming feeling washed over me.

I am here now. I told myself. *Spiris and I are here now and we will not be going back.*

"I think it was a snap decision," Spiris said. "Because he gave no indication of a plan to take you. I was surprised when you showed. You were rumored to be extremely powerful, Iniq. If I hadn't seen your face, I would have known you by the rumors and been just as surprised... it was impossible to think someone like Baecos could use his power on you like that."

"It's because I was the stupid one. Weak. I let him in to my life and when he saw his chance to take my power... he took it," Spiris pushed me away from him and looked into my eyes with a hard look.

"Don't say such horrible things about yourself," he said. "Remember who the bad guy is here."

"I understand why Cruor didn't come for me now," I told him. He frowned at my words. "She thought I ran off with a friend."

"If she knew you at all she would have known that wasn't like you," he fought. His fingers trailed patterns into my side.

"You're the one that said I run headfirst into danger. You

really don't think that sounds like something I would do?" I
asked him.

He looked like he was about to argue but there was a knock
that came from the open door. I was in such a rush to get to
Spiris that I forgot to close it and Aselia now stood in the
opening with an annoyed look.

"Can you hurry up? I made some good progress yesterday
and wanted to show you," she said with a small frown on her
face.

As much as the Baecos situation rained havoc on my psyche
I could recognize when something more important needed my
attention.

"Is this how you ask me for attention?" I teased and detangled myself from Spiris. He followed closely behind me to as I
walked with Aselia out of the room. "I didn't know you liked me
that much."

"I don't," Aselia shot back but there was a small blush on her
cheeks.

Aselia indeed had come further than I had thought she could.
She could now cover two people and conceal their magic for a
total of ten minutes. We would need to work on her stamina,
but it was at least some progress and it was news that I desperately needed.

It came easier for me to cover the entire group. I practiced
on Ash and Felix even though I knew they probably would not
be coming with us but if I could use them as practice, I would.
Anything to aid me in building the power.

The issue now was concealing noise from people outside the
confines of my magic. Everyone could see each other now after
a bit of trial and error but concealing our presence wouldn't

work if they could still hear us talk. If Baecos came, how would we ambush him if he heard our footsteps?

Even after hours of practice, I could not get anything to work. Aselia had already been able to hold her power for an additional twenty minutes by the time the sun was beginning to set but I was still floundering.

"Let's go take a break," Spiris said and helped me stand up from my place in the grass. "You have already done so much, don't get discouraged."

I gave him a smile on the outside, but on the inside, I was raging.

How could I not get discouraged? I either get the magic down or the person my past self had once called my friend would take his chance to drag me back into my own personal version of hell. I wanted to believe that the trip would go smoothly but there was no way I could leave our encounter with Baecos up to chance. Hell, even the Earth king. If we entered his barrier, he would no doubt call in the Baecos to come get his 'goods'.

"Do you know how to undo the seal on my powers?" I asked Aselia as Cruor guided our group to the mess hall. My stomach was twisting painfully and begging for food. I hadn't eaten anything that day and I could already feel it wearing on my body.

"No clue," Aselia said. "I am guessing when you ascend the universe will take it off for you, but I have never met a person who deliberately sealed half of themselves."

"It slipped before I came to the Other World," I said but stopped in my tracks when Felix's gaze met mine. We had already taken our normal seats and that meant that he was almost right across from me. His eyes would be the hardest to avoid.

"Ah yes, that was a show," Aselia said. "Maybe it only happens when you are in danger," she supplied.

"Wait you saw that?" Spiris asked Aselia but was interrupted by Felix's snort.

"So then throwing her to Baecos would solve all out problems." Felix muttered.

"Don't," Cruor snapped at him. Surprise at her response to him flitted through the table. "Iniq did what she had to, I realize that now and everyone else should. I loved them both but... we can't hold onto this forever."

"It's been four months, Cruor." Felix said with a growl of his own. "Were you not the one just asking the elders to forgo torture of Callum? Why is Claire any different?"

"There is no difference," Cruor said. "She would be well within her right to have defended herself."

Felix's chest rose and fell with the violent pants that passed through his snarling lips. I could feel the magic around us build. Ash sent us a panicked look before trying to place his hand on Felix's shoulder but Felix only smacked his hand away before it made contact.

"You are right to be angry," I told him. His gaze snapped towards mine and I was half prepared for him to shift right there and attack me. "Claire deserved better than what I had given her."

"You raised her, Iniq." Felix spit at me. "I don't care what type of person she turned out to be but couldn't you feel it when you looked at us? Couldn't you feel how important we were to you? How come you can remember people like Spiris and Cruor but the pups that spent more than half their life with you are suddenly gone to never reappear?"

"You were once fighting for her against Claire and Callum," Ash reminded him. "And she has no control over her memory loss."

"Like hell she does." Felix stood up. "It was her choice not to remember us. A selfish choice and Claire paid the price for it."

No one uttered a word as he left, instead they all looked at me. Waiting for a reaction, I realized. I grabbed food from in front of me trying to ignore the stares that made my eyes burns.

"I won't make you relive my trauma, don't worry," I told Ash and Cruor. Aselia let out an awkward laugh.

"I watched you do that, I just didn't know what you were showing them that made them freak so hard," she said. "Very efficient."

I ignored her and focused on the food in front of me.

CHAPTER SIXTEEN
INIQ

"I would rather skip the café today," I told Cruor as I met her once more in the front of the castle. She gave me an understanding smile and held her hand out to me. I took it and we were engulfed in shadows.

This time it was short, and when the scene appeared in front of me, I couldn't stifle my gasp. We were on the highest point of the castle and I could see the entire grounds and even over into other dead forest. It was a breathtaking view, but I was more scared of falling to my death than really caring about anything in front of me.

"I had guessed you would say that," Cruor said and twirled me around to look at an iron table and set of chairs that stood in the middle of the small enclave we were in. "We are on the west tower, it's a small place we carved out for ourselves so we could get away from the hustle of the castle."

"There is no door," I noted. She gave me a smile and led me to the table. There was the same coffee as yesterday in the café waiting for me and this time there was a sweet looking pastry for breakfast.

"That's the point," she said. "No chance of being bothered." She pushed my food towards me and took her own seat. "Eat."

"I hope Fye won't be offended," I told her, she shrugged.

"Just make good on your promise to come back," she said.

We ate in silence. It was nice actually, to not have to say anything and be so at ease. The bond was not pulling as violently as it once was, which I was thankful for but that didn't mean that the brush of Cruor's ankle against mine didn't affect me more than it should have. I was just able to control myself better now. I had also gotten used to being up so high and a calm descended on me in a way that I hadn't felt in a long time.

"Thanks for this," I told her. "It's nice that no one can reach us here."

"You would get antsy before too, sometimes," she said. "Not wanting to be around too many people at once. We would retreat here for a few hours at a time to recharge."

I nodded, a movement from far off caught my eye. I made out Ash and Felix in their hound forms in a field of flowers. They seemed to be sparring, or at least I hoped that's what it was. Felix's hound form was easily distinguishable with his scares and as I took a sip of my coffee, he lunged towards Ash bringing them both to the ground.

"Felix is not wrong," I told her. "And he has a right to hate me."

She followed my gaze to them and watched them as they continued to roll in the field of flowers crushing them underneath their bodies.

"He doesn't hate you," she said. "You heard his words last night. He was just upset that he had been forgotten."

"I have been able to gather that they came here when young, but what happened to their parents?" I asked her.

She grimaced. "They were a pack of Hell Hounds that lived in a cave in between my kingdom and the Dark Kingdom. There are some people in this world that like to skin the Hell Hounds and use their fur as a way to power their own magic. They make coats and shawls out of them and suck the magic from their skin. Its why hell hounds are so hard to find in other kingdoms."

I let out a harsh breath. Those poor children.

"So, their parents were all killed?" I asked.

"I assume so, they wouldn't go into too much detail. Even to this day they refuse to but I have a feeling that their parents gave themselves up so the children could escape. We found them trying to get into our barrier screaming bloody murder," she recalled. "I don't even remember their exact ages but young enough that their bodies were still underdeveloped. Magic control sucked and not all of them could shift."

"I was closest to Ash and Felix," I said on a hunch.

"They were the ones that claimed you," she said with a small laugh. "They may be in my court but I bet you if you asked them to join you in the Other World, they would drop everything to do so."

"I wouldn't do that to you," I told her and took a sip of my coffee.

"Why not?" she asked, her eyes drilling holes into the side of my head. "I would deserve it."

"I can see why you reacted the way you did. Since I was friends with him, I mean, and there was no indication of what he really wanted," I told her. Her eyes widened. "Not that I forgive you," I added quickly and continued to watch Felix and Ash. "But it does make me understand your motives a bit better."

Cruor cleared her throat obviously uncomfortable by my words. There was a small blush that played at the tips of her pointed ears.

"Let's go train," she said and stood up without looking at me, I let a smile grace my face at her actions.

They were waiting for us when we finally touched down on the soft grass that surrounded the castle. I had expected Spiris to eye us with careful apprehension, but he just smiled when he saw us, even as Cruor's hand brushed my shoulder.

The relationship between the three of us was weird but in a world like this filled demons, stolen memories, and High Kings. I couldn't really be bothered with the mortal idea of monogamy. If it worked, it worked, and this had been the first time since I came into this world that I had felt like I had really gotten somewhere with Cruor. Looking at her now though, I couldn't help but think that it was never her that had changed but me. I learned more about his world and how to navigate the constant wave of doom and unknown.

"What's on today's agenda?" Aselia asked with a smug smile. She was standing next to Felix who had his arms crossed and his eyes downcast. I was surprised to see he even still came today given his outburst.

Every time I looked at him guilt burned in my gut. It had lessened the more I heard the others support, especially Cruor's, but that didn't reverse the damage. I couldn't remember watching the hounds grow up, nor could I feel the bond that we were supposed to have... but the guilt I felt when I saw the hurt look on Felix's face told me that it had to be true.

"The same thing just focusing on sustaining it," I told her. "I will figure out how to silence the group under my magic."

Aselia took Ash and Felix by their arms and dragged them at least twenty feet away before firing up her magic. Felix growled at her touch, but the action only made Aselia smile at him. I looked over to Spiris and Cruor to realize that both their eyes were on me.

"What?" I asked feeling self-conscious under both their piercing gazes.

"Nothing," Spiris jumped in before Cruor could speak. "Let's see if you can impress us today."

I couldn't help the smile that tugged at my lips. I would do way more than impress them.

After a grueling two hours I had finally gotten a hold of my magic strong enough that I was able to muffle their voices, but it came at the cost of my magic being constantly connected to them. I could silence them from everyone if I cut off my magic to them but for us all to hear each other I would have to be connected to them.

Aselia had been keeping up her magic with no break since we started. She lay down on the grass with her eyes closed and didn't move. The only indication that they were still behind me was the soft chattering, mostly by Ash. I wanted to be proud of her, I was proud of her... but it felt like her success only showed my weaknesses at that point. It was a selfish thought, one that made my magic quiver as a result.

I let go of my magic completely and met both Cruor's and Spiris's eyes with a small frown.

"If I have to keep a constant stream of magic going, I will lose power very quickly," I told them.

"Well, isn't the biggest thing our signature?" Cruor asks. "Can't you just use it only when needed?"

"If Baecos or the Earth King sneaks up on us it would be too late. What's the point of half-assing it?" my voice came out almost in a whine. Spiris's lips twitched as if holding in a smile.

"Let's rest for today," he suggested. "There is no use burning out all your magic if you feel as though you hit a wall."

I nodded but still felt the sense of discomfort in the pit of my stomach when I realized that we didn't have that much longer to get back to the Dark King. I only had so little to prove myself with and it all rode on whether or not I could get a magical mirror to him. The more I thought about the mirror the more antsy I felt. I wanted to know what it had in store for me. My past that had seemed so tightly locked away seemed dull in comparison to the mystery that surrounded my future.

Would I become a King?

Would Nitri bar me again?

Would he finally have enough of my disobedience and kill me?

There were too many questions I needed to answer but I was glad that none of them involved Baecos. I was curious about what his father had done to make my mother strip the magic away from them... but I had more important things to deal with than being stuck in a never changing past. At least if I didn't like what I saw in the mirror, I had a chance to change that... but the past was already set in stone and there was no way to run away from that pain.

"Can Iniq and I use the hot spring?" Aselia asked startling me as she came up from behind me. The two across from me had let me think in peace and I hadn't even notice that Ash had stopped talking. "I'm not sure if I can stand smelling her for much longer."

I rolled my eyes but let the smile show on my face. "Like you are any better, I could smell you from across the field."

Cruor stopped Aselia from continuing with a wave of her hand.

"Please do, you know where they are."

A sigh escaped my lips as my sore and magic depleted body sunk into the steaming water. The bath had a nice floral scent that invaded my senses the moment I entered this area. Cruor's kingdom had a whole underground area filled with them. I politely declined Aselia's attempt at a shared one and chose to pick the single one for myself. The area it was in reminded me of the Dark Kingdoms room, looking like the stone was scooped out and a hot tub placed directly in the middle of the room with barely anything else on the sides.

It would have been a lie to say I wasn't enjoying myself. There was a different kind of guilt that filled my heart when I thought of how I was here relaxing while people out there continued to die due to what *my mother* had chosen. It was holding hands with the fear of not being able to ascend and the fear that Baecos would infiltrate this kingdom in a moment's notice. Both weighing down threatening to sink me in to the spring.

This life was not far. It never was.

The more my mind thought through the last few months the more I realized just how screwed up the world really was and that I was actually *lucky*.

Lucky to be alive. Lucky to have Spiris by my side. Lucky to have been born from a king, even if I couldn't even remember her face. It felt like everyone knew her except me. That's how my whole life felt, everyone knew everything there was to know about my past, but no one was willing to just sit down and explain it to me.

"Not that there is time in between running for my life," I muttered with a huff and sunk further into the water.

Would my mother have chosen differently if she had known the life I were to live? Kneku said that they saw the future, to an extent, and she was the one who told the dark king that I would be the one to destroy the world as we know it. She had to of known that I would be stuck with such a life... shouldn't she?

Even though I do not remember her I remembered the comfort of the unknown figure that hugged me in the door and pushed me into the Other World. Was that really her?

She probably thought I was crazy for what I was doing here. I wouldn't blame her for it cause honestly, I had no idea what to do. Now that my magic had hit the wall, I was not sure how to grantee the safety for myself and the people around me.

Spiris's possible death passed through my mind with a jolt. It was a painful memory that made my chest tighten. I would be responsible if anything ever happened to him... and the others. The memory of Cruor fighting for her life right before my suicide during my first life passed through my mind.

Everyone was a liability. Everyone was at risk. I couldn't stand if they got hurt... because of me.

I leaned my head against the cold stone, looking up at the rough ceiling. The rocks resembled the way icicles used to form on Vein's mortal house in the winter. They threatened to snap off and impale me right then and there ending the six-hundred-year battle for my life with ease.

A memory hit me hard, one of the very room I was in. It was so sudden that I jerked when the ache that followed it exploded across my forehead. I was in the same position that I was now, but I was no longer alone. Cruor stood in front of me completely naked and panting lightly. Her wet hair was slicked back showing off the tattoos around her face. Her red eyes were hooded, and her plump lips were reddish and hung open slightly given me a view of her pointed fangs.

"God," I said with a moan and covered my eyes with my hand.

The memory made my already hot skin turn sensitive. I couldn't help the wandering of my mind. The way her hands felt against my body before I had left that world. The way she dominated me in every way possible. The glint in her eyes when I gave the exact reaction she wanted.

It was hard to forget that part. Even if the bond wasn't an issue, I knew that her touches would haunt my mind but now that the bond tugged painfully at my stomach it almost felt unbearable being in the warm pool. I thought I was warm before all the thoughts but now it felt like my insides turned to goo. The feeling shot through my body and I could already feel my core ache, begging for her touch.

How could a memory make me so wanton already?

The bond had to be on some other level because even last time, it wasn't as bad. I had thought after spending time together the feeling would leave me, but here it was coming back even stronger than before.

I let my hand trail from my neck and teasingly run across my chest. I was not about to go beg Cruor to bend me over, but there was no way I would be able to leave the room without some type of release. My breath caught as my fingers trailed around my erect nipple. I tried to like it, it was pleasurable as my hand trailed down to my legs, but it was also wrong. Even as I rubbed circles on my clit I could not stop myself from imagining a different hand rubbing me.

I let out a moan as the idea of Cruor standing in front of me overtook my once rational mind. It echoed in the room, and I swore I could hear Cruor's dark chuckle. I froze suddenly in the middle of imagining her fingers plunging into me as I heard footsteps coming towards my secluded room. I cursed and tried to sink back into the water hoping that they would not come in.

That daydream was crushed when the crack of the opening door filled the room.

"You always like this one. Far away from the others," said the very same devil that I was just fantasizing of. "Can I join you?"

No. My rational side said.

"Yes," I told her. I sat up and turned towards her. There was a white towel that sat on her hips baring her perky breasts to the world. Her tattoos that were once hidden by clothing wrapped around her arms and torso, adding to the delicious looking curves that I had traced with my tongue just a few months ago. My mouth dried at the sight. She met my eyes with a smile and dropped her towel, I averted my gaze quickly, not wanting to lose myself in what felt like a stupid lust filled haze.

The water splashed lightly, and I let out a sigh of relief when she stayed on the other end of the spring. Her feet brushed across mine in the water and I pulled them away.

"Did I do something wrong?" she asked. The water sloshed as she moved closer to me. "Not like the coffee this morning?"

"No," I said still not looking at her.

"Was I not friendly enough to Spiris?" she asked as her foot came to brush mine again.

"That's not the issue," I muttered and tried to turn so I wouldn't be tempted to look at her but my body stayed frozen. My clit throbbed, reminding me of my unfinished business.

"Then why won't you look at me? You have seen this many times before," she said with a slightly playful tone. I knew that tone. Learned it all too quickly when she teased my reactions in bed.

I gulped and took the chance to look at her. She moved her black hair out of her eyes, it was slicked back and wet. The water rolled down her face, her neck, and down to the curve of her breast. Her breasts were just under the water, hiding nothing from sight. I couldn't pull my eyes away from them. She walked slowly over to me, giving me another look of the beautiful body her clothes hid so well.

Her hand pushed my chin up to meet her eyes.

"Now you can't stop from staring," she joked softly. "Why wouldn't you look at me before?" Her breasts and her toned flat stomach were almost at eye level. "Embarrassed?"

"I remember this hot spring," I told her.

The smile on her face intensified and a small twinkle showed from the depths of her red eyes.

"What do you remember about it?" she asked. I ran my hand across my face not liking the way my body urged me to reach out to Cruor.

"I'm not playing this with you," I told her. "Sit back down please. I told you I didn't want just a sexual relationship."

And it seemed the moment I was starting to understand her that it just turned to sex.

She let out a chuckle. "What's wrong with this, hm? And it's not *just* sexual, don't misunderstand," she moved so she stood right in front of my knees. I wanted to open them and let her do exactly what the memory had shown me, but I forced down the want and stood preparing to leave.

Her hand grabbed my wrist stopping me from leaving. I was now exposed to her, and the chill of the air hit my body.

"Cruor," I warned.

She pushed me to sit on the cold rocks while my feet and calves stayed in the hot water. I met her eyes and regretted it immediately once I saw how dark they had gotten. Heat flooded my body. She positioned herself in between my open legs and pulled me closer to the edge of the spring, almost falling off.

"Spiris gave you permission to do whatever you wanted so don't use that as an excuse," she said and trailed her hand up my thigh. Her body leaned close enough that her breasts rubbed across my stomach and mine across her chest. I gasped at the feeling. She leaned close, her lips mere centimeters away from mine, eyes daring me to make a move. "Why are you denying yourself something we do so well together?"

"*Did* well," I corrected. She smiled down at me.

"Did you forget about the Water Kingdom?" she teased.

She trailed a finger up my side, drawing meaningless patterns on my ribcage. My already erect nipples seemed to harden at the action and shivers ran through me. She leaned forward and placed a kiss at the edge of my lips, then my chin.

I swallowed and leaned my head back slightly to give her access to my throat, I felt her smile as she kissed me. She left another one in the middle of my chest, then one on my left breast right above my nipple. I couldn't help but arch in anticipation.

"Do you still want to deny yourself this?" she asked and

trailed a finger across my stomach stopping at my hips to drag it up between my breasts. Her finger circled around my other nipple teasingly. I sucked in a sharp breath.

"I am not denying anything," I said through gritted teeth.

"So, it's okay if I do this?" and her tongue trailed over my hard nipple, circling the area the same way her finger did. I let out a strangled moan and in repose her mouth covered my nipple entirely and she began sucking.

I hissed and gripped her short hair harshly, pulling her closer. She pushed her body flush against my own and counted to suck and bit lightly. She began kissing the way to the other nipple, stopping to meet my eyes before continuing.

"This one okay too?" she asked while watching me as her mouth descended on the other one.

I moaned and bucked against her, the throbbing between my legs intensifying.

When she removed herself, I harshly crashed my lips to hers and wrapped my legs around her. I needed her closer, needed to feel her soft skin against mine. She wasted no time in forcing her hand between us.

"What about this?" she asked against my lips as her fingers ran across my folds. "Is this okay?"

"Fuck, Cruor," I moaned against her as she brushed my clit. She entered two fingers in me without warning. I let out a cry against her lips. She pumped them in and out rapidly, the sounds of the wetness echoing in the small cave.

"You know I have been dreaming about this," she told me as she thrust harder into me. I had to let go of her and lean back into the ground to brace myself against the power of her hand thrusting into me. I threw my head back as her other hand met my clit. The moan that forced its way through me bounced off the walls. "Ever since I had you after those painful years. I couldn't wait to see this look on your face."

"Cruor..." I was cut off by the orgasms crashing through me fast. I was caught off guard.

"That face," she said with a small moan of her own. Her actions did not cease making me breathless as I panted through her thrusts. "I think about it. Every. Waking. Moment. Tell me I am not alone in this. Tell me how much you missed this."

"Cruor I—" I was cut off as her teeth came down on my nipple. "Of course, I've wanted you."

"Then why do you continue to refuse me? Put distance between us when you obviously want this so bad?" she commented. "Lay down."

I lay down on the rocks without a fight. Cruor leaned over my body and pounded into me at speeds that made me grip onto the rocks below.

"Cruor, god," I moaned against her as she made hard circles on my clit.

"Will you continue to deny this?" she asked and left small kisses trailing down my stomach. "Promise me you won't, and I'll give you the best orgasm of your life."

I orgasmed again, feeling myself clamp down on her fingers.

"I won't. I won't I promise. I won't deny you anymore," I panted on the floor, thankful for the break until I felt her suck on my already abused clit. "Oh my god," I gripped at her hair harshly. "Fuck Cruor, I can't—"

My eyes rolled in the back of my head when she penetrated with her fingers again, curling them inside me. I bit down on my closed fist to stop the scream from coming out of my mouth. She forced me to ride wave after wave of pleasure without stopping as if making up for the months we were separated.

"Why did you do it?" she asked as she pulled away from me. She helped me into a sitting position and gripped my face between her hands, pulling me close. She gave me a passionate kiss before pulling back with a smirk. "Did you forget this so easily?"

"No, I just... didn't know what I wanted. Didn't know what I was allowed," I told her. I let my fingers trail over her pointed ears, down her jaw, her neck. I wondered how many times I had done the same thing. How many times had I sat there with her while I trailed my hands over her body? Her skin was slippery because of the water. My fingers slipped across her chest with ease.

"You are allowed whatever you want, High King Iniq," she said with conviction.

"What if I don't want to choose between you two?" I asked, watching her reaction. She just smiled. "What if I want to be selfish and keep you both by my sides? Will you still allow it?"

"We will set a rotating schedule," she said. "If you promise to come back, you will hear no complaints from me."

"What if I can't come back?" I asked her in a whisper. "Nitri has very strict rules."

She placed a small kiss on my nose.

"You always find a way to break them," she said with a smile. "Now where were we?"

CHAPTER SEVENTEEN
SPIRIS

*I*niq was back in the field once more just like every day before.

Her hair was pulled up into a bun on the top of her head but there were still small strands that stuck to her sweaty face. She had taken one of my turtlenecks and cut the bottom of the shirt and the sleeves clean off, she paired them with loose pants that tied at the ankles. *A crop top* she had dubbed it. I shook my head at her actions, but as ridiculous as they may have been, seeing her like it was everything that I could have asked for in life. I had never recalled a time where her eyes were so full of life.

There were very few times where I had the gift of seeing Iniq in her past life. At a party Baecos would allow me to attend usually, but even then, there was always an air of melancholy around her. I don't know what had happened back then to make her the way she was, but I would be damned if I'd let it happen again. We had come so far. Survived everything that was stacked against us even if it was impossible. There was no turning back and I would gladly give my life *again* if it meant she could keep that smile on her face.

I watched as Iniq threw her head back, her laugh traveled

across the grassy plain to my spot on the ground. Aselia delivered a punch to her ribs and began blushing furiously. They had been trying for the better part of two hours to turn the hounds invisible. Iniq was perfect as always, but Aselia was still struggling.

Iniq linked her arm with Aselia and waved her arms around wildly no doubt trying to explain how to make them disappear. Aselia pretended to pout and not listen, but her eyes washed over the hounds and took in every word Iniq said with a nod. I didn't miss the way she leaned into Iniq's touch. The way her eyes followed her fondly when Iniq wasn't paying attention. Aselia may have been over nine hundred years old but there was no mistaking the child like response she had to someone being unapologetically nice to her and to expect zero in return. Nitri had to have done a number on her. I still couldn't wrap my head around how much of a monster he was to do that to his own children.

Iniq tugged playfully at Aselia's long hair much like I had seen Aselia do to her in the past. Aselia swatted her hand away, but her face softened all the same. Iniq had a way with people. No matter the life, we were drawn to her. Even in the darkest of times she would be there like a beacon of hope. It was a horrific part she had to play, but this time she wasn't alone.

I wished more than anything that she could realize how powerful she could be and stand above everyone like the King she was. Even though she was something akin to a god, there was always a moment where she would fluster and look to me to help her. She still had trouble getting food for herself at the table. I wanted to tell her that if she commanded myself or anyone else, we would do anything to make her comfortable. Don't like the amount of people in the dining hall? We'll tell them to leave. Miss mortal food? I would gladly open the door to the mortal world in an instant and track down whatever food she wanted.

Yet she lived in the world as a guest. She walked through the halls like she was not the sole person that held the fate of the world in her hands. Like she was not a person that could move mountains and darken the sky with a wave of her hand. Did she know that she had more magic than the Dark King and Baecos combined?

Iniq may not have realized it yet, but I had yet to meet someone who saw magic like she did. Understood it in such a way that if she saw someone use it once, she could replicate it in a matter of days. As a child we worked tirelessly for years to get up to a level that Iniq got to in a few days. Iniq obviously did not see herself in the light that others did.

"I don't remember a time where she looked like that," Cruor said, walking to my side.

Iniq was laughing again while Aselia yelled at her for doing so. Ash's head was missing now. My lips twitched at the sight— her laugh was contagious.

"I have not had the pleasure of seeing her happy," I told her. "From the beginning, I was never able to see this. Even last time when she didn't realize what was happening, it was like her sadness clung to her like a disease, even though death."

"What do you think changed?" she asked and sat down on the grass.

It was a simple answer, so simple it hurt. Hurt because it could be so easily broken and force her to go spiraling back to the blood crazed person she was before the door opened.

"She's healing," I said. Iniq let out a triumph sound as Felix fully disappeared. "She hasn't had a nightmare since we came back from the Dark Kingdom."

Cruor didn't reply at first and instead we just basked in the light laughter that surrounded us. Felix's hound form came back into view with a bored expression. He was another one drawn to her. He may have been hurt and angry, but he still volunteered to help. Still showed up every day to aid her in her training. His eyes met mine as if he knew I was thinking about him and let out a huff through his large jaws before turning back to the girls.

"I didn't know she had nightmares still after she left for the Other World," she said.

"They never stopped," I said with a sigh. "She tells me it's Baecos. And even after months she still dreams of my death no matter how many times, she wakes up to see me next to her."

I don't know when the animosity between us disappeared. Maybe when we figured we didn't have to fight over Iniq. Maybe we just both realized in the moment that the only thing we really wanted to see was her happiness. I could not speak for Cruor but seeing Iniq like this was the best gift I could have asked for.

"I'm sorry, Spiris," Cruor said in a whisper. My eyes shifted to her. She was picking at the grass. "I know I should have been there. I knew I should have dragged her out of that house when I had the chance. I know in the end it was my fault that she had to watch you die like that. I … didn't think you would come back but I am glad you did. For her at least."

I had never expected a sorry from her, it made my chest tight.

"It was Baecos fault in the end," I told her. "You were right though. It is better like this. If I had not been brought back, she would have been alone in the other world." *And Nitri would have no doubt destroyed her.*

Iniq took that moment to look towards us, searching until she met my eyes with a smile. My heart skipped a beat. That smile would be the death of me. I smiled back at her.

"She loves you," Cruor summarized. There was a slight bitterness in her tone.

"And I her. I always have," I told her and stood. I turned to her and extended my hand to her. "Let's go help them out."

Cruor nodded and accepted my hand.

"Spiris! Come test this!" Iniq yelled as we approached. I wanted to clutch my chest at the feeling building inside me.

I only prayed it could stay like this forever but as I felt the weight of the demon card in my pants pocket return once more, I had a sinking feeling that it would not.

~

We had come far in the week that we had been training but as the clock against time began ticking, a nervousness hung over the group.

"We can't keep up the four of us and the hounds," Iniq told us as we sat in the study room that we had to overlook the map. "If we cannot cover us the entire time, or at least the majority of it we cannot bring them."

"But without them we are at a huge disadvantage, if Baecos finds us," Cruor pushed back.

"We are more powerful than him and his court," Aselia said with a hiss.

Iniq shifted in her seat but didn't say any more.

"You are," I told Iniq, everyone's attention snapping towards me. She gave me a wounded look. "They took advantage of your lack of knowledge last time. This time you are more prepared."

"I… don't have all my magic back yet," she said. "I can feel it, just beyond the seal. I can access it sometimes, but it is unreliable."

"What you have now is enough," Aselia said. "More than enough. The magic will come when we need it."

"You have too much faith in something that has no reason," Iniq told her with a sad smile.

"It has reason, when you need it, it shows up, right?" she said. "That simple."

Iniq rolled her eyes but did not fight back.

"We leave tomorrow before the sun rises. I recommend we

all sleep early in case we do not have time to sleep much on our journey over."

Iniq joined me in bed that night before the sun was even down.

I lifted up the covers and she curled into my side immediately and let out a loud sigh. I clutched her closer and buried my face in her hair. Her small body molded perfectly against mine as she pushed us closer together. She had been silent for longer than normal today and I could only guess what her mind was worrying her about.

"I'm worried Baecos will show up," Iniq murmured against my chest.

"We will do what we can to stop that," I told her. "You have trained hard. We are prepared."

"And if he does show up?" she asked.

"Then we kill him," I told her. "We kill him, take the mirror, and leave this world to reclaim your throne."

She nodded against me. Her thin hands trailed patterns on the back of my shirt. It was comforting, or at least it should have been if I didn't know her so well. She was thinking hard. I buried my head in her hair and inhaled deeply, enjoying her scent.

I was scared too, but I wouldn't admit it to her. I was tempted beg for us to stay here. She was at least happier here, but I knew in my gut that she had accepted her fate as a High King and it would be wrong for me to bar her from something she wanted so badly.

"Would you take over the Light Kingdom if I asked you?" she pulled away to meet my eyes. Shock ran through me followed by ice cold panic.

Let her leave this world without me? She would be in the other world alone. Who would be there to look over her?

Who would be there when she had nightmares? What if Nitri tried to pull something? I told her I would be by her side forever and now she was asking me to stay so far away from her. My hands tightened around her. I couldn't imagine a life without her and now she was asking me to accept it for a kingdom that was in ruin. A kingdom that was a disgrace to us all.

It's not like that. Her voice said in my mind. I hadn't even felt her enter. *You are just the only person I trust.*

"Do you understand why I would refuse?" I ask her. She nodded.

"I had hoped you may have but I am trying to not let my personal feelings for you sway me," she said with a sad smile. I was glad. It made the panic subside, just enough for me to feel a warmth bloom in my chest but not enough for me to believe I was out of the woods.

We would have to figure it out at some point. We couldn't just have a kingdom with no king. What would happen to the people? While I might have felt no tie to that kingdom I was not as cold to wish death on all those with Light powers.

A selfless thought, I realized. I wished she could be more selfish. I gave her a kiss on the forehead and pulled her closer once more.

"Let's cross that bridge when we come it."

It's okay, I would be selfish enough for the both of us.

"I am going to travel us there," Cruor said the next morning as we left the castle. The sun had still not shown its' face, leaving us surrounded in darkness. "Try to get us as close as possible. I am hoping that will cut the time off as much as possible."

"How close do you think you can get us?" Aselia asked and opened the map that she had been storing in a sack she brought along with her. I had a sack of food and water on my back as well just in case we were unable to enter the kingdom.

"I am shooting for here," she said and pointed to an area near the edge of the Earth Kingdom. "We would still have a day's travel ahead of us and that is only the assumption if the barriers allow me in. If not, we would take the forest path and there is no saying how long that would take."

"That will take all of your magic," Iniq said, her face twisted in protest but the rest of her sentence was cut off.

A swirl of shadows behind Iniq seemingly appeared out of nowhere. I dove forward and pulled Iniq to my chest to get her out of the way of the whatever it was that choose now to come and threaten us. The magic around us rose sharply and Aselia leaped into action standing in front of Iniq with her arms out as if to take the attack instead.

Iniq squirmed in between us and peered over Aselia's shoulder, but I kept my hands firmly on her not allowing her to move from the spot between my arms. This was the safest she would be, sandwiched between two demons who would tear into whatever threat showed itself to us.

Felix was the first to shift, he covered Aselia's side, the size of him almost blocking the intruder from my view. Ash remained in his demon form looking shocked while Cruor let out an exasperated sigh as another demon that I did not recognize made himself known.

The man's long brown hair whipped around him as the shadows disappeared. His red eyes looked panicked as he registered the scene in front of him. He was a hell hound, that much I could tell from the tattoos that covered his body, but nothing else gave away what he was doing here. A growled pushed its way out from my chest.

"Calm yourself," Cruor said, shooting the group a look. "He is a friend."

"Fye?" Iniq asked and pushed her way out of my arms and

around Aselia's still body. Aselia's hand clasped her wrist before she could move towards the man she dubbed as Fye. Iniq sent Aselia a narrowed eye look. "There is something wrong."

"Minnie, Cruor, I came as fast as I could." Fye said and tried to gather his long hair, but his hands were shaking so violently he settled for pushing it roughly out of his face. "I was sleeping when I heard the commotion and I tried to get here as fast as I could. By the gods, it's horrible Cruor!" Fye rushed towards her and gripped at her shirt. Cruor met him with wide eyes. "The town's people. They are going insane. Children, they are gone!"

Iniq freed herself from us and turned Fye to so that he could look at her. "What's happening with the town?"

"I don't know." Fye sputtered, tears were welling in his eyes. "There was a commotion that woke me up and then when I looked outside.... chaos."

"What kind of chaos?" Cruor asked.

"The people they... are going on some type of rampage." He explained. "Breaking into houses, burning buildings. Slaughtering children in the street. Forcing themselves on the helpless while other watch on. I didn't know what to do Cruor, I have never seen them act like this I—"

Iniq shut him up with a harsh slap that echoed through the still morning air.

"We will go with you," she insisted and looked around at the group. "All of us."

"Iniq, I don't like this," I said as I stepped around Aselia's frame. Aselia and Felix still seemed to be on guard, they were right to. "This sounds like something a powerful Light Magician can do."

I didn't have to utter his name but recognition passed through the group. I had seen him use the same type of magic before, it was heart breaking and disgusting to watch as he pushed people to their breaking point. Iniq was not the only person he had tested his magic on in the last few hundred years, towns people, guards, or really anyone that angered him could be subjected to the mental assault he loved so much.

"Then more reason to go," she pushed. "If Baecos is in the kingdom we need to push him out."

"What does Baecos have to do with this?" Aselia asked.

"Did mother not teach you what light can do?" Iniq asked. "To a person's mind?"

Aselia shook her head.

"He can put ideas in their head," Cruor explained, but she didn't know how wrong she was.

"No, he can call forth a deep desire. A light," Iniq said. "Something that always existed. Something you've always wanted. Making it all you think about."

"The darkness—" Aselia was cut off by Iniq's growl.

"Is the same," she said. "Except it is much more sinister especially when paired with light," Iniq gave her a look that told her not to talk any longer, but she did not listen.

"We can use this time to go to the Earth Kingdom." She suggested. "Where we know that he cannot follow as fast."

"Don't you dare think I will sacrifice my people for that," Cruor growled.

"Stop fighting," Iniq commanded. "We go, now."

CHAPTER EIGHTEEN
INIQ

*S*creams surrounded us as we traveled to the town.

The once calm and majestical city filled with smiling people was in chaos, just as how Fye described. Multiple buildings were caught in flames that shot into the early morning sky causing a red hue to overtake the area. The smoke hung over everyone and stuck to our skin and clothes. I had to cover my mouth to block the smoke from entering my lungs.

The scene was horrific. There were dead bodies littered the ground in various stages of abuse. A mother covering her children and wailing as she clutched mangled bodies to her chest. People were running all along the streets breaking the glass on the store fronts and throwing things into the street. There were shouts of anger and whoops of triumph following by a blood curdling scream.

It was a stark contrast to the happy and peaceful town she had once visited. The same people that smiled to us as we passed their shop now began tearing down their neighbor shops, pulling out the owners, and bashing their head in with whatever was closest. It is just proof that no matter what someone shows on the outside, they will always have some sort of dark violent thoughts that live deep inside them.

"No," I whispered as I watched a man force the grieving woman away from her children's body and onto the ground. He laughed at her face and began unbuckling his belt. "Stop!" I called to him but when he met my eyes, he only gave me a disgusting smile. My magic rose around me widely wiping around me like a harsh wind. I couldn't take the sight of his dirty hands on her and the people by my side seemed to be in such a state of shock they didn't know how to proceed. "Regain yourself!"

This time my words were filled with as much magic as I could pack into it. I knew what I needed to do, and it came easier now that I knew what I was capable of. The man froze against the women in shock and then leaned back on his heels blinking rapidly like he had just woken up from a bad dream.

"I didn't know what came over me," he whispered. The women scrambled away and grabbed an object I was unable to make out, but before I could call upon her to stop, she smashed the heavy object against his head. He fell to the ground with a thud, his body did not even twitch as the blood from his head spilled onto the ground.

"Pure madness," Aselia whispered by my side.

The women forgot the man and scrambled back over to her children's lifeless bodies.

"I can't feel Baecos's magic," Spiris said from behind me. His hand was on my shoulder anchoring me to this world. "He may have caused this and left."

"I doubt that," Cruor muttered.

"Get me to the highest point in the town," I told Cruor. Without any questions she led the group further into the city. Each turn was a step further into the madness. I wanted to stop every one of them but I had to ignore them until we got to the highest point, maybe then would I be able to put a stop to this. I would need to reach as many people as I could with my magic and there was no way I could save everyone if I ran through the whole city.

When we passed a group of men that formed a circle around something unseen to us, Fye jumped into action and began pushing himself through the group. Only then did I see the face of a badly beaten child.

"Go help detain those men," I told Felix's hound form and Ash. They followed my command without hesitation and jumped on the men throwing them to the ground. "We continue!"

I didn't care that it was Baecos's magic that drove them to this. Those thoughts about a child were unacceptable. I did not care that this was Cruor's kingdom, I would be a disgrace of a King if I just let the monsters continue to live with thoughts like that. This would be the one slip up that could cause them to get a taste for the violent behavior.

Cruor led us through a maze of windy roads until we reached a budling that was engulfed in flames. Up until now a handful of buildings only had small fires to put out, but this one almost covered the entire three-storey building. We all stopped in our tracks as the screams reached our ears. I swallowed thickly trying to control my breathing. I wanted to dive into the flames and save whoever was in there, but we needed to hurry or this would last forever and even more lives would be lost as a result.

"I'll stay," Aselia volunteered and ran to the shop. She put her hands out in front of her and water flew from her palms. There was a loud hissing sound as fire met water and black smoke filled the air around us.

"Stay with her," I told Spiris. His dark eyes were unreadable as he looked over me. "Find us after you save them, they will need a lot of healing."

He looked to Cruor, debating my words.

"I've got her," Cruor assured.

With a short kiss to my lips Spiris left my side and dove straight into the burning building. I turned to Cruor with the screams of the fire victims still weighing in the air around us. With a pained look towards the building, she continued to lead me further into the city.

This is messed up. I thought. *I knew Baecos was horrible but this... it's insane. More than I thought he was capable of.*

"I can guess what you are going to try," she said breathlessly. We had been running on an incline and I could see a small clock tower ahead. It would be perfect. Not only was it on a hill that overlooked the town but even staring up at it there was no building that even came close to its height. "I hope it works."

"Me too," I muttered and coughed into my elbow as the smoke felt like it was overtaking me. She grabbed my arm roughly and traveled us. I was roughly pulled in all directions. My eyes blurred and I had to screw them shut in order not to unleash the contents of my stomach onto the floor. The trip was over quickly, the only sign we had moved was the change in air that surrounded us. My eyes cleared and I met the burning town. Even from here I could hear the screams and the heat seemed to reach up towards the sky. Even if this worked, we would have a long way to go to save the town from utter destruction.

Without wasting time, I gathered whatever magic I could find inside me forcing it up and out of my body. I would need every lick of it I could get. It would severely delay the trip in finding the mirror, maybe we'd even run out of time if I used too much... but it would be worth it to save the town. If I needed to, I would find a way.

"Give me time," I told Cruor. When there was no response, I looked behind me to see what she was doing but the roof was empty. Where the fuck did she go? I tried not to let the panic fill me, there were bigger things than a missing King. Hundreds of screams reached my ears as if to remind me of the situation at hand. "I got this."

I continued to gather the magic, closing my eyes as I did so. Trying to focus on grabbing everything I could. I didn't mean to panic at the feeling of my magic being drained to me, but I couldn't get the idea of a life without magic out of my head. It would make me a target. I would be weak, everything Nitri told me I was. Not to mention Baecos would have a better advantage than he did now.

I couldn't think of that. Not while those people were begging for help. Not while Spiris, Aselia, Fye, Ash, and Felix were working so hard to protect the people of the town. People that had no connection to them yet they were risking their lives out there.

If they could do it, so could I. I inhaled. Then exhaled and inhaled again.

"Regain your control," I spoke. My words vibrated the air around me and sounded like a thrum of a deep instrument instead of actual words. "Remember yourself. Shake off the magic."

I continued to chant my words over and over again as I fed them magic. I could feel the waves push itself out, like a hand reaching out over the town. The fingers reaching until they couldn't reach any further. When they stopped, I would push more magic into them while chanting to get just a foot more, then an inch.

I could feel the change in the atmosphere but the strain on my magic caused the breath to be sucked out of my lungs and caused me to fall to my knees. Not only did the screams continue but I could *feel* him now. Could feel the blanket of magic he laid across the town. It was as thick as a snow fall and as sticky as glue. Even as I pushed my magic to the limit, I could still feel the remnants of his power. It was too strong. My magic was not up to par and he had poured so much magic into the town that it felt impossible to scrub it clean.

I sucked in a deep breath of air feeling like my lungs would collapse if I pushed myself any further. My body was ready to fold in on itself and even just standing there was enough to cause tremors to shoot up my body. I tried to push more magic but my reserves were gone and the only small amount of magic left felt like the only thing keeping me alive. I had never realized how much my body had come to rely on the magic until it had no more to fuel itself.

There was a shuffling behind me. I couldn't feel the magical signature due to my magic being almost completely spent but I could still feel the malicious sensation that rolled off of the person in waves. I knew who it was before I even turned. The same person who had forcibly tied me to a table and stripped my magic away as I screamed stood there as if it was the most relaxing scene in the world. His hand buried itself in his pocket and his posture was slouched lightly with a lazy grin currently spreading across his face. The deadly purple eyes that I once thought looked so mesmerizing glowed in the dark with something close to blood lust. His long blond hair was tied at the nape of his neck. The only thing off was the blood that was splattered across his white shirt. It looked like he had taken some time to himself to partake in the town's descent into madness.

Vitos stood behind him in the shadows. His body was so hidden from view it was almost like he was cowering behind Baecos. The morning light hit his face in just the right way to show me that his lip was split open and there was a bruise blooming on his neck, almost in the shape of a hand. His eyes shifted when I looked to him, and his head hung as if he was ashamed.

I didn't like the look on his face. Inside I knew I should feel satisfied by the look of him so beat up... but I couldn't wish it on anyone. Even someone as vile as him.

"You always looked better on your knees," Baecos mused. He took a step forward, but I scrambled up and away from him. "How do you like my present?"

"Don't talk about people's lives like that," I hissed at him. The fear may have paralyzed my legs, but the anger was alive in my heart and it wanted to *destroy* the man in front of me. "This is no present."

"But it is," Baecos said with a small pout. "A perfect diversion to take you back with me."

"Where's Cruor?" I asked panic filling my chest when I realized that he had me right where he wanted. We fell into his trap. He must have been watching the Fire Kingdom and knew that we were still inside, this was his only way to force us to a place where he could corner us like animals.

"That was not my doing," Baecos said with a smile, he took another step forward. "She left you here all on your own. Works out better this way."

I had nothing to fight him with now. The door was nowhere to be seen and there was no thrum of magical power bursting from my mind.

I was alone. Completely and utterly alone. Cruor left me, the door left me, and the rest were helping the townsfolk. If I was going to live through the assault, I would have to fight through it myself.

"It won't work," I told him, trying to fake my confidence. "You're out numbered."

He ignored my comment and came to my side staring at the burning town in front of us. There was no smirk on his face, instead it was a crazed smile.

"Isn't it magnificent?" he asked as his hand clamped down on my shoulder and he turned me to face the town. "This is what a *real* god can do." His voice was a whisper in my ear as he spoke.

"Bend people to your will. Make them kill each other. Make them finally have the courage to relive their darkest desires. You think your puny powers can stand up to this?"

"Don't touch me," I hissed as his wandering hand came to my hip. I would stab it with a dagger if I could conjure it.

"I've wanted to show you this for so long," he cooed, his teeth tugging at my ear lobe. "You really think you are the only one in this world that has the power to become a god? Look around you, this is nothing for me. I can do this without a second thought."

I needed to pull magic from somewhere. I didn't know how but I knew it was the only way to get out of this. Vitos was unlikely to help but if someone, just anyone could come and get Baecos off my back long enough to supply me with just an ounce of magic I might have a chance.

But you are still alone. A voice whispered. *No one will come save you.*

"So, you just want to prove you're better, is that it?" I asked him and tried to push whatever I had out in hopes of finding a signature I recognized. "Is that what this is all about? The kidnapping? The magic stealing? All so you prove your strength?"

I prayed he couldn't tell I was stalling. Just as I thought I felt the edge of a familiar demon my magic flickered out like a light, leaving me alone with the feeling of Baecos against me.

"So, I can become the god you failed to be," he said with a harsh whisper and began dragging me backwards. I let out a scream but was cut off by Baecos arm to my throat. "The god my father tried to become until you *bitch of a mother* murdered him. I'll take her precious daughter once more and prove that I was the one that was supposed to be victorious."

I kicked and failed against him, but it was no use, his arms were wrapped around me too tight.

"He probably deserved it," I spit at him. His response was to choke me harder. "I'm going to kill you," I could already feel myself getting lightheaded. It was the fatigue mixed with the way he was blocking my airways. He just let out a low rumbling chuckle at my actions.

"Find Callum and let's leave," Baecos ordered Vitos. Vitos left without a sound.

Take his magic. The voice from the door told me. *Drain him.*

Finally, the door had showed up but it was too late. I wanted too badly to listen to it. To fight against the one person who has fucked over my life again and again, but the will to fight was seeping from me without Baecos coaxing it. Even as I bucked wildly against him, there was no escape.

Iniq, take his magic. The door growled at me. *Take it. Take it. Take it.* It chanted in my mind each one getting louder and louder as my consciousness began to fade.

Baecos let up for just a second to bring my face to his and cover me in violent kisses that left my lips bleeding. He looked satisfied at my lack of energy and my lost will. It was what he always wanted. He needed to be in control, needed to dominate everything.

Now. The door yelled so loud I flinched. I was hit with in onslaught of information that made my head explode. I couldn't make sense of most of it with my head feeling the way it was but I could do one thing. I lifted my shaking hands up to his face just like I had done to the shadow Baecos in the forest. He had the same reaction, a cocky smile and a look on his face that told me he knew it would happen.

I felt his magic play under my fingertips. I called it forth from my mind and imagined the various strings of his magic leaving his body and coming into mine, filling my empty magical core. He gave me a confused look when he felt the first burst of magic and then in just a moment his expression changed to a murderous one. He tried to push me away but he could not, not when I was still sucking out his magic, it fused my hands to his face.

The more his magic filled me the easier it was to understand exactly why he took mine. It was an intoxicating feeling with it leaving a sweet taste on the tip of my tongue. My previously exhausted body came to life and felt like electric shock waves made their way through my body. Baecos's knees buckled and he dropped to the ground in front of me.

"You look good kneeling," I told him with a purr. My lips curled into a dangerous smile, and I felt his magic nestle inside me. It was pounding against my skin causing my body to warm, but in a pleasant way. I let out a content sigh.

Baecos's mouth was stuck in a silent scream. A feeling of triumph washed over me.

I could end this. I could end this right now and be rid of this monster. All this time, this was all I had to do. It was a cruel way to die, I could feel his body tense and his eyes were losing their glow. It must hurt, but I am happy it does.

"Any last words?" I cooed at him.

CHAPTER NINETEEN
SPIRIS

*I*t was happening again. I could feel it. Just like the last time she had disappeared from this world I felt her magic tickle my sense as if to give her final goodbye. It was so light, barely there. Like a ghost of a tap on the shoulder but when I turned, nothing was there. The last time I had a bad feeling about the magic, and I got there far too late to save her. Her body had already gone cold. I couldn't let that happen this time.

"We have to go!" I called to Aselia. She was crouched in front of the family that we had pulled from the fire, healing them but when she heard my tone her gaze snapped up to mine immediately. She whispered something to the family, but I didn't stick around to hear her, instead I ran full speed in the direction that Iniq's magic had come from.

It was not long until I found myself looking up at a clock tower. I reached my magic out to feel if she was up there, but it was only Baecos. Lead formed in my stomach but the new heaviness of Iniq's possible death did not stop my legs from pushing themselves into the clock tower and up the stairs.

This couldn't be happening! My mind screamed at me. *We were supposed to be safe here. He wasn't supposed to get through the barrier.*

I growled and skipped to the ledge a few stories above me that I could make out. I could not skip to a place that I have not been, but if it was in my sight, I could do it. It was faster than running anyways. I continued to skip myself up the winding stairs breaking into short runs when I could not make out a place to land. It was exhausting but I had to push myself, needed to get to her. There was no time to rest.

My chest burned when I finally reached the top of the tower. I kicked the door to the roof open and it flew off its hinges clanging to the ground of the roof. In front of me was a sight that shocked me to my core and froze me in place.

Iniq was in front of a kneeling Baecos with an insane smile on her face. Her hair was whipping around her wildly and there was blood splattered on the front of her shirt and face. Baecos's body was taunt and unmoving. I could see the strings of his magic floating around them and turning to bury themselves in Iniq's skin. I had never seen magic come out like that before.

Aselia crashed into my back sending me flying forward. I could hear her angry intake of breath, but she paused when she took in the sight before us.

"This can't be," Aselia whispered horrified. "How is she doing this?"

I wanted to ask the same thing but had no chance to as a ball of silver rushed at Iniq and tore her away from Baecos. The magic strings snapped between them, and I caught a glance of her blood-stained palms as she was thrown to the ground.

"Iniq!" I scrambled over to her and pushed the ball of fur off her. Callum attempted to snap his large jaws at me but with my demon strength I was easily able to push him out of the way. He let out a loud growl but instead of fighting back he went straight to Baecos.

"Don't move." The familiar voice of my brother said as I

wrapped a dazed Iniq in my arms. My head snapped over to the group and saw that Vitos stood between a still kneeling Baecos and Aselia with an ice sword. Vitos held out a sword of his own toward her with an unsteady hand.

He looked downright pitiful when my eyes washed over his form. The light was almost fully over us now giving me a good look at how many cuts and bruises were on his face. It broke my heart to see him like that way. It was not the brother I knew, not the same one that would stand up to the other children for me while they bullied me senseless. Not the same one that promised me we would be okay after our parents died.

He was a weak version that had gotten so lost that he didn't even look human anymore.

Callum shifted, showing his panicked, naked self, and before anyone could stop him, he grabbed both Baecos and Vitos, and in a flurry of shadows, they left their place on the tower.

"Callum!" Cruor's voice yelled as she raced to their now empty spot. Rage boiled inside of me at the sight of her. I was about to let go of Iniq and pound my fist into Cruor's face but Aselia beat me to it and placed her sword directly under Cruor's chin. Cruor gave her a wide-eyed look.

"Where were you?" she questioned. Her red eyes narrowed, and her teeth barred at Cruor's crouched form. It was a mix of disgust and anger that was splashed across her face so obvious it was like it was painted on.

"We got separated," Cruor said he throat constricting as she tried to swallow against the pointed blade. "I was helping townspeople."

"You left her alone with Baecos," I hissed.

Iniq was gripping tightly onto my shirt, still wide eyed and daze. She took deep gulping breaths as if she could barely breathe.

"I didn't feel him," she excused. "And you got here in time."

Aselia pushed the sword into her neck but a groan from Iniq stopped called our attention.

"Now's not the time," she panted and I helped her into a standing position. She faced towards the still burning town and he magic flared around her. I had to grit my teeth to stop the pained moan. It was far too strong to be so close to it... was this what those strings were? A high king power maybe?

I couldn't make out the chants she spoke but I could feel the magic pour out of her.

"His magic is almost gone from the town with his departure but it will take too long," she stated through locked teeth. "We don't have time to waste."

After another moment the magic snapped back to her and she sagged against me. I couldn't feel Baecos's magic before but now that it was gone it felt like a weight had lifted off the town. Slowly the fires began to put themselves out, I am assuming by the towns folk that regained their control.

"You consumed his magic," Aselia said from behind us.

"I think some of his soul too," she said. "Or I at least got a taste of it."

"It looked like strings; I've never seen that before," I told her as I walked her back to the group not sparing a look at Cruor. The only thing making me from snuffing out Cruor's existence was Iniq as she clutched onto me. She would be less than happy if I killed Cruor so soon after I agreed they could be together.

"The door helped me again. I didn't know what I was looking for, still don't, but I'm just glad I didn't lose all my magic," she straightened her back and gave me a small smile. "We leave tomorrow for the Earth Kingdom."

"Absolutely not," I fought her. "You need to rest."

"No," she pushed back. "Baecos is at a disadvantage now that I took so much from him. It will take him awhile to recover."

There was an unspoken *I hope* that hung in the air around us.

"She has a point," Aselia said. I felt her prod at my mind.

I want to leave Cruor's kingdom. Iniq will not mention it but the fact that she left her so easily makes me uneasy. She gave no indication that she was in my mind instead just sent warning glares at Cruor as she brushed off her pants.

This is not the first time she did this. I told her. *I was hopeful she changed.*

"Let's go check on the town and the hounds," Iniq said while looking towards Cruor. "Can you travel us there?"

"Of course," she said with a strained smile. She was lucky Iniq did not have a bad temper, if it were me, I would have felt betrayed. I would demand retribution.

With a wave, shadows engulfed us and we were right back where we were when we first broke up as a group. It was quick work to find the others and thankfully, they were all in one piece. Iniq gave them all a sympathetic hug. Felix hugged her for a moment longer than necessary, but no one mentioned anything.

Cruor spoke in front of the people taking all the glory for herself. The only thing she did correctly was give Iniq credit for saving the entire town. They cheered and many came to give their thanks by pulling her into a hug. Iniq accepted them all and made sure they were okay before we left. There was a handful of people that we had rounded up as prisoners. There was a line they crossed, Baecos's magic or not... some things were unforgivable.

"Let's send part of the guards to rebuild the town and take the prisoners," Cruor said to Ash when we traveled back to the castle. "We will be leaving tomorrow so send only enough to cover then main damage. We need some to patrol before we leave and check for any holes in the barrier."

"How did they even get in?" Aselia asked, her voice had an accusatory tone to it. Cruor paused and shifted her eyes to the floor.

"I am suspecting Callum led them in," she explained.

"He's still accepted by the wards." Felix said. There was no question to his tone nor malice, it was spoken as if it was just a statement of truth.

"Yes," Cruor answered curtly.

"So, you purposefully let Baecos's minion a free pass through the wards," Aselia said her voice in a hiss. She stalked towards Cruor, but Felix caught her wrist before she could do any damage. "Did you not think that once he left to block him from the wards as well?

"Let's not do this," Iniq said her strained voice freezing everyone. "Is it wrong to have hope that a person you love will see the error in their ways?"

"It's more than that, Iniq," Aselia sent a glare to Cruor. "I don't believe her excuse about leaving you alone for one minute."

"You left her?" It was Ash who asked this time, his voice was pained and rose an octave with each word.

"I can take care of myself. Did both of you not see the way I almost took his soul? Don't act like I am incompetent," Iniq hissed. "Plus...I told her she could go. The townspeople were more important."

Lies. Lies. Lies. Why would she lie like that? To me? To Aselia?

"Iniq," I said in a low voice. She sent me a pained look as if begging me to drop it. I would do it, for her. "Let's eat and rest in bed until it's time to leave."

"I would like that," Iniq responded with a light smile, this time it was real. She dragged me down the hall leaving the others in a tense silence.

We repeated the same process as the night before just this time instead of Iniq asking me to take over the light kingdom she just slept deeply. The whole ordeal with Baecos must have taken more out of her than she let the others believe.

During the meal she barely spoke only focused on her food and then we left without a word. She barely spoke to me even as we showered together. Even as she pulled me closer and touched my body in a way that made her hard to resist. I knew when she needed a release, I could understand that she needed it now more than ever, but I was unsettled by her silence.

I wanted to hear her talk before the journey. Baecos would no longer be a problem, but the Earth King would be. I do not put it past him to be just as malicious as Baecos which meant there was still a chance she could get hurt... *again.*

"I love you," she whispered against my chest. I jolted, surprised that she had awoken from a deep sleep. "Don't waste energy thinking. Your King took care of the biggest one." There was a smugness to her tone.

"And she did wonderfully," I said against her hair.

"Sleep," she commanded, "We have a long day ahead of us."

I nodded and closed my eyes. Even as she fell back into a deep sleep, I could not brush off the feeling that tomorrow would be worse.

"So, you can bring us right to the Earth Kingdom's edge," Iniq reminded Cruor of our conversation the day before as we all stood sleepily outside the castle. Waking up before dawn was fine for one day, but two and after such a horrific event, was a bit much. I shifted, hiking up the backpack that I had brought with us. Just in case the mirror was as powerful as they claimed it to be I wouldn't dare risk any one person holding it for too long.

As I shifted, I also felt another weight in the back of my pants. It was the demon card once more that had wormed its way back into my clothing. It made me uneasy to think it still followed me. I didn't know what kind of magic Kneku put on it, but it didn't feel like a good sign.

"I have also been practicing since you've been gone, Iniq," Cruor said with a smile that showed her fangs. I hated it. "It's the same distance from here to the edge of the water kingdom. I have made the trip there and back just before you arrived last month," Iniq looked taken aback.

"So, someone like you can be affected from a death," I deadpanned. She gave me a glare.

"A lot of things could have been avoided if I could travel a further distance," she replied. "Felix, Ash."

The two boys in question stepped up and stood in front of her, ready to take orders.

"Protect the kingdom while I am gone. Get Fluvis if anything happens. If he feels you near the barrier, he will come to you."

"We will be okay, like Iniq said Baecos is weak he would not dare pick a fight now," Ash grabbed Cruor's hands anyways, becoming serious. "Take care of yourself Cruor. Don't go dying yet, you have no offspring to take over the kingdom if you die."

She rolled her eyes but dismissed him with a nod.

Ash turned to Iniq. His face held an obvious frown.

"Will you come back?" he asked, his voice breaking softly. It must have pained him to meet her again when she didn't even know who he was and then when he finally got her back, a happier version, she was ready to leave him once more.

"Next time you see me I will be a King," she said with a playful smile. "I expect a feast and celebration."

Ash pulled her to him tightly, his fists were balled and almost white as he did so. Iniq gave him a hug back and rubbed his back softly.

"Don't forget your patrols," she muttered softly. "And take care of yourself while I am gone. I won't be able to watch over your eating habits anymore."

Ash eyes widened and filled with tears.

"You remember," he said and nuzzled his face into the crook of her neck.

"I remember enough to know that you are a grown hound now and you must take more responsibility," she said in a playful tone.

Ash nodded and pulled away from her. The next surprise was Felix. He hooked his arm around Iniq and pulled her in for a hug. His face was a stone as he did so. Iniq's hands clenched into fists, not once, twice, a third time, before returning his hug.

"Take care of yourself," he told her while holding onto with a heavy look in his eyes. He held onto her longer than the day before after her run in with Baecos.

"Do I get a goodbye hug too?" Aselia asked breaking the heavy attention around us.

Ash laughed and went to go hug her, but she held her hand up.

"I mean from the tall hot scarred man," she said. Ash looked dejected and Felix had the hint of a smile on his face.

"Let's go," Iniq said pulling away from Felix, her expression turning serious.

Cruor nodded and with a look back to her only two remaining court members her magic rose sharply. I tasted the ferocity of it on the tip of my tongue.

"Cover μs," she said to Iniq.

Iniq nodded and with a wave of her hand I felt her magic wash over us. Aselia's joined after hers and by the intake of air from Ash I assumed that we were now invisible to their eyes, but we could all clearly see each other under the shared blanket of magic. Iniq hard work had paid off beautifully.

"Prepare yourselves," Cruor said and without any other warning, the scenes around us flickered and twisted. The world around us darkened and I could feel us being thrown in all different directions even though I never felt my feet leave the ground.

I focused on my breathing and reached out to Iniq. Her hand grabbed mine harshly.

I did not know how long we were stuck in the void, but when it spit us out, I felt like my stomach had been twisted and thrown to a pack of wendigos. I leaned over while placing my hands on my knees taking a deep breath.

"It worked," Cruor said in a pained voice. "We made it inside the barrier."

Blinking a few times to clear my blurry vision I could make out that we were in the middle of two large mountains. There was a dark dirt path underneath our feet and every few feet, there were patches of bright white flowers that swayed in the wind. The air was sweet here, clean; it filled my lungs easily.

"At least there is no one around," Aselia said with a moan of discomfort.

"We should keep up the magic just in case," Iniq said. "I'm surprised we fooled the barrier."

"Only time will tell," Cruor said. "I suggest we get going before we find out."

"You know where to go?" Iniq asked and jogged to keep up with Cruor's pace. I matched my strides to match hers and wrapped my hand protectively around hers.

I had a bad feeling about this. The kingdom. Cruor. The mirror. Looking between the group I couldn't tell if they felt the same way I did or if they were just already on edge because of the trip.

"Of course," she said. "The Earth king and I were friends for many years. Even after Baecos took you we never fought... but I also didn't realize how deep he was with Baecos until Fluvis told me he was at the party we tried to rescue you from."

"The Earth and Air King visited the Light Kingdoms many

times," I told them. "Baecos used to have magic sharing parties with them."

It was a disgusting ritual full of vicious men who got hard-ons for pain. They loved the idea that the magic they were consuming came from unwilling victims. They would play their fantasies out loud after their head swam from the high the magic gave them. Both Vitos and I had refused to partake in his parties no matter how many times Baecos had asked.

"Please tell me it was his own magic he shared," Iniq said with a grimace.

I didn't want to tell her that it was hers. That Baecos had stored as much of her magic as possible and used it not only for himself, but to get the other corrupt kings on his side as well. It was a great tactic, no one could resist the temptation to feel the magic of the most powerful warrior in the world and in return they would be tied to Baecos forever because of the severity of their crimes. If the High Kings were still walking the land, they would not stand for such behavior. I wondered how scared they would be when Iniq was finally king and came back for vengeance. It was the ultimate insult, and a King of her caliber would have no choice but to punish them for their actions. I hoped she would gouge their eyes out.

"I would take the silence as a no," Aselia said. "Disgusting magical kings and their god complexes."

"How did Baecos even know about it?" I asked her. "The pathetic excuse for a magic drain?"

"How would I know," Aselia said with a huff. "Weren't you there with him his entire life? Wouldn't you have known if he had contact with a High King?"

"He never did. Besides Iniq as far as I know," I told her. "That's why it's weird that he is trying to emulate Nitri."

"Wait," Cruor said stopping in her tracks. "Nitri consumes magic?"

A pregnant silence fell over us. Iniq and I both looked to Aselia.

"Yes," she said. "But a god can take your whole being. A god can consume your entire magic and soul. When they are done it's like you never existed. Like Iniq said yesterday... she tasted *Baecos's soul.*"

Cruor thought over the information.

"Baecos wants to be a god," Iniq explained. "He wants to prove that he is more powerful than me." Her voice trailed off as if she wanted to say more but she shut her lips tightly.

"Did Baecos ever act weird around you?" Cruor asks me. "Like was there ever a dramatic change? When he was around us *as a friend,* he never showed any malice towards Iniq before. Ever since he took her, I was wondering if there was a trigger or something."

Every word out of her mouth tested my patience. Not because it was regarding Baecos but because here she was acting like we were all bosom buddies after she also abandoned Iniq.

"I told Iniq before that he kept her relationship with him secret from us," I told her, feeling irritated. "But his father did commit suicide leaving him alone with the kingdom. He was still young then though, so it is to be expected that it affected him greatly."

"He told me..." Iniq's voice trailed off again. "How young was he when that happened?"

"He was twelve, if I remember correctly," I told her.

"That's the same age you were when you joined us in the fire kingdom," Cruor noted.

"Let's not talk about this," Iniq said stopping all conversation. "I need to preserve energy, as do you."

I felt Iniq probe at my mind.

Are you okay? I asked her.

He let something slip last night. About my mother murdering his father. I think that is where it all started but I still don't understand the change. He was with us for hundreds of years before the first attempt.

I swallowed thickly.

Let's not make assumptions. We can ask the Dark King about what really happened when we are done.

You're right. she said and left my mind.

The sun over the earth kingdom burned hotter than anywhere else I have felt. Unlike the Fire or Light Kingdom, there were barely any trees here to cover us with shade. I had been so happy to feel the sun beat down on my skin when coming back to this world but the more the sun heated my hair and burned my skin, the more I wished for the eternal night of the Other World.

The walk through the mountains turned rocky and the mountains that had once seemed so far away from use slowly encroached in on us. After a while we were forced to walk in a single line between a skinny windy path that led us through a mountain. We were walking at an incline and a small sweat had broken out over my skin. I made sure to have a hand on Iniq at all times but as the road got stepper and rockier it was hard to maneuver myself.

It was in-between those large rocks when I got my first hint of the salty air. It was fresh and reminded me of my childhood. Mother and Father would take me and Vitos to the beach often to train. That's where they taught us to harness our light power, take it from the sun and learn to store it in our bodies. Then when we were overheated, we would jump into the ocean to cool off only to start again as soon as the ocean had brought down our body temperatures.

Vitos was such a happy child back then. He would take the role as a big brother, always making sure that I was taken care of. He would also always try to teach me the magic that he learned, I pretended many times to not know a thing when he taught me. He was too excited to take care of his brother and I was more than happy to be his center of attention.

It's all about intent. Came from him long ago. I had known that whatever I willed would happen but until those words fell from his mouth, I had never been able to put such words to the feeling.

It changed when our parents were drafted into war for the light kingdom. Wars rarely happened, that war was one of the last that we had in our world. Both of my parents ended up dying on the sword of the enemy and overnight we were wards of the Light King.

I was too young to remember who we were fighting against and mourned my parents' death the best I could. It was Vitos who was forever changed. The smiling kid turned sinister. His pranks became a little too hurtful, and when Baecos took over as king...

Baecos only ever fed my brothers horrible habits. Baecos brought out the worst in him and now he has been used as Baecos's personal toy. The Vitos who seemed to exude bright light and happiness was now a black hole. My heart hurt for him, and I couldn't help but feel responsible for pushing him so hard into his arms while trying to escape with Iniq.

"We are not far," Cruor said from in front. She was leading the group and was panting hard. She had convinced us that she would have enough power to sustain us for a trip and back, but it was obvious how much she was struggling. I couldn't help but think of the magic she may have spent yesterday, but if she wasn't fighting Baecos... then who?

"Is it really filled with dangerous creatures?" Iniq asked. She was also breaking out into a sweat. She and Aselia had been the ones pushing their limits this entire time. I had a feeling that the reason they were not talking wasn't because they didn't want anyone from the earth kingdom to overhear us, but because they couldn't bring themselves to without losing concentration.

I felt useless. I had no magic to contribute, and I had no idea where we were going.

"We will see if they are still there," Cruor said. "The last time I came was over fifty years ago."

"Were you unsuccessful?" I asked her.

"I saw my future and then I put it back," she said.

Iniq let out a small gasp, "What did you see?"

"I don't know, truthfully," she said. "The mirror doesn't give you much context. And it's only a few seconds before it turns back to a normal mirror," she paused for a moment. "I think it was a thread breaking."

"That's ominous," Aselia muttered under her breath.

There was a break in the mountains in front of us and I could hear the ocean waves from the back of the group. It only took a few more steps until we filed out onto a sandy beach. The ocean waves were loud, and I felt the spray of the water as they hit against the shore. The sand was light golden, and I already felt some worm its way into my shoes. I took a deep breath, almost losing myself in the beauty of the sun hitting the blue waves.

I missed this.

Iniq's hand tugged at mine. I met her eyes; she gave me a small smile.

"It's beautiful here," she said. "When this is over, would you like to visit the ocean with me? Mortal oceans may not hold a candle to this, but I still remember a few I could show you."

"I would love that," I told her around the knot in my throat.

"This way," Cruor said and walked down the left side on the beach. "There is a cave here and at the end is where we will find the mirror."

The entrance of the cave was easy enough to find. There was nothing special about it from the outside. It had an inch of water at the bottom that sloshed into my shoes and wet my pants as we trudged through it. The inside of the cave was dark and damp but was big enough to fit us side by side now.

"Why did you not keep the mirror for yourself?" Aselia asked Cruor.

"I do not want to see my fate," she said. "Even after I saw the thread break, I found myself wanting to keep it even though I came with no intention of doing so. That feeling alone scared me enough to put it back."

"Why did you come?" Iniq asked.

Cruor gave her a look and reached out to squeeze her hand.

"I wanted to see if you were still alive."

CHAPTER TWENTY
CRUOR

The words were true, but I selfishly hoped that they would have a bigger impact on her. Hope that a spark or I don't know... romance, or love would be there.

After my disappearance yesterday I could feel the wall between us now. I knew I shouldn't have left her... but as soon as I had felt Callum's magic, I had to go to him.

I ran as fast as I could into the forest surrounding the town. I had felt it as soon as I touched down on that roof. It was just a waft of his magic but it was enough for me to pinpoint his exact location. I felt Iniq's magic explode behind me, but I did not look back because just as a weaved around a large tree I saw him.

Callum looked the same as he used to, which gave me some hope. It was a relief that he was not being treated the same as Spiris' twin. He wore a light tunic, and the staple leather pants. His eyes widened as he took in my form and his muscles tensed as if he was about to bolt.

"Don't run... please," I begged my voice coming out hoarser than I intended. "I can take you back to the kingdom."

He shifted on his feet and his eyes darted away from me.

"Are you not going to ask what I am doing here?" He asked looking up at me with his head still turned downward. Like a guilty puppy.

Which meant he knew what he did wrong, and if he knew what he did wrong...

There was a chance.

"That's not important right now, Cal," I said in a soft voice. "Just come back home with me, we can figure this out."

His eyes snapped up and he peered behind me. There was a spike of magic from far behind us, I could recognize it as Spiris's brother which meant Baecos would not be far behind.

"You left me in the dungeon," Callum accused, his voice hollow. "Even after I begged you and apologized over my sisters' dead body. And you still locked me up."

"There is price to pay for treason," I told him. "But you have served your time. We can go home and think of a better solution so long as you promise your loyalty to me." He gripped at the hem of his shirt still not able to fully meet my eyes. "I promise, Cal. I will forget all of it. Every transgression. Just please allow me to bring you home."

It was Baecos's magic that now exploded in the area. I jumped at the power of it and my heart started pounding in my chest. I needed to get back to Iniq.

Callum finally looked up but just as he was about to open his mouth a sickly skinny and pale version of Spiris appeared next to him. He gave me an unreadable look as he reached out to touch Callum.

"If you play around in the forest for any longer, history will repeat itself," Vitos said, and in a flash of light, they were gone.

History will repeat itself? My blood turned cold. Iniq!

I should have stayed with her, I knew that. But the chance of getting Callum back had to be taken. He grew up in my kingdom just like the other hounds... if he was sorry and could see the error of his ways, he deserved a second chance.

Aselia had seen through it right away. I deserved her verbal assault. After Iniq left the dinner table last night to rest, Aselia turned to me and delivered the biggest tongue lashing I had received in centuries. Felix was the one holding her back trying to calm her, but it did nothing to quell her anger.

It wasn't just her though, Spiris watched me like a hawk. I knew he wanted to say something but just like everything else in his life, Iniq took precedent. If Iniq didn't want to mention it, he would comply even if I could feel his glare the entire trip through the earth kingdom. He watched all of us in a stoic silence, but I could feel the heat behind his stare when it was directed at me. I was worried he would sway Iniq. Convince her to leave me for real this time. The bond had gone crazy ever since last night. It would tug at my chest begging me to go to Iniq, but I knew that I could not. It would have to be up to Iniq to accept me after leaving her to deal with Baecos.

She protected me from them, saying that she had told me to leave but no one believed it. The eyes were what gave it away. When she looked at me there was so much disappointment in her face, I couldn't stand it. And just like the knight in shining armor that he was, Spiris saw her intention. Saw what she needed. And then promptly took her away from the situation. Those actions were what would forever set us apart.

I saw it for the first time when he filled her plate of food. I remembered the same look in the Water Kingdom. She would stare at her hands, and you could almost see her brain searching for something, but it never came.

During the same time, I had asked her what she wanted to do and was met with the same look. A look I couldn't understand. Spiris knew the look even before asking. He saw it and made the changes right away. It was I who was lagging. It was I who couldn't read her. After six hundred years together, it was as if I could still not understand the thoughts running through her head.

What even happened to us so long ago that caused this? We were perfect, weren't we? Happy together as a family, with a kingdom to rule. What else did she need? I gave her everything. I built a library for her, let her visit that stupid café almost every day, I didn't say anything when she brought Baecos over to the

Kingdom even though the way he watched her made me rage with jealously. What else could I have done to keep her by my side?

"There is a barrier we must go through," I told them after Aselia paused to catch her breath. The magic was wearing them down, fast. "We can remove the magic there."

"The mirror protects itself?" Iniq asks.

I nodded. "I have never had a problem entering but while in there it feels like the cave is cut off from the outside."

"Where do the creatures come in?" Aselia asked wiping sweat from her brow as she straightened herself.

"You'll see."

I led them through the cave, slowly being careful of any possible escaped creatures. Mire Drakes. Disgustingly slimy creatures with skin as grey as the cave walls and row upon rows of teeth that could literally snap off your leg if you got too close. The only colored part of them were the yellow lines on their bellies that led around their mouth and their long red tongue. They had multiple sets of legs; the last one I was able to count had six in total. Made them a hell of a lot faster.

I was worried about seeing the mirror again. Worried about the future. I had lied when I told them what I had seen. I did see the thread, but I also saw something else. My kingdom, destroyed. The castle was nothing but debris, there were bodies everywhere. I could not make out who in the area was killed and the image had only stayed there for a second, but it was enough to chill me to my bones.

There was nothing else though. And there was no time in which this happened, the mirror was funny like that. It never gave you an idea *when* it would happen, only that it would and it was up to you to change the course of the fixture.

I had yet to proven that it could.

The blue shimmering barrier came into view, glowing softly at the end of the cave. I could just barely make out the underground lake that held the mirror. The water was calm, and I could not see any movement from its depths. It was odd and caused me to stumble as I moved closer. Last time I had seen hundreds of those slimy Mire Drakes they swam around the entrance of the barrier, snapping at whoever got close.

But now there were none.

I held my arm out to stop them from going further. I conjured a sword at my side with my fire magic. The others paused but followed suit, Aselia with an ice sword, Iniq with a bow, and Spiris with a crystal-like sword.

I slowly walked closer to the barrier peering in, the coast seemed to be clear.

I stepped through and could now clearly see what the barrier had been hiding. The slaughtered corpses of the Mire Drakes were littered across the floor. Their purple blood splattered all over the walls and into the water. I swallowed thickly. The mirror was placed in the middle over a pile of their slimy corpses.

This wasn't right. The mirror should have been at the bottom of the lake for protection. I had made sure to put it back there when I was finished with it.

I waved my hand and pointed to my head. I felt the intrusion of both Aselia and Iniq immediately.

Is Spiris in here too? I asked.

I'm here. Came his voice.

This is not right. The mirror shouldn't be out in the open like this.

Not to mention that the Mire Drakes have been slaughtered. Aselia commented. *I have only seen this creature once before and from what I could see, they were not easily overthrown.*

I cannot see anyone else here. Iniq said.

Can you use that dark power? Just in case something is hiding?

I'll try. She said.

She waved her hand around the area. The scenery didn't change.

We are clear. Aselia said.

She separated herself from the group and walked towards the mirror. She hesitantly picked it up, jerking violently as the magic it exuded started to run through her veins. This was how it worked... it pulled your magical essence from you and in return it provided those few seconds of the future. Through the mental bond I could see flashes off what the mirror had chosen to show her.

Her in an all-black robe, just like the one she had showed up in the first time she came to my kingdom. Her hair that usually sat on top of her head was down and her black horns were decorated with golden leaves. She was in the middle of an empty throne room there were three other seats placed besides her. She sat in the largest one and even through the mirror you could feel the power that she was exuding. Her eyes shifted around the empty throne room before the scene changed.

No. Her mind whispered. *I don't want that.*

The next scene was what looked like the dead forest but instead of the branches being bare and gnarled they begun sprouting colorful glowing leaves and fruit began growing on them in a matter of seconds. It was a beautiful sight, one that would have taken my breath away... if not for the person that was slumped against one of the trees. It was a beautiful man, he had long blond hair and golden eyes. His body was in a similar black robe to what Aselia was wearing in the previous scene but this time, there was no throne beneath him. His head was leaned back against the bark of the tree and the light in his golden eyes slowly disappeared as he watched the leaves burst into life. He let out a final sigh before those eyes finally became empty.

Then there was nothing.

Father. Her mind was a flurry of panic before she withdrew her mental link.

That was Nitri she saw? The king of kings, a demon that was

no more legend dead at her feet. How was that possible? Who would be strong enough to do such a thing?

She looked at us with scared eyes. Iniq walked over to her and put a hand on her shoulder.

"It is your right. This is what was always meant to be," Iniq said with conviction. "We will talk about this later," Aselia nodded and handed Iniq the mirror. Iniq did not look at it, instead waved Spiris to come over and take it from her.

It was what I had been seeing up until now but didn't fully comprehend and not it only enraged me. They were always putting the wants of the other before themselves. They were utterly obsessed with each other, and I could never beat that.

Before Spiris could touch the mirror, loud footsteps came down the cave.

We all jumped into action.

Iniq placed the mirror back in the center of the Mire Drakes corpses and motioned for us to step as close to the wall as we could.

Stay quiet, I will cover you. her voice told us.

I was the furthest away from the group and the closest to the incoming intruders. If anything happened, I would be the only one able to escape while the others would have to fight their way out.

"I think the mirror is broken," said Callum's familiar voice. "I couldn't see anything, just blackness."

"Maybe you were too stupid to use it," came Vitos's response. He sounded better than yesterday, his voice less hollow, his steps heavier.

Their bodies slowly pushed through the barrier. Callum had his hands in his pockets as if they were on a nonchalant walk in the woods, the conflicting emotions that I had seen him go through yesterday were absent. Vitos as well had his bruises and lip fixed but his skin was still almost translucent and the bags under his eyes were stained dark purple. His once curly hair laid limp around his head.

Now that they were both in the cave, I could feel their magic. It was intertwined with Iniq's. They all went back to the Light Kingdom and replenished themselves with her magic. Took from her just like she had taken from their king and if they were able to recover with the help of her magic then...

I shot her a look, but her eyes were already narrowed in their direction. A bone chilling laugh followed them down the cave. I didn't need to see Baecos's face to know it was him. Even though Iniq was able to drain him, he was already bouncing back to his normal self. Why was he here? I thought I was the only one that knew about the mirror. My eyes caught Callum's face... he wouldn't tell Baecos would he? He of course had known, we talked about it but I never thought he really would lead him here.

Stay still. Iniq told us. *Aselia, pay extra attention to our magical signatures.*

What are you going to do? Spiris asked, his voice panicked.

I am going to end this.

Don't, I pushed back. *Let's figure out how to leave. We cannot risk it now that he is replenished.*

Baecos entered the cave, he had a glow to his skin that made my stomach twist. He wore the smirk that always seemed to get right on my nerves. He literally just strolled in like nothing was wrong, like his head was not almost snatched from his body.

"That's not nice, Vitos," Baecos chided playfully. His arm came to wrap around Vitos's neck. He flinched at the contact and cast his eyes downward.

"*Kill yourself,*" Iniq's magic filled voice filled the cave. My heart pounded in my ears, and I conjured my sword, preparing for their attack. There was nothing they didn't seem to hear her words. Her magic must have been disguising the noise. I shivered at the action. This was not what I wanted to see but if it would get us out of here, I would suffer through it. *"Kill yourself. Conjure the sword and kill yourself, now. It's the only way to redeem yourself."*

I was watching Baecos's back as he passed me. He wasn't affected, neither was Vitos. They just continued to lazily stroll to the mirror. I watched as Callum jerkily moved forward, as if being held back by an invisible force. His head twitched to the side, and I watched in muted horror as he conjured a sword.

It was never for them... it was for Callum. Taking out the weakest first. My muscles tensed ready to run to him... was this why Callum saw black in the mirror? Was it because Iniq was going to kill him here?

No, I commanded Iniq in my head. *No, Iniq! Stop this! Not him!*

She didn't give any sign that she heard me, just continued to stare at Callum as he struggled against her magic.

Stop Iniq! I yelled again, *We raised him! We raised all of them! I know he betrayed us, but this is too cruel!*

Nothing, not even a twitch. Callum, unbeknownst to Baecos and Vitos raised the sword to his neck. Each movement was like it took him an immense amount of strength to pull off. His eyes were wide as he tried to fight. He readied his sword across his neck.

The years I had with him flashed through my eyes. He was such a volatile pup. He would walk around yelling and fighting whoever made him angry. If anyone dared to hurt his sister, he would challenge them to a battle so he could reclaim her honor. He would spend hours arguing over meaningless stuff with the other hounds... but it was all a front. A front so that he could keep their attention. He just wanted to be seen, I knew that... that's why I gave him such leniency throughout the years. All he wanted was to be a part of something.

He wasn't a bad person. He couldn't be. I knew deep down that Callum would have never fallen so low if not for outside influence. I still believed in him. Even as he was held in the dungeon, I knew that one day he would come around. He would have no choice; he was family and he would never just give up on his family. Not after he fought so hard to protect us.

Just like Ash, Felix, and even Claire. We were a family. Iniq and I raised them as weak pups into strong men and women who would do anything for their kingdom.

I refused to let this be the end.

"No!" I yelled and lunged forward to grab Callum's hand. He let out a loud gasp, his hand fought against mine as I tried to pull the sword away from his nick.

Baecos and Vitos turned to face Callum and I.

"Release your power!" I yelled at Iniq. "Please I beg you, don't make him do this!"

Baecos and Vitos watched Callum struggle. I was sure now they had not heard me or could see me. They continued to look at Callum like he was insane.

"If you wanted to kill yourself so bad, you could have just asked for help," Vitos commented snidely.

"Why can't you remember what they mean to us?" I yelled at Iniq. I felt Callum's hand push his sword closer to his throat. I was losing the battle. Baecos shifted while watching us curiously as if not knowing what to make of the situation.

"This is not about remembering," Iniq said though baited breath. "This is about life or death. Look at the situation in front of you, Cruor."

"We will die if we don't kill them first!" Aselia growled. "The only reason you are still alive is because of Iniq and I right now!"

"Please, Iniq," I looked at her tears filling my eyes. "Please don't kill him, please I can fix him. I beg you."

"It is too late, Cruor," Iniq hissed. "Let him go, you saw what he has done to the kingdom. Look who he is with, you really think he had no part in yesterday's massacre?"

"What are you still doing?" Baecos asked and tried to take a step forward towards Callum, but I dragged him back. There was a shocked expression that washed across Baecos face.

"Don't do this," Iniq growled.

"I will take him back to my kingdom," I told her. "I will leave the barrier with him and take him right back to the kingdom. He will be far enough away that your magic cannot reach him, only then can he live."

Iniq stood up as straight as a pin. "You are leaving us here? With Baecos?"

"Are you out of your mind?" Aselia yelled.

"Cruor don't do this *again*," *Spiris* begged.

"I'm sorry," I said and continued to drag him towards the barrier. "I can't let you kill him, Iniq."

"If you do this Cruor, I am breaking the bond," she said. "And if I get out of here alive Cruor, I will come back and make you regret this."

I paused and considered her words. I was leaving her again, right in the path of danger. I had a choice now. Her or Callum. I swallowed thickly and met her angry eyes. Spiris had a hand on her shoulder, he was glaring just as hard as Iniq was.

You are a coward. I heard that glare tell me.

I know. I am a coward; I always have been. The reason I had so easily believed that she had left me for Baecos was the very same reason I could not stand here and fight against him. I feared the failure that awaited me. Scared of the looming threat of death, and I couldn't handle the thought of it. With a shaky breath I continued to pull him out as Baecos and Vitos stared at us, still not sure what was going on. It was only when I reached the barrier did I look back to Iniq, her eyes filled with unshed tears.

I'm sorry.

Time slowed. Baecos began stalking towards us, but time had slowed so drastically he paused mid-step. Iniq was the only person who remained normal speed. Between us there was a glittering thread. It was beautiful. Strong and white, it glittered and quivered between us. The breath was stolen out of my lungs when looking at its' beauty. It wasn't of this world; it was too pure to be.

"I wished this could have ended differently Cruor," she said. "I did have love for you. I wanted to see you happy. I wanted to fight for the life we could have had, but I see now we have different goals here."

Before I could respond her hand came down on the thread, and as if it was as thin as a spiders' it broke clean in half.

There was a pull in my chest, not painful but enough to jar me. My breath stopped, and it was like a veil had been lifted. I still saw the same Iniq in front of me but the urge to run to her, the urge to apologize, the urge to protect her from Baecos. It had left with the bond.

It made my decision all the easier.

I hoisted Callum outside of the barrier and commanded my magic to take us as close to home as possible.

*T*rusting her was the biggest mistake I made in my entire existence.

Not just in this life, but it seemed like all the ones that had come into contact with her, she had left me in a predicament that led me to my death.

I watched in muted fury as she dragged Callum over the barrier and traveled away with him. Leaving us alone and trapped in a room with the most dangerous person on the planet.

The bond had called to me the way Kneku had mentioned. When she stepped in to stop Callum, I felt it strain. Even the bond knew that there was no coming back from that one. It tried hard. It was so desperate to bring us together while we were in the castle. It made it known that if we did not solidify it then, there was no going back. As soon as she touched the barrier is when I felt it and pulled without a hesitation. If I was to choose between her and the two people behind me who had proven to have my back against all odds, it was obvious who deserved my loyalty.

I meant every word I said. I could have loved her; I did at one point. But not after this.

I once thought it was I who was the coward. The person who never wanted to fight for themselves. The person who always just went with what other pushed them to do. My cowardice used to be just submitting to whatever the fates had decided for me., until the day I walked through that door.

I would not be that person any longer.

I raised my bow and readied an arrow towards Baecos's turned back.

"Get ready," I whispered to the two by my side. I took a deep breath and infused my arrow with as much magic as it would take. "Spiris, grab the mirror. Aselia, call the door."

"Are we not going to kill him?" she asked next to me.

"We don't want to chance him being reincarnated," I told her. "I thought about it after I tasted his soul, there is no guarantee he will not come back even if his soul is gone."

I sent my arrow flying towards Baecos's back. In an instant his head flopped back, and an evil grin spread across his face. His free hand came up and stopped the arrow in its path, right before it impaled his left eyeball.

"That's a neat trick," he said and made a show of snapping the arrow clean in half. I didn't allow him to talk anymore. I pushed my magic to the brim and bolted towards him trying to keep my magic cloaked on me while I moved. It was already straining against me, fatiguing me but if I gave up here everything, we had done up to this point was useless.

I conjured my sword and thrust it straight towards his torso. His hand snapped down hitting my shoulder just as the sword was about to make contact and deterred it just far enough to the right that it only caught just the edge of his trunk.

His hand tried to grasp at my shirt, but I poured magic into my hand, making the ball as big as I could. I kneeled to get away from his open hand and slammed the swirling ball into his hip.

He wasn't able to brace himself and stumbled backwards. I would have been proud of this move if it didn't take so much magic that I was now semi visible to them.

Vitos stood still as a statue. I sent him a look. I felt bad for the man he has become. I had been under Baecos's wrath for a combined total of two and a half years, while he had suffered through six hundred. No matter how horrible he was to me back then... no one deserved that.

Good kings have their people in mind when ruling. All of their people. Remember that if the throne is really the path you have chosen. Kneku's words flitted through my head when Vitos's wide eyes met mine.

I am not sure if Kneku foresaw it, but it was obvious what I needed to do.

If I promise to take you to the world beyond, will you be loyal to me? I sent to his mind. His eyes widened. Baecos studying himself after tripping over a dead creature's carcass.

"Iniq, look at you learning new stuff," Baecos said with a laugh. "And you are hiding your magic from me? Let me guess, you are not alone? Is Spiris here? Or was he the one that dragged Callum out of here? No, that had to have been Cruor, she has a thing for that hound it would seem."

Vitos's hand twitched. I had seen the memories from Spiris's head and now looking at Vitos I could see the resemblance of the happy go lucky kid. Just now, he had been beaten down so hard he had no other choice.

Your brother misses who you used to be. I told him. *And you are obviously unwell. Let me help you, in return I demand your loyalty.*

He's my mate. he said it with pain in his voice. Years upon years of sweet moments filtered through his head.

I conjured a dagger and chucked it at Baecos before he could take a step forward. He caught it with ease and smashed it against the cave wall.

"I have been around a long time, Iniq. These tricks don't fool me."

Mate bonds can be broken. I told him. *I did it. I can help you too. The sweet moments do not outweigh the cost of the abuse.*

Those words were what sent him into action. He looked at Baecos, but Baecos didn't pay him any mind. Instead Baecos's hooded gaze lingered on my form. It was the same one I had seen so many times before and it just proved to Vitos that it was never him that he wanted.

"We are ready!" Aselia yelled from behind me.

I lifted my hand up, towards Vitos.

Now or never.

"Iniq, no!" Aselia groaned from behind. "Leave the fucker!"

Baecos's eyes widened. I took the moment to cover both myself and Vitos fully. Baecos growled and tried to grab onto the spot where Vitos was. But I was too fast for him. I shot my hand out to Vitos's half raised one and pulled him out of Baecos's way.

"Don't think you can do this Iniq!" the demon's voice bounced off the cave. He turned in circles looking around for us. I backed us away from him and towards the towering door that covered the back of the cave wall. "You think you can run from me? You will pay for the sins of your Kings! I will rip that magic from your body and overtake you as the new god!"

Spiris had an unreadable look and Aselia was glaring daggers at me.

Baecos began throwing corpses around the cave trying to find us.

"Let's hurry," I said and we all piled into the door leaving a furious Baecos in the cave behind. us. I grabbed Spiris's hand as we entered holding on tight to both the brothers.

We stopped walking once the noise from the cave disappeared in the background. Aselia turned on her heels and marched up to me, poking her long finger at my chest.

"What the fuck do you think you are doing?" she asked. "This isn't a pity party for sociopaths! I have seen what he has done to you! And you are saving him from the punishment he deserves?"

"How do you even know what happened in the Light King-dom?" I asked.

Vitos's hand became slack in mine.

"Eternity Fountain," Spiris murmured. "I used it to check on you after I died... I didn't know you were interested in Iniq even then, Aselia."

"Of course! A new king doesn't just happen! I had to see for myself, and you know the first thing I saw? This fucker pounding into Iniq!"

Vitos tried to remove his hand from mine, but I held firm.

"You will get lost in here if you let go," I told him. The dark-ness had already started fluttering around us. I could feel the various magical signatures floating around us, curious as to what we have brought them for entertainment.

"He is dying, Aselia," I told her. "He has barely a signature left. And the more we take from Baecos the easier it will be to destroy him."

"Let him rot!" Aselia screamed.

There was a pause.

"Was he consuming your magic too?" Spiris asked.

"Yes," Vitos answered hesitantly.

"So?!" Aselia's hands flew up into the air and she paced around the dark space. "He is a magician, it comes back!"

"Sorry to break it to you but I am almost as good as a mortal now," Vitos said. "My magic has been resisting to replenish. Iniq may have done the honor of saving me but whether I stay with Baecos or leave with you, I will be dead in a months' time."

Spiris stiffened next to me at the news of his brothers deteri-oration.

"Enough talk of this," I told them. "Aselia, open the door near the dark kingdom."

She grumbled a protest but continued to walk forward into the abyss. I followed after her with both of the boys' hands in mine.

Iniq. The familiar voice whispered. *Let's talk.*

A warm hand found its way to my shoulder.

"Aselia," she stopped in her tracks and turned, no doubt to yell once more but she dropped to her knees when her eyes zeroed in on the person behind me.

"High King Neia," she whispered.

I snapped my head back. There was a woman much taller than me in a pure white robe. Her grey hair cascaded down her back in waves and black horns decks out in golden chains curled on top her head. Her golden eyes were warm, and she had a kind smile on her face. We had matching tattoos and I at once saw myself in her features. Our noses, our foreheads, our lips.

"Mother," I whispered.

Spiris gave a sharp intake of breath besides me. "I have seen you once before, in the light kingdom... I never knew."

She gave him a small smile but did not respond to him.

"Give your companions to Little Aselia, Iniq," she said her voice akin to the sound of bells ringing. "I would like to catch up."

I didn't need to hand them off because Aselia was already taking their hands and I let myself fall into my mother's warm embrace as she dragged me away from the group. I inhaled deeply and found her scent to be something akin to honeysuckle.

I remembered the smell. I remembered the way her fingers threaded through my hair. The way she would whisper to me in the night when I awoke from a bad dream. I remember when she played with me and Father in the hills outside of our house in the light kingdom. Father's smiling face stuck out to me the most. He had hair dark as night and eyes the color of a setting sun. He would look at mother with such love that as a child it made me wonder what type of love awaited out there for me.

"I remember you," I whispered against her robe, tears falling before I could even realize I was crying. "How could I forget this? How could I forget you? How could I forget father?" I looked up at her. "Is he here with you?"

"Later darling," she said and rubbed in between my eyebrows removing the tension. "We need to talk about you."

"What about me?" I asked her. "I still don't remember much about my past lives."

"That is for the best," she had a sad smile on her face. "The memory of death creates a trauma not easy to forget. You will need all your strength for what is ahead."

"Did you do that? Seal me?" I asked her. "Was it always you guiding me?" I gripped her hand not willing to let go just yet.

"Yes, it was I," she told me. "Sealing was the right idea but after failed attempts I could not just stand by and continue to let this tragedy befall you again and again. Listen Iniq," she gripped my shoulder tightly. "You remember what Aselia saw in the mirror?"

I nodded to her.

"She takes the throne."

"She takes *Nitri's* throne, child." Mother corrected. "This is the path we have been chosen for. Everything I have done has been another step closer to this very moment."

"Did you know you would die?" I asked in a whisper. So, she did know what my life would have turned out to be. She did this all for a reason.

"Yes," she replied. "I watched you earlier, you are on the right track but let me tell you, there is so much more to this. When you talk to the Dark King tell him you met me in here. Tell him the destruction is Nitri, persuade him to trust you."

I swallowed thickly at her words.

"Is it Baecos's father? Was he the one to kill you?" I asked.

"It is a memory I can help you with," she said and leaned down to plant a kiss on my forehead. "When you enter the next word, you will remember. But Iniq, do not let this deter you from your goal."

"I don't understand my goal, mother," I told her. "I don't understand anything the fates want from me."

"You are change, Iniq," she said sternly. "You are the change the universe needs. You have been bogged down again and again but like a weed you will grow back stronger than ever."

"I don't know what change you are talking about," I grumbled.

"You will dethrone Nitri." A rough voice said from behind my mother. I was met with my father's broad form. He put a tender hand around my mother's shoulder. "Honey, now is not the time to be cryptic."

More tears streamed down my face at the sight of him. I pulled him in for a hug, his woodsy scent filling my senses. He let out a laugh and patted my hair.

"I didn't think you would be strong enough to be here," I said against him. I remember now, my father was not strong... he was normal magician in the Dark Kingdom. He shouldn't be here.

"The universe did us a favor. A gift for our work." Mother said.

"You have done so well, Iniq," he said. "You are so strong. You are wise. You have more power in you and more drive than I have seen even in the kings. Hold on to it. It will guide you."

"You have to go, Iniq." Mother said. "You have stayed here too long."

"Can I come back to see you?" I asked them meeting their eyes. Their sad smile told me all that I needed.

"This is the only time, Iniq." Father said. "The fates have been watching you. As have we. We will continue to watch you through on your journey, but this will be the last time we meet in this lifetime."

I buried my head back into his chest and pulled him and my mother close to me.

"I love you guys. I am sorry I forgot about you for so long," I told them.

"We were always there, darling." Mother said sweetly. "You just needed to know where to look."

"Go now." Father said. "You surprised even us by saving that boy, but the decision will pay off."

I nodded and reluctantly pulled away from them.

"Go on." my mother said. "And don't look back. Remember my words."

With one last look at the couple who know stood hand in hand, I turned with a heavy heart and ran back to my group. They looked at me with questioning faces but did not asked when I pushed them forward.

Aselia opened the door once more with ease and stepped out. Spiris reached out to me taking my hand in his. I paused feeling the need to look back to find them once more but he tugged me forward.

"Let's make this worth it," he said with a whisper. I nodded and followed him out of the in-between.

CHAPTER TWENTY-TWO
INIQ

"*F*ather please!" *The blonde boys voice was hoarse as he struggled.* "*I'm sorry, I'm sorry. I'm sorry!*"

No matter how the boy screamed his father would never let up. His father, who looked just liked the adult the boy was to grow into would smile down at him with an almost sad smile.

"*This is what you were born for Baecos.*" *He would coo to him. He would wipe his tears once he was done carving his skin, but he was never done for long.*

The memories unfold in front of me like a bloody blooming flower. They were more horrible than any nightmare and more gut wrenching than I had ever felt. This was what true evil was.

They came as if I was watching through my mother's eyes. This had to have been what the universe had showed her because after the images flew past me, I was face to face with Baecos's father. He was on his knees in front of my mother, a sadistic smile plastered on his face that I had seen Baecos wear so often.

"I warned you, Acidos," I felt my mother say. With her power, the world expanded just like it had when Kneku had lent me his power weeks ago. The thoughts ran past me with ease giving me a clear view of what it was all *really* about.

Acidos loved the feeling of his son's magic flowing through his body. He loved the way his own child would scream at him to stop, beg him. I watched in his mind as he ushered the young Spiris and Vitos away from the door where he had just brutally tortured his own son.

"Just some training." He told them with a smile. *"Go now."*

The children were too young to understand what was happening behind that door. They would go outside and play among the trees while they waited for Baecos to show up again. Acidos had watched it all. He became obsessed with Baecos's magic, his life. He wanted to control him in every way possible. This is when he began taking him for "kingly" lessons. To everyone else they would just assume his father was preparing him for his rise to the throne, but they were wrong. So very wrong. Only Acidos and Baecos really knew the awful things he would do to the young boy behind closed doors.

"I did not kill him, *High King Neia.*" Acidos spit her title like a curse. "Though, that's not really your position anymore is it though?"

My father, who had been standing behind Acidos, holding his hands behind his back, gave my mother a look. He looked rough with dark circles under his eyes and his normally tanned skin seemed a few shades paler.

We must act now. His gruff voice said in my mother's mind.

Even though my mother knew what was going to happen I could not stop my subconscious from screaming. With a wave of my mother's hand, she had singlehandedly changed the entire fate of the world. She cut off the magic to the Light Kingdom as if it were no harder than cutting tissue paper. She cut it straight from the depths of the universe. The only indication that it happened was the pain that radiated through my mother and

Acidos. They both clenched their hearts and crippled at the feeling of the magic being stripped away.

I love you. My mother sent to my father. I had already seen it unfold in my mother's mind but no matter what I said I had no effect on her. I could not stop the nightmare that was about to happen, because it already had.

"Father?" A young Baecos called from behind the group. "What are you doing to him?"

In the second it took for my father to meet Baecos's eyes, Acidos jerked back and conjured a spear with the only remaining magic that resided in his body. In one swift movement he stabbed the spike into my father's neck and with all his strength, sliced it open.

There was a yell that I recognized to be my own from behind my mother.

"Daddy!" I screamed.

I will see you both in the in between. My father's voice flitted between our minds. *I love you Iniq, remember that.*

The wound was too severe to heal and with a feral Acidos guarding his body, there was no way he would survive. His magic was gone faster than his blood could stain the carpet.

"Mom, save him!" my younger self screamed at her; I didn't understand yet that this had been planned. I didn't understand that the wound was far too deep, that this would be the last moment I would see my father.

Acidos pointed the bloodied spike at my mother. "I will come back for your daughter; you will watch as I devour her magic and defile her body. I promise you that I will be more powerful the next time I come back."

"You cannot reincarnate with half your magic missing." my mother told him with a sad voice. "And even if you had managed, I promise you that I will be there to stop you from ever entering this world again," she said.

There was another plan that came to light in her mind though, it was heart breaking.

Acidos gave her a daring smile. "We will see if you can beat me, Neia."

Without another word the Light King slit his throat much like he had done to my father. My mother held in her tears as she faced the two pale faced children.

She came over to me and placed her hand on my forehead.

"You will forget this, until we meet again, dear Iniq. Please believe me when I said I had no other choice. That this was so we can rebuild our kingdom. Every points in your history will lead you up to the moment of Nitri's fall. This is in your hands now," I watched through her own eyes as my body slumped to the ground, tears still falling down her face.

"What did you do? This is your fault, isn't it?" Baecos growled at my mother and hit his tiny fists against her legs.

She caught his fists in her hand and bent down to meet his angry eyes.

"What your father had done to you is unspeakable, Baecos." She whispered. Baecos flinched at her words. "You did nothing to deserve it. You were born to a father who could not see beyond his own desire to become a god."

"A god like you," Baecos spit. "he told me you were here to look over us! Why did you let him do that?!"

My mother cupped his cheek, wiping tears as she did. She hated the thoughts going on in Baecos's head. She could see the monster he would become.

"I killed him, Baecos," she uttered the words the universe had pushed her to. "He was nothing but a pawn to this world, just like you, just like Iniq. Iniq will grow to be strong, you must stay by her side."

There was a sour feeling in her mouth as she said the words. The bitterness and hatred for Iniq had already begun to sprout. Over the next few hundred years it would become unbearable as he spent the days with myself and Cruor, pretending to be friendly but in reality, he was just waiting for his chance. A chance where he could finally follow in his father's footsteps and do the only thing that his father ever failed at. He would take the magic of someone born from a god in attempt to defy the universe and become a god himself.

There was a push, like a ghost of a hand, or maybe a whisper. The one you think you hear in the middle of the night but when you look over your shoulder, there is nothing but darkness. It was time, the universe had spoken. Neia did her job.

She left the boy stunned as she walked to the pile of dead bodies, she gripped her mates' hand as she conjured her own weapon, this time without hesitation she stabbed it directly into her still beating heart.

Iniq, your journey will be full of bloodshed and heart ache. I pray the universe is not wrong about this. I pray you are strong enough to overthrow Nitri once and for all, build a new world, build a fair one.

Darkness came over her, she couldn't help but smile at the familiar feeling. She was done fighting. After so many thousands of years, after the world had forgotten her, after meeting her mate, after fighting evil Acidos, she could rest now.

CHAPTER TWENTY-THREE
CRUOR

*A*s soon as I traveled away from the cave Callum had stopped struggling. Iniq's magic had left both of us and we were exposed. There was a slim chance that they would follow us but the dead forest gave a little protection if anyone were to chase us. I pushed Callum away from me. He stumbled, but when his eyes met mine he fell to his knees.

"Have you dragged me back to kill me?" Callum asked.

"If I wanted to kill you, I would have left you in that cave," I told him with a hiss.

I don't know how Ash and Felix did it, but I thanked whatever fates that existed when their shocked faces were the first I saw running towards us. I was still far from the kingdom but the jump had taken the majority of my magic so I would need their help to make it back.

"We felt your magic...," Ash started to speak but stopped dead in his tracks when he saw Callum's form kneeling on the forest floor.

"What is the meaning of this, Cruor?" Felix asked. His eyes were hard as they looked over the situation. They reminded me of Spiris's, and I felt the immediate need to explain everything to him.

I swallowed thickly.

"He was going to die. I had to save him," I rushed out. "I know he's not what the council says, I know he can be redeemed. Baecos must have put him under some sort of spell, I could not just let him die in that cave."

Felix's jaw flexed and Ash took a step back, his face had turned pale.

"Baecos was there," Ash said. There was no question in his tone, he had already put the pieces together. "With you, Spiris, and Iniq. And you took back Callum…" He steadied himself on the tree next to him. "But there is no one else by your side. Please tell me they went to the Dark King. Please, Cruor."

"How did you retrieve him, Cruor? Where are the others?" Felix asked, his voice had an angry tone to it. He strode over to my spot and grabbed the front of my shirt. His hands were shaking with anger.

I searched for words to tell them, but I could not find a better way to say that I had left them in a cave with Baecos and Vitos that was smaller than our dungeons. Ash leaned against the tree next to him, hand clasped over his mouth.

"They are literal High Kings, they will survive," I told them. "Bring him back, this time put him in a room and chain him to something."

Neither moved at my command.

"Please don't tell me you left them there with Baecos," Ash begged. "Please don't tell me you left them with the person that has literally killed her six times over. Please don't tell me that after a hundred years of preparation, when Iniq is finally back with us, you leave her with him again?"

"I gave you an order!" I hissed at them. "I am still your king, go now."

They looked at each other in a horrified silence that made my blood boil but after a moment they turned to leave.

CHAPTER TWENTY-FOUR
SPIRIS

*I*niq had begun crying right after the door closed behind us. I tried to bring her into my arms and ask what happened, but she shook her head and told me that it had to wait. By the devastated look in her eyes, I knew it had to be more than just seeing her parents.

The realization that I had seen a High King so long ago weighed on me heavily. She had looked the same in the door as she had when I saw her walking through the Light Kingdom. Iniq was not with her then, she was alone and standing in the rose garden much like Iniq would do when she returned to the Light Kingdom. She had given me a small smile and her eyes told me that she was a person I could trust, but before I could run up to the mystical woman, she turned and walked back towards the mansion, her robes swaying around her as she walked.

She was gentle while her daughter Iniq was poised to kill. Iniq had her sides, saving Vitos was proof of that, but when she looked into the eyes of someone who stood in her way, she was not going to hesitate.

I shifted Vitos against me so that I could help assist him up the mountain to the Dark Kingdom. The door had spit us out a lot closer than last time and I could feel the barrier work against us. Vitos shook against me as he tried to push himself up the rocky path. Not only was his fragile body not built for climbing, but the shadows were slowly encroaching on him and I knew sooner or later he would succumb to the same torment that Iniq had. I was not sure if my heart could take it.

I had been resigned to forget about my brother. When I saw his face before I died I never thought that I would see him again, and I was happy with that. Then when I first woke up, I was enraged. I couldn't believe he would let me go like that. Couldn't believe that he would make himself out to be such a perfect villain.

But after a while I began to miss the person he was. Miss the bright smiling brother that would try and shield me from the cruelty of life. Then when I saw him again for the first time in all those months... looking like *that*.

My gut began to twist. I began to think of all the rotten things Baecos had forced him to do in our absence. I could only guess at what Baecos was using him for. My parents would be disappointed in me to see what I had let him become. They were probably staring down at us from wherever their resting place was and shaking their head in shame. Even if they weren't, I could be disappointed enough for the both of them.

"You will start to see some pretty nasty things," Iniq said, her tears now dry. "I'm not sure if it's better to just knock him out and carry him up the mountain."

"Like a scrawny thing like you could carry me," Vitos spit. He cast his eyes down. He had to be ashamed of the way he looked now, at who was helping him. His pride was too big sometimes.

"I will do it, Vitos," I told him. "It would be better this way."

He sent me a look, but before he could respond Aselia waved her hand. She had cut off his air supply and he struggled against me for a moment before passing out. He quickly became purple.

"Aselia, let up," Iniq hissed at her.

Aselia gave us a pout but listened anyways and I felt Vitos relax against me instantly. I lifted him into my arms and cringed when I felt how light he was against me. While he had still remained as tall as me, he had lost all his muscle mass.

I am dying whether I go with you or stay with Baecos. His words rang in my head.

"Are you ready?" Iniq asked. I nodded at her.

"You still have the mirror, right?" Aselia called

"In the backpack," I told her. The backpack seemed to weigh a thousand pounds more on my back with the announcement.

We stayed mostly silent as we walked up the mountain until Iniq stopped in her tracks and let out a laugh.

"I am so stupid," she said and waved her hand in the air.

Nothing happened at first but slowly a door appeared to our far right, then another, and another, and another. All the doors were scattered around sporadically and there was no sign what they led to.

"I wish I thought of that," Aselia said with a grumble. "How do we know which one leads to the throne room?"

"I asked only the ones that led straight to the Dark King to show, so I hope that I did this correctly."

She walked a bit further up to the closest door and opened it without hesitation. I could make out a dark cave like room but nothing else. She poked her head in and then waved for us to follow. I ran to catch up, jostling Vitos in my arms.

When I passed the threshold, I was painfully aware that we were not in the throne room. What stood before us was a large bed that had piles of furs and blankets on it, much like the one we were given during our stay, but this one was twice as large and there were also chairs and a small table that littered the room.

"First you force your way into my throne room and now into my bedroom?" the Dark King spoke as he left from a door that materialized out of thin air. He was just as frightening as when we first met, and I felt his magic prod at my sides. His red eyes lingered on my unconscious brother. "Leave him on the bed."

I nodded and carefully set him down on the bed making sure the blankets covered his frail body. With a final look I faced towards the group again, all of their eyes on me.

"I saw my mother," Iniq told him. The Dark King's gaze snapped towards her. "And father."

"Let's talk in the throne room," he said and waved his hand, another door appearing out of thin air.

"Will he be safe here?" I asked him hesitant to leave Vitos alone.

The dark Kings gazed washed over me and a small smile tugged at his lips. "Should I be offended that you doubt me so?"

My heart skipped a beat and I looked down at the stone floor. "I did not mean it like that."

"He will be fine, child. Do not worry."

I nodded to him.

"Spiris, could you get the mirror please?" Iniq asked as she shot me a small smile. She did that to comfort me, I know. It was I that should have been comforting her. Our minds were still connected when she broke the bond. Not only that but she had been forced to come face to face with her dead parents and Baecos as we tried to flee for our lives. Yet here she was showing me it was okay that my brother was slowly dying in my arms.

I nodded against the thickening of my throat and opened my pack. I followed them through the door and I searched blindly for the mirror. I felt for the mirrors' cool surface and pulled it out quickly, not wanting to stay under the Dark Kings questioning gaze.

I didn't mean to look into it, I was content not to. I didn't care what my future held because I knew that as long as I could stay with Iniq, I would be happy. And now that I had my only blood relative by my side, there was nothing else I could want. I saw the mirror as something akin to a bad omen. I knew that there was nothing that it could show me that would be good. Life had taught me that much. Time after time the forces in my life had ripped the people I have loved from my hands and made me watch as they perished, why would I expect the mirror to be any different?

But even in the second it took for my gaze to slide over it, it awoke. It felt like my mind was sucked into it and all I could see was the gruesome image that shook me to my core. My gut felt like it had been punched and the air evaporated from my lungs.

"Spiris?" Iniq's voice called out, but I didn't pay her any mind.

In the mirror was me and Iniq. I would have been ecstatic to see us still together in the future, but this was different.

Blood was streaming down her face and her expression was set with a look of pure agony. She was straddling over me, her arms raised. There was a dagger in her hand that already shined with blood. Under her I lifted my hand to stop the blow, but she didn't falter. Just as she was about to bring the knife down to my face the mirror was grabbed from me. I tried to hold onto it tighter, I needed to see what the outcome would be. I needed to be sure that in the future the one person I loved the most was not about to end my existence. But the force against me was too strong and the mirror slipped out of my fingers, the future going with it.

Everything slowed as I watched the mirror plunge towards the hardened cave floor. The seconds turned to minutes but even as it slowed my body wouldn't move, the only thing that continued to work properly was my mind and even that was a mess of thoughts.

This whole journey was for nothing. The mirror would be destroyed, and the Dark King would refuse us. This whole time

I had been fighting for Iniq was for nothing, because in that mirror she had been so ready to end it all. The look on her face told me that she meant to kill when she raised her arms. Why would she try to hurt me like that? There must be a reason, she couldn't change like that overnight.

She said she loved me, and I loved her.

Was it something I did? Was I the cause for my own death? But I would never do anything to harm her... I knew that. She knew that too, right? Even in our darkest times together I had never seen such an expression on her face before.

The hands I now recognized as Aselia's floundered to catch it before it hit the ground. She was too late. The mirror hit the ground with a crash and shattered into a million pieces across the hard cave floor.

It was just like the scattered souls that I had thought of long ago. There was no putting it back, at least not completely anyways. The shards scattered across the dark floor and reflected my horrified expression back to me a million times over. There was a moment of silence before the frenzy.

Rough hands grasped at the front of my shirt and Aselia's face came inches close to mine. A growl forced its way up her throat. Her eyes were wide, almost like she was terrified, but I knew by her tone that she was angry. Maybe it was both, her future had not been any more pleasant than mine.

"Do you just realize what you did?" Aselia growled at me and shook me violently. I let her—I was too stunned to fight her off.

"I'm sorry," I whispered to her. My eyes sought Iniq, she had a sad smile on her face.

It's okay. she told me in my mind. Her voice resembled a mother who had just seen their child make a mistake. The tone lacked any anger but was filled with understanding which made the whole thing more confusing. And painful.

A million questions ran through my mind.

What was that I just saw?

Did she see it too?

Why would she try to kill me?

I waited with bated breath for her response, but she was already facing the Dark King who sat on his throne with a grim expression. I had only seen her this serious a handful of times in my existence. There was no smile on her face. No tremor of excitement in her hands. This was a person who knew what they wanted and came to fight for it.

"It's okay, my mother already told me what I needed to know," she said to him her eyes darted to Aselia. "The mirror has shown us what it needed to."

"You cannot see the dead, child. Do I look like such a fool?" he asked.

Aselia pushed me away with disgust and turned to the king. I wished in the moment I could just disappear into the shadows, never to be seen again. A part of me wanted to take Vitos and run away from my future death, find solstice in the mortal world... but the other part, the bigger part, could still not believe Iniq would do such a thing to me.

"Souls lie in the door between this world and the next. She saw them, we all did," Aselia vouched for Iniq.

The King searched Aselia in a scrutinizing manner, no doubt diving into her memories to prove if she had been lying. She puffed out her chest and put her hands on her hips and if daring him to prove her wrong.

"Memories can be falsified," the Dark King said after a pause.

"I would not come to you with such foolishness," Iniq insisted. "The mirror may be broken but my own memories are pure and untampered."

"Tell me with your words. What did they say?" He asked Iniq after a pause, not like he didn't already hear in her mind.

"First I will need you to promise you will not breathe a word of this to anyone," Iniq said.

If the King could lower himself to roll his eyes, I felt in that moment he would.

"I promise," he said, his voice echoing in the empty air of the room. Only now did I see his shadow people shiver besides him.

"We are going to kill Nitri," she told him. He sat straight up in his seat. "That is the destruction my mother saw, the one that she put into motion. She was the one that chose her death, she was the one that removed the magic from the light kingdom, and she was the one that set forth this destruction, not I."

The dark king paused before letting out a bark of a laugh. I could understand the humor in this yet I couldn't bring myself to even smile. As messy as this was, this is the path the fates have chosen for us. For *her*. "Nitri will have your head for this you know?"

"Which is why we need your help," Aselia said. "You need to lend us your knowledge. We cannot go into this empty handed. If we show up on his doorstep without this knowledge we might as well be dead."

"You can help us hide our mind from Nitri," Iniq said her eyes glanced towards me and I remember the conversation we had with Kneku in the library. It was all leading up to the moment happening right now. The demon felt like it was burning a hole in my pants pocket. I hadn't meant to hold onto it, but it seemed to follow me wherever I went, finding its way into my clothing when I least expected it. It served as a reminder from High King Nitri.

Don't forget who you are, Spiris. Love is a beautiful thing but obsession can be dangerous. Did he know what would happen? Was this the obsession he spoke about?

It couldn't be. I refused to believe that anything less than perfect could come from mine and Iniq's union.

"And I don't suppose it will be Aselia who is next in line for the crown." The Dark King mused snapping me out of my thoughts.

"I will be," she said. "The mirror foresaw it."

The Dark King's eyes met mine for a moment.

And what role do you play in this? He asked in my mind,

I swallowed thickly, not able to keep the image of Iniq trying to kill me out of my mind,

I do not know, I told him. *But regardless I will stick by her side to help her see this through.* He took this as an answer and faced Iniq once more.

"I will teach you. In return, I expect something from you when you become king," he said to Aselia.

"Anything," she vowed.

"Unite the worlds. This one and the other world," he said. "You are right about one thing. I am tired of being the only demon in the realm… and I would like to see my mate once more."

"Deal," Aselia said.

And with that, my fate was sealed.

ACKNOWLEDGMENTS

I would like to thank you, the reader who just finished this book. I cannot begin to describe how surreal it is for me to be able to do what I love and it is all thanks to your continued support.

Also as normal, thanks to Madli for this beautiful cover! Working with her has been an absolute pleasure and I can't wait to work with her again. If you would like to commission her, go to www.madli.eu.

You can also reach her on her social media at https://www.instagram.com/madliart/

ABOUT THE AUTHOR

Elle is a native Californian who has lived in Los Angeles for most of her life. From the very start, she has been in love with all things fantasy and reading. As soon as Elle found out that writing books could be a career, she picked up a pen and paper. While the first ones were about scorned love and missed opportunities of lunchtime love, she has grown to love the fantasy genre and looks forward to making a difference in the world with her stories.

Loved this book? Please leave a review it really helps Indi authors like myself get more readers!